B L I S T E R

CONRAD JONES

GerriCon Books Ltd

CHANDLER
BOOK DESIGN

First published in Great Britain in 2009
by
GerriCon Books Ltd
Orford Green
Suite 1
Warrington
Cheshire
WA2 8PA
www.gerriconbooks.co.uk

A CIP Catalogue of this book is available from
the British Library

ISBN: 978-0-9561034-4-4

First published by GerriCon Books Ltd. 05/2009

Cover Photos: ©istockphoto.com

Cover designed and typeset in Meridien 11pt
by Chandler Book Design
www.chandlerbookdesign.co.uk

Printed in Great Britain by the
MPG Books Group, Bodmin and King's Lynn

CHAPTER 1
Blister Agents

The city of Liverpool was once the busiest port in the world, and the centre of the terrible human slave trade. Most of the historic dock buildings are long since gone, but some of them remain and have been turned into a tourist hub along the banks of the River Mersey. The Terrorist Task Force are also based on the riverbank. They occupy the top floor of a fortress-like building known as Canning Place. The remaining lower floors of the building are occupied by the county's uniformed police divisions. Today the taskforce had been called to an emergency meeting. They were sat listening to Chen explaining the properties of blister agent weapons.

"The sulphur mustards, of which mustard gas 2-chloroethyl sulphide is a member, are a class of related cytotoxic, vesicant chemical warfare agents. They have the ability to form large blisters on exposed skin, both internally and externally. In spite of the name, technically they are not actually gases, but are liquid chemicals which turn into vapour when they are released," Chen smiled at the gathering in the room. He took a sip of water and then continued with the brief.

"Pure sulphur mustards are colourless, odourless, viscous liquids when they are at room temperature. However, when used in impure form as warfare agents they are usually yellow-brown in colour and have an odour resembling mustard plants, garlic or horseradish, hence the innocuous name. Mustard gas was originally assigned the name *LOST*, after two men called Lommel and Steinkopf, who first proposed the military use of Sulphur Mustard to the German Imperial General Staff during the First agents that had been summoned to an extraordinary meeting.

Chen was of Chinese origin, and was an information guru for the Terrorist Task Force. The taskforce was set up as an elite counter terrorist unit that operated outside of the usual military jurisdiction, and they answered directly to the Minister of Defence. When incidents were escalated to the level of the Terrorist Task Force involvement, then all other avenues had already been exhausted.

"Is there a reason behind the chemistry lesson?" John Tankersley asked impatiently, rubbing his aching neck. He had been lifting heavy weights in the station gym prior to the meeting, but he had pushed his limit too far and torn a muscle. It was Chen that had been spotting him as he lifted the last heavy set, and he had failed to provide enough support, which had caused the injury. Tank was pissed off with him.

"Please be patient Tank, I'm getting to the point but you will need all this background information to understand the implications of what I'm about to tell you," Chen replied holding his palms downward in a calming motion.

John Tankersley was the lead agent of the taskforce. He was an ex-Special Forces operative and had been decorated more times than an artificial Christmas tree. John Tankersley was a brute of a man, six foot tall and seventeen stone of solid muscle, it wasn't difficult to understand why his colleagues shortened his name to 'Tank'.

"Okay, but get to the point please, the German High Command are not really on my need to know list," Tank snapped back. The muscles in his wide jaw twitched and the veins in his massive neck throbbed visibly as he spoke.

"I'll be as brief as I can," Chen smiled and his oriental features were exaggerated. He had deep brown eyes and high cheek bones. His smile was brilliant white and had a very disarming effect on everyone he met, especially women.

"Will you get to the point Chen," Tank said under his breath. He rubbed his hand over his shaven head.

"People exposed to mustard gas rarely suffer immediate symptoms, and mustard-contaminated areas may appear completely normal, victims can unknowingly receive high dosages.

2

However, within six to twenty four hours of exposure to mustard agent, victims experience intense thirst, itching and skin irritation which gradually turns into large blisters filled with yellow fluid wherever the mustard agent contacted the skin. There are many recorded incidents of the thirst being so intense that it causes a type of delirium, or madness. Victims can become extremely violent," Chen smiled again as he continued the presentation. He could see that Tank was becoming agitated, which amused him. Chen often teased him that if Tank's brain was as big as his bicep, then he would be a genius.

"At very high concentrations, if inhaled, mustard agent causes bleeding and blistering within the respiratory system, damaging the delicate mucous membranes and causing the victim to drown on their own bodily fluids. Severe mustard gas burns are usually fatal. Furthermore, mustard gas is a persistent agent which would remain in the environment for days and continue to cause sickness. If mustard gas contaminated a soldier's clothing and equipment, then other soldiers or medics he came into contact with would also be poisoned," Chen sat down at the long meeting table and looked at the gathered agents. The gathering remained silent. No one was quite sure where the meeting was heading.

"Thank you Chen, most interesting, and also very concerning," Major Stanley Timms broke the silence.

The Major was the director of the taskforce. Before he had been selected to operate the covert unit, he had been a high ranking officer in the Royal Marines with a military record that would make Rambo blush.

"I'm sure that you can appreciate the implications of a blister agent falling into the wrong hands, MI5 has received information that a right wing extremist group is intending to attack the 2012 Olympics with such a chemical," the Major explained. Anxious looks were exchanged around the room. The taskforce knew that the forthcoming Olympics could be a target for a hundred different terrorist organisations, but this was the first tangible plot to surface.

The credit crunch of 2008 had sent the economy into melt down, which had pushed unemployment up and house prices down, leaving many in a desperate financial position. The effect increased racial tensions nationwide as immigrants were still flooding in and taking indigenous British jobs. It was fuel to the fire for the right wing fascist parties.

"How solid is the information?" Tank asked. The intelligence agencies often scare mongered. The greater the perceived threat, the higher their government budget was.

"Solid enough to have been put onto the Minister's desk," the Major replied.

"What do we know about the protagonists?" Grace Farrington asked. Grace was the taskforce's number two. She was of Jamaican descent and looked more like a pop star or a beauty queen than a Special Forces operative.

"We don't know a great deal about them at all I'm afraid, except they preach the usual anti-immigration nonsense as the rest of the neo-Nazi groups," the Major answered. He stood up and walked to the head of the table. On the wall behind him was a bank of screens. He picked up a remote and the largest screen flickered into life. The face of a handsome young man appeared. The photograph looked like a school portrait.

"This is Christopher Walsh aged sixteen, and this is the most recent photograph that we have of him. He is now twenty seven years old, and a very successful business man. He was an eminent scientist in his field until he began to diversify his business interests. The information that the intelligence agencies have received puts Christopher Walsh on centre stage as the brains behind the proposed attack," the Major sat down again.

"What is his background?" Grace asked.

"Chemicals, believe it or not," Chen answered the question.

"Well, chemical weapons to be more precise," the Major added. "We think that one of his associate companies was behind selling mustard gas formulas and production methodology to at least half a dozen rogue governments, and God forbid, several extremist organisations, but nobody knows where he is or why he would be involved in an attack on the London Olympics."

Tank picked up a paper file from the desk and flicked through the pages. Chen had compiled some of the basics about chemical weapon production. He stood up and walked toward the meeting room window. The chemical formulas and technical information blurred on the page. It made no real sense to Tank, but he knew that to some people it would be only too easy to manufacture chemical weapons. Tank looked out of the window. The River Mersey was only a stone's throw away from the taskforce headquarters. It looked dark grey and angry as it flowed on its way to the Irish Sea. Across the road hundreds of tourists ambled around the historic Albert Docks, once the centre of the slave trade, the ancient buildings had now become a huge tourist destination. Tank wondered just how much of Chen's blister agent it would take to attack a 'Soft Target' like the docks.

"How easy would it be to manufacture this stuff," Tank asked, placing the file down on the window ledge.

"It would be difficult," Chen answered. "All the ingredients required for the manufacture of chemical weapons and homemade explosives are monitored. So if someone bought enough of the individual ingredients required then the intelligence agencies would be alerted."

"We think that Christopher Walsh is involved because he may already possess the ingredients required, therefore no one would be any the wiser if he made a chemical agent. Every chemical plant with any association to him is being investigated by MI5," the Major said.

Tank looked out of the window again. It had started snowing again for the third time in a week and the sky was obscured by dark low clouds. Over the last month or so they had seen the heaviest snow fall in a century. The Liver buildings on the riverbank looked bright and clean against the grey clouds. There were two huge bronze birds perched on top of the building. They had become the emblem of the historic port.

"We are looking into how easy it would be for anyone to get hold of a blister agent, but my concern is this," Chen approached the bank of screens and the school portrait changed. The black and white image of a naval ship appeared. Judging by the style of the uniforms worn by some of the sailors in the picture, Tank reckoned that it had been taken during the Second World War. The deck of the vessel was covered with artillery shells. There was barely an inch of the deck that didn't have ordinance on it.

"This is a British Royal Navy vessel shortly after the allied invasion of Italy during the Second World War. I can't tell you what it was called or exactly when the picture was taken because the information relating to this vessel was so classified that it was destroyed. To all intents and purposes this picture is the only evidence that this ship ever existed." Chen moved across the room and the picture changed again. Two mini submarines appeared on the smaller digital screens. Tank was reminded of deep sea salvage documentaries that he'd watched on television. The submarines had robotic arms and grabs.

"The ship in the picture was carrying an unknown number of mustard gas shells," Chen looked sternly and allowed a pause for the information to sink in. The room remained silent and a nervous tension began to build.

"In your files are the details of a chemical weapons disaster which occurred during the Second World War in the Italian port of Bari, 1943. The incident was so bad that the allied leaders conspired to destroy their entire stocks of the chemicals. The British Government scuppered this ship, amongst others, and pretended that it had never been contemplating the use of chemical weapons against the Germans. They scuppered a total of sixteen similar vessels at various points around the British Isles," Chen explained.

Tank could see what was coming. The mini-submarines in the picture had either been stolen or purchased by someone on the MI5 watch list, and when you combined that information with the fact that a known chemical weapons dealer had been implicated in a terrorist plot then it all added up. Someone was trying to recover mustard gas shells from the bottom of the ocean.

CHAPTER 2
December 2, 1943 Bari, Italy

Jimmy Lyons watched as the port cranes moved methodically to and fro unloading the armada of ships that had arrived over the last few weeks. The Italian armed forces had surrendered and the allies had the German army on the run. The allied Italian campaign had begun with a fierce battle for the capital city of Rome. Men and munitions were arriving every hour to bolster the allied mission. Driving the German army out of Italy northward would need hundreds of thousands of men and millions of tons of supplies. The port of Bari had been identified as one of the main arteries that would be needed to support the allied invasion.

Jimmy took a cigarette from his soft packet of Lucky Strikes and placed it into the corner of his mouth. He nudged his pal with his elbow and offered him one too. The sailor took one gratefully and followed suit by placing it into the corner of his mouth. His fellow shipmate, Mark Brown, lit a match with his thumbnail and they both smoked in silence as they watched the armada of vessels being unloaded. Jimmy and Mark were American sailors aboard the USS Bistera which was part of an allied convoy of heavily armed cruisers. They had been sent to protect the convoy from a German counter attack against the port. It was getting dark and as the sun went down there was a chill in the air.

"Did you get a letter from Jackie yet?" Mark asked.

"Yes, I got one in the mail run yesterday," Jimmy shivered. He wasn't sure if it was the cool evening air that had made him shiver or the thought of his wife thousands of miles away.

"The kids all okay?" Mark tried to make conversation, but it was always difficult. Men at war had to try and desensitise themselves. Worrying about getting home to their loved ones would drive them mad if they allowed it to. It was a constant mental and emotional battle dealing with being torn from their loved ones.

"They're fine, she said to say hello," Jimmy said patting his shipmate on the back. They had been at sea for months and to quell the boredom the sailors often shared their letters with their friends. The sailors got to know each other's families intimately by reading and rereading their letters. The sailors rarely received letters at sea as they had to wait until they made port, and so sharing their post passed the time. It created a bond between naval men that couldn't be matched by the men in land based forces.

"Be sure to say hello back to her from me," Mark laughed. Jimmy laughed at Mark laughing. Mark had a laugh which sounded like a cross between a donkey baying and a sea lion barking. Whenever Jimmy heard his laugh he couldn't help but laugh too. He shook his head as they chuckled, and took another soothing puff on his cigarette. It was a precious quiet moment.

Jimmy stopped laughing suddenly as an air raid siren in the distance beyond the harbour began to wail. He dropped his cigarette onto the deck and crushed it with his boot as the first siren was joined by a second, and then a third. Within seconds there was a deafening cacophony of a dozen or more sirens blaring. The sirens were joined by the distant hum of German Junkers Ju 88 long range bomber engines approaching.

"Get on that forty," Jimmy shouted to Mark.

The naval vessel was armed with 40mm Bofors anti-aircraft guns. They were fitted together in fours and welded to a carriage that could rotate to track enemy aircraft. Jimmy could hear the approaching bombers but he couldn't see them yet. The evening sky was darkening quickly which made spotting the enemy even harder. He looked around the overcrowded harbour and he had a gut wrenching feeling. There were so many ships crammed into the port that even a blind bomber pilot couldn't miss hitting something. The scene was one of blind panic as soldiers and sailors ran to arms, while civilians and port employees scrambled for cover. The port had no anti-aircraft system of its own, not even barrage balloons. Jimmy knew that they were sitting ducks. He tensed his neck and gripped the handle of the Bofors as he waited for a target to aim at.

"Take my letter Jimmy," Mark said. His voice was breaking slightly as fear took hold of him.

"Keep it in your pocket Mark. You're going home with me my friend," Jimmy said. Mark pushed the letter back into the breast pocket of his sweat stained shirt. The letter was for his wife if he died. Most soldiers and sailors at war carry a final letter for their loved ones, as a way of conveying all things that they wished they had said, but never got around to.

"I've got a bad feeling about this Jimmy," Mark said. His eyes were watery, as if he were about to start crying.

Jimmy grabbed his friend's wrist tightly and held him. "We'll be fine Mark," he said, but he didn't believe it himself. He felt sweat trickling down his spine, despite the chill in the air. They stared at the dark sky in silence. The noise of the sirens began to quieten and one by one they stopped wailing. The noise of the approaching bomber squadron grew louder. Jimmy could feel his blood pumping through his heart and he wiped sweat from his brow as the first bombs began to fall.

The horizon illuminated, and a huge red fire ball climbed toward the sky. An enormous tower of curling black smoke engulfed the port's cranes. Mark Brown triggered the Bofors gun into life, firing thousands of 40mm shells into the night sky. The deafening sound of the anti-aircraft weapon was joined by a hundred others as every naval vessel in the harbour returned fire onto the German Luftwaffe. The two frightened shipmates loaded and fired their weapons for what seemed like a life time. The harbour became a scene of carnage.

There was a sudden huge explosion close to them. The blast wave knocked Jimmy off his feet and he cracked the back of his head against the metal hull of the ship. Mark sprang to his aid and placed a piece of shell wadding over a small cut on Jimmy's head.

"Get back on that forty, nail the bastards!" Jimmy shouted over the deafening roar. He looked toward the source of the explosion. There was a troop carrier in the water close by that had taken a direct hit. It was listing dangerously to starboard. The decks were covered in bodies and the water around it was full of human flotsam. Some men were alive and screaming for help and others were floating face down, beyond help.

Another deafening explosion came from behind them. Jimmy stood up and looked toward it. A US cruiser had been hit mid ship. The bomb had penetrated two decks before exploding in the munitions store. The sky lit up like a Disney fireworks display as the ship was torn apart by its own exploding ordinance. A thousand tons of shredded steel was launched into the air, showering the surrounding ships with a deadly metal rain.

"Get down!" Jimmy shouted. He crouched down and covered his head with his hands. There was a shower of red hot metal shards clanging against the bulkhead of the ship. A three inch spike pierced Jimmy's forearm and the red hot metal seared into his flesh. He screamed as he grabbed at it with his fingers. He pulled at it but it had welded itself to his skin. He choked as he pulled harder still. The spike ripped free, taking a lump of skin and muscle with it. He closed his eyes to shut out the pain and rested his head against the cold metal bulkhead. He felt a hard wet slap across his face and it shocked him back to reality. He touched his cheek with his fingers and then stared at them. There was a greyish sticky fluid on his fingertips and the piece of slimy intestine which had slapped him in the face was lying across his shoulder. He recoiled from the stinking viscera and knocked it onto the deck as if it might bite him.

"Jimmy, help me," Mark gurgled. Jimmy looked at his friend and his mouth opened in shock. Mark had been pinned to the metal bulkhead by a wide piece of shredded metal. It measured three feet long and the edges were charred and jagged. The shrapnel had hit the ship at such a speed that it had disembowelled Mark Brown and then penetrated the hull. There were coils of visceral intestine hanging over the metal and dangling onto the deck. Jimmy wretched and the taste of acid vomit filled his nose and mouth. He staggered to his feet and grabbed at the offending metal fragment.

"Help me Jimmy, please help me," Mark whispered as his life slowly spilled onto the deck.

"You hang on there, Mark, hang on," Jimmy started to panic and grabbed at the metal again. It was still red hot and his fingers burnt on it. Mark's body slumped down against the red hot metal plate and his face started to sizzle against the plate. Tendrils of smoke drifted from his face and Jimmy nearly vomited again as the smell of burning flesh drifted toward him.

"Get back on that forty sailor," a voice boomed over the noise of the battle. Jimmy turned and looked at the senior officer in disbelief.

"What?"

"I said get back on that forty sailor, your friend is dead and we will be too if we don't drive these bastards away, look around sailor we're being annihilated down here. Now I'm ordering you to get back on that forty," the officer seemed to be cool and calm and well in control of his faculties. His calm persona rattled Jimmy to the core and he saluted the officer before taking up his position on the 40mm Bofurs gun. He glanced at his dead friend and tears filled his blue eyes as he pressed the trigger and unleashed its deadly load skyward. It was nearly an hour before he stopped firing and the sound of the last bomber's engine whined off into the distance.

Jimmy Lyons had to wiggle his fingers to get the blood flowing back into them. The vibration of the Bofors gun combined with the cold night air had taken its toll. He sat down on the cold metal deck and stared at the ruined body of his shipmate. Mark Brown was still pinned to the bulkhead with his guts spilled over the deck around him. Jimmy knew that he had to retrieve Mark's farewell letter from his shirt pocket, but he didn't dare go near him. He looked around the harbour and was totally in awe of the devastation that was before him. The water around his ship was full of bodies, and some of them were still alive. The sight of so many of his countrymen in dire straits shook him to his senses. He suddenly came to and ran to his dead friend.

"I'll tell Carla you were the bravest man I ever had the honour to sail with Mark Brown," he touched his friend's face and was surprised how cold he felt already.

Jimmy grabbed the letter from his breast pocket and folded it safely into his own. He saluted and ran toward the deck rails to help recover the dead and injured from the water. He looked over the rails and thought that he could be looking at a scene from hell. Jimmy and his shipmates worked tirelessly through the night pulling survivors from the water first, and then recovering the dead. A total of seventeen vessels had been sunk in the harbour, which equated to thirty four thousand tons of cargo. The closest ship to the harbour wall was the munitions transporter vessel U.S. Liberty ship John Harvey. It had been bombed to the stern igniting its load of artillery shells, which had torn the ship to pieces and fractured an oil pipeline. The heavy oil poured unhindered into the harbour water.

The problem was that nobody except the captain of the John Harvey knew that the artillery shells were each packed with 11kilos of mustard gas. Churchill and Roosevelt had allegedly conspired to use the chemical against the Germans if things in Europe went badly. Their plan was to strike terror into the German troops by using the appalling weapon to kill and maim and to contaminate land so that the Germans couldn't remain there. Unbeknown to the Germans or the allies, the Luftwaffe had destroyed the entire arsenal of chemical weapons, releasing the vapour into the harbour water and across a wide area of the heavily populated port. The amount of vapour released into such a concentrated space meant that the terrible effects of the blister agent were magnified tenfold.

Jimmy could smell a powerful odour, similar to garlic. Although he thought it was odd he didn't pay it any attention. He rushed down the gangway and began to help his shipmates hauling survivors onto the deck. The harbour water was covered in a thick layer of engine oil which clung to the survivors as they were pulled on deck. It also clung to the rescuers that touched them. Jimmy and the rescuers noticed that many of the survivors were badly blistered.

"We need medics brought aboard to deal with these burns," Jimmy said to a senior hand.

"The bastards must have been dropping incendiaries," the charge hand replied.

"Can you smell garlic on them too?" Jimmy asked. He swallowed and his throat felt like sandpaper. He reached for his canteen of water and took a long gulp. The liquid offered him little relief and the thirst returned in minutes.

"Can I have some of your water?" the charge hand reached

for Jimmy's canteen. Jimmy recoiled and snatched the canteen away from his senior officer. His eyes were stinging and he wasn't feeling well, but he needed his water to quench the raging thirst that he had.

"I haven't got much left," he snapped, lifting the canteen to his lips and draining it.

"Don't drink it all you fucking bastard," the charge hand shouted at him angrily.

He reached for the canteen and grabbed it away from Jimmy's lips. Jimmy curled his hand into a huge fist and punched the officer in the mouth. He staggered back and tripped over a stricken survivor who was laid out on the deck behind him. Jimmy put the canteen to his lips and emptied the liquid greedily. He swallowed the last drop as the officer tackled him hard around the waist. The wind was knocked out of him and the force of the blow carried both men backward toward the guardrail. Jimmy hit the rail hard and he desperately tried to maintain his balance, but the momentum was too great. It seemed like an age between hitting the railing and then falling into thin air toward the contaminated sea below.

Jimmy Lyons and his senior officer were never recovered from the harbour. The concentrated blister agent was stuck to the surface of the ocean by engine oil. It was a slow and painful death. Over one thousand allied servicemen died in the harbour that day, along with two thousand civilians in the surrounding suburbs. Many of the deaths that day were recorded as victims of fire caused by the German bombs. The truth was that there were no fires, and the victims were covered in chemical burns, but because no one knew that the blister agent ordinance was present the medical staff members were oblivious.

By the time Jimmy's ship the U.S.S. Bistera reached portside to unload the dead and wounded, the entire crew were affected by the blister agent. Most of the crew were completely blinded, some recovered but some did not. Their injuries were recorded as a mystery illness that swept the ship. The truth about the mustard gas artillery shells was highly classified, and the authorities ashore had no knowledge of their existence. This increased the number of fatalities, since the physicians could not prescribe the proper treatment for those suffering from the effects of mustard gas. Eventually the physicians themselves became infected from contact with the skin and clothing of those directly exposed to the vapour. The records of the incident were destroyed and the only surviving records of it were not declassified until 1967.

CHAPTER 3
The Terrorist Task Force-2009

"Do we know where the dump sites are?" Tank asked. If they could identify where the mustard gas artillery shells had been dumped then they could put the areas under surveillance and wait there for the terrorists to arrive.

"No and no one working within the government today has any idea. The records were completely destroyed after the war," Chen answered. It was sixty five years since the chemical artillery shells had been sent to the bottom of the ocean. The remaining survivors from that time would be well into their seventies. The Ministry of Defence had to make sure that the truth was never discovered. If superpowers like America and Britain were suspected of contemplating the use of chemical weapons then they could never take the moral high ground again. It would give rogue states carte blanche to use chemical weapons against their neighbours.

"What do we know about how they were dumped?" Grace interrupted.

"What do you mean Faz?" Chen used her nickname.

"You said earlier that the ships were scuppered at sea. So how were the ships sunk? Did they use remote charges or mines? If we knew how they were sunk then we can trace exactly who sunk them, and from there we can find survivors and ask them where the ships are," Grace explained her theory. Tank eyed her too long, although most of the taskforce had an inkling that they were an item, Tank still tried hard to keep it secret. He glanced around the table to see if anyone had noticed him staring. No one had.

"That's a very interesting point," Chen said beaming from ear to ear. He flicked through his file of data looking for something that he may have overlooked.

"Pass me some of the file Chen and I'll help," the Major said. Chen handed him a manila file a few inches thick. The Major began thumbing through it. Tank looked at the contents over his shoulder and a question sprang to mind.

"Where did these files of information come from if everything was destroyed or never recorded in the first instance?" Tank mused. Everyone stopped looking and turned toward Chen for the answer. It did seem to be a contradiction in terms.

"These files were composed by a man called Geoff Evans. His mother was told by the ministry of defence that his father was killed in action by a German U-boat in 1943 however he believed that his father was killed while on an operation to destroy a cache of chemical weapons," Chen stood up from the table and passed Tank a hand written letter. The letter was yellowed with age and ripped at the edges, but it had been laminated to prevent it deteriorating any further. Tank read the letter and shook his head in disbelief. Able Seaman Evans had written a brief letter to his wife expressing his concerns about a secret mission they were rumoured to be embarking on. Whispers of a secret cache of chemical weapons were passing around the ship and the crew had been stripped to the bare minimum number of men required.

"It was the last letter Mrs Evans ever received from her husband," Chen said as Tank was reading it. "Her son never let go of the idea that his father had been killed whilst on this secret mission and that the war office had brushed his death and the mission under the carpet. Over the next three decades until he died in 2002, he compiled these files of press cutting and snippets of research that he'd gathered, and he constantly bombarded the government with his concerns." Chen shrugged as he explained. The files were full of newspaper cuttings and library information containing the last known whereabouts of Able Seaman Evan's shipmates.

"Don't tell me that his concerns fell on deaf ears," Grace said sarcastically.

"He was considered to be another conspiracy theorist," the Major added.

"Look at this," Chen said. His eyes widened as he spoke and he picked up another piece of paper as if he were crosschecking both for details. He passed the paper to the Major and the major studied a bundle of envelopes. They looked unopened and were marked for return to sender.

"What is it?" Tank asked. Chen passed the papers to him. Tank looked at them quickly and the handed them to Grace. She shook her head as she read them.

"Evans's son had sent over a dozen letters to this man, all of which were returned unopened," Chen said.

"Which wouldn't be so remarkable except that he was a Royal Naval submarine Commander," Tank added.

"And we all know what submarines do best, don't we?" Grace said.

"They torpedoed ships and sent them to the bottom of the ocean never to be seen again," the Major nodded his head thoughtfully. The group remained silent for a while as they contemplated the information that had been gathered over a period of decades by an aggrieved son who was campaigning for justice for his dead father. It was a terrible scenario, but there was little or no evidence there to take the investigation forward.

"So we are presuming that Evans believed that his father's ship was loaded with chemical weapons, and that it was torpedoed by the Royal Navy at sea?" the Major summarised what he had just read through.

"Yes, but this file indicates another sixteen vessels were disposed of in the same way, and off British coast lines," Grace said astounded. "We can't seriously believe that the Royal Navy sent its own men to be torpedoed by their own submarines."

"What if the submarines didn't know they were British ships?" Tank said.

The group exchanged glances again as they each mulled over the possible scenarios in their own mind. They needed to identify the possibility of mustard gas shells being recovered from the bottom of the ocean, and in the process they could be stumbling into an incident of international proportions. They may have found physical evidence that the allies were prepared to use mustard blister agents in the Second World War, and that they were prepared to slaughter any witnesses to the disposal of them to protect themselves from international condemnation.

"We need to find this submarine captain. If he's still alive then he could be the only person that can tell us where the dumps sites may be," Tank said as he picked up the telephone. "We need to start with this address and follow the trail from there," he added pointing to one of the returned letters that had been written years before by the son of able seaman Ernest Evans.

CHAPTER 4
Liverpool Bay, December, 14th 1943

Able seaman Ernest Evans heard the ships engines quieten. The pilot of the ship sent the message to the engine room to put the engines into idle and the vessel slowed to a drift stop. Ernest Evans, Ernie to his shipmates, looked at the night sky to orientate himself, but the stars were cloaked in dark clouds. They had been sailing for six hours and as far as he could tell the ship had been steered in a huge circle. There were no twinkling lights to be seen on the shore because of the blackout. The port of Liverpool had been subjected to heavy bombing raids by the Luftwaffe. Civilians hung blankets and thick curtains over every door and window to stop their gaslights and candles from betraying the city's position. Air raid wardens were appointed to patrol the streets and they were given the responsibility to enforce blackout conditions. It made it difficult for the German pilots to navigate from the air, but it also made it impossible for seamen to navigate using the lights of habitation to guide them up the coastline. Ernie couldn't be sure, but his sense of direction told him that they were somewhere in Liverpool Bay.

"I'm not happy about this voyage mate," a signalman joined him at the rail. They stood next to each other and stared into the inky darkness. The ship swayed gently as she drifted on the ocean swell.

"I've not been happy about this mission since the first time it was mentioned to me. It's a bad one and I've known it since day one. When have we ever been ordered to sail in a circle on a ship with no name?" Ernie scowled as he spoke. He was known to his shipmates to be a harbinger of doom. His glass was always half empty instead of half full. This time though he had his shipmate's ear.

"What do you mean the ship has no name?" the signalman was confused. He had noted that the name of the ship had been painted over when they had boarded, but that was often done to confuse the enemy U-boats. The name painted out had seeped back through the paint, and the signalman recalled that it was just readable as the HMS Ely.

"Did you see the name when we boarded?" Ernie whispered, as if Hitler himself could hear them. He was always full of gossip and conspiracy theories. If there was ever dissent amongst the able seamen then you could guarantee that Ernie had a hand in spreading the tales around the ship. Ernie was well respected by his shipmates because when he did have a theory he was usually right. He was also an exceptionally brave sailor. His superior officers would have given their brass buttons to have him in their crew.

"Of course I did, she's the Ely."

"Oh no, she isn't," Ernie whispered again. "The Ely was a new class frigate launched from Plymouth Hoe in forty one, and this tug is definitely not a frigate. This is a merchant ship that's been painted to look like a warship. Look around you man she is not a frigate." Ernie huddled closer to his shipmate. "Now you tell me why anyone would dress up a merchant vessel as a warship unless they were up to no good?"

The signalman turned his head ninety degrees and studied the deck and its fittings. The more he looked the more convinced he became that Ernie was right again. The skeleton crew had been forbidden to venture below decks on this voyage, apart from the engineers who fired the ships powerhouse. That in itself wasn't unheard of. Sometimes a valuable cargo or passenger was hidden from the crew by restrictions on access around the vessel, especially when a head of state was on board. The admiralty couldn't risk the Germans finding out that they were carrying a high risk target when there were so many U-boats at sea.

"Look at that foredeck gun turret," Ernie gestured with a gloved hand. The signalman had been in the bridge for most of the journey and hadn't had the opportunity to study the vessel in detail.

"I haven't seen a gunner like that before," the signalman admitted with a slow shake of his head.

"It's a merchant ship I'm telling you, and that cannon is from the deck of a German U-boat. It must have been captured and then refitted onto this merchant ship. This is not one of her Majesty's warships mate," Ernie rubbed his chin and looked out to sea again. One of his pastimes on the long voyages that he had been drafted on was the study of the Royal Navy's vessels, from aircraft carriers to the smallest launch. He knew them off by heart, and he knew where they had been in action and the details of how some of them were lost during the war years. The HMS Ely had been lost in the South Atlantic Ocean some months prior. Why the war office would go to all this trouble was beyond his comprehension, but it added fuel to the flames of rumour that the mission was to transport chemical weapons. The fact that the crew had been banned from descending below decks reinforced the point.

"It's a strange one sure enough," the signalman agreed and took out his pipe. He filled the wooden bowl with fresh tobacco before lighting it. The smoke drifted toward Ernie and he welcomed the comforting smell.

"What do you think we're doing out here then? The ship is drifting," Ernie asked as he filled his own pipe with his favourite blend of Condor tobacco.

"I think this is a rendezvous point, and we're here to meet another vessel, maybe the rumours are true and there are chemical weapons below, who knows?" the signalman speculated.

"I'd agree with you except all the hatches are welded shut," Ernie lit his pipe and puffed on it to make the tobacco burn.

"The hatches are welded shut, why the bloody hell would they do that if we're delivering something?" the signalman asked incredulously.

"That's my point, every hatch is welded closed. Whatever is in those holds isn't coming out again without the help of a blowtorch."

"Maybe they don't want anyone prying into the cargo."

"Maybe, but I'm not sure that I want to be a part of whatever it is that they're up to," Ernie replied.

"Ours is not to question why, ours is but to do or die Ernie," the signalman patted him on the back as he puffed his pipe again.

Ernie heard a deep whooshing sound coming from the darkness. It was a sound that only a few sailors had witnessed and then lived to tell the tale. It was the sound of torpedoes approaching the drifting vessel at speed. The two shipmates stared into the blackness and they froze with fear as the white tracks of two torpedoes appeared in their range of vision. Ernie dropped his pipe and watched its red glow disappearing into the ocean below. Seconds later two huge explosions ripped the stern apart. Ernie grabbed the deck rail instinctively and held it as tight as he could. The concussion wave from the explosions hit them milliseconds after impact. Ernie felt his eardrums burst and the world went quiet instantly. He turned to his shipmate only to see that most of him was gone. His left arm was still gripping the rail but the rest of him had been blown overboard. Ernie noticed that the signalman had been wearing a wristwatch that his wife had sent to him for Christmas. It was a rare thing to see a wristwatch on anyone below the rank of captain in those days, and so it stuck in Ernie's mind. Ernie felt the ship lurch violently and the rail he was holding buckled. His shipmate's arm dropped off the rail into the bubbling water. He darted away from the rail and grasped a canvas sheet which covered one of the ship's life rafts. The raft had been bolted to the deck in three places. Ernie shouted at the bridge but his cries went unheard. He knew that bolting lifeboats to the hull was only done when a ship was being scuppered. If there was no floating debris then no one would ever know where the ship had been sunk. Ernie turned and prepared to throw himself off the stricken ship into the sea when a third torpedo hit the stern and shattered the steel hull into metal confetti. Ernie was shredded by a wall of flying metal shards. The ship tipped almost vertically before slipping beneath the waves taking with her the deadly secret cargo that she carried, along with fourteen of her Majesty's finest seamen.

CHAPTER 5
Sunnyside Rest Home, 2009

The Sunnyside Rest Home was a modern red brick building with a black slate roof. It was two storeys high and had been built in an L shape. The reception area was similar to that of a motel, except the receptionist was wearing a crisp white nurses' uniform. Beyond the reception desk was a small arcade of shops which serviced both the residents and their many visitors alike. Security was as tight as it could be considering that it was a busy residential home. It was a private concern which was open to the public. Each resident had their own one bedroom apartment which offered them their independence, but they were under the umbrella of a full time medical team that supplied and distributed all their required medication and care. Some of the elderly residents were bedridden while others used the facilities' gymnasium every day. One of the fitter residents was eighty four year old Billy Wright.

Billy had joined the Royal Navy when war broke out in nineteen thirty nine. He trained with thousands of other sailors at HMS Indefatigable. His father was an old seadog and he used his influence to convince his young son to opt for a career beneath the waves as a submariner. The logic was that Hitler's navy would be less likely to torpedo him if he were deep beneath the surface, and the chances of him returning home to his family would be greatly increased. Today he was excited because he was to be visited by a journalist from the Royal Navy who was coming to interview him as one of the few surviving submariners from the Atlantic fleet. He was immensely proud of his war record. Billy had been eighteen when he climbed into his first submarine as an eager junior officer. By the end of the war at the tender age of twenty four he was the navy's youngest submarine captain. The British submarine fleet were responsible for the destruction of two million tons of enemy shipping, the sinking of fifty seven warships and thirty five German U-boat submarines. Submarine Commander Billy Wright had kept his ship's log which documented every encounter he had ever been involved in throughout his naval career. He once had to turn over all the sub's paperwork to the navy's record officials, something to do with the 'Official Secrets Act', but Billy always documented everything in duplicate so he'd retained his duplicate log for posterity. The log had remained Billy's secret for decades and it had never once caused him any issues for years, until he began to receive letters from the son of a naval man who had been lost in the war. Billy read the first letter which disturbed him so much that he never read anymore of them. He marked them with 'return to sender' and never gave them a second thought.

Billy had dressed in his Sunday best, suited and booted with his medal ribbon shining proudly on his chest. He sat and fidgeted nervously as he waited for the journalist to arrive. He was a punctual man and he was annoyed that the journalists were already half an hour late. They had probably been delayed by the snow and he would be alerted as soon as they arrived. The reception desk had a policy of checking visitor's identification and then contacting the residents to let them know that their guests had arrived.

His telephone rung and it startled him. He leapt to his feet and eagerly picked it up. He polished his medals with his sleeve nervously.

"Hello Billy, your guests have arrived and they apologise for being late but they were delayed by the snow. Shall I send them down to you?" the medical receptionist sounded cheerier than usual.

"Guests, in the plural? I was only expecting there to be a journalist," Billy said sounding surprised.

"Well he has photographer with him too," she informed him curtly, reverting back to her usual grumpy personality.

"Oh. I see, well you had better send them down here then," he said running his hand over his thinning silver hair instinctively. The mention of the word photographer invoked a natural vanity.

"They'll be with you any second, enjoy," she warbled. Billy looked at the handset as he heard her disconnect. She had either had a personality transplant or she had gotten laid, one or the other.

A loud knock at the door disturbed his thoughts and he looked in the mirror and straightened his tie before he headed for the door. Billy approached the door and was slightly irritated when his guests knocked loudly again. Before he could reach for the handle it was turned by someone from the outside and the door was flung open.

"Just a minute, how dare you?" the old submariner bumbled as two burly men burst into the apartment. "When I was in the navy we were taught to wait until a door was opened before we were invited into.....," Billy didn't finish his sentence.

The first man into the room had long hair swept into a dark ponytail. Billy instantly knew that he was not an enlisted sailor, journalist or otherwise. The man with the ponytail hit Billy square in the face. The thunderous blow floored him and broke his nose. The man's huge fist split his top lip and cracked two teeth and his jawbone simultaneously. Billy could taste the coppery flavour of his own blood running down the back of his throat. He wanted to cry out but he was losing consciousness and could only manage a throaty gurgle. The man with the ponytail stamped down hard on his stomach. The vicious stomp crushed the wind from his lungs and Billy felt like he was going to suffocate. The second man grabbed him by the ankles and dragged him across the carpet. Billy grabbed at the furniture as he passed trying to break free, but every time he gained purchase ponytail stamped on his fingers. Billy could feel his skin being burned by the friction on the carpet and he arched his back to escape the agony. He dug his fingernails deep into the pile but the man was too strong and Billy was too old and frail to break free. Billy felt his index fingernail being ripped off as it stuck in the carpet pile. He tried to scream again but could only manage a garbled cry. Ponytail kicked him hard in the face. The impact shattered his cheek bone beneath the left eye socket and all but put paid to his feeble resistance. Submarine Commander Billy Wright lost consciousness.

CHAPTER 6

Liverpool Bay, December 14ᵗʰ 1943, 2ⁿᵈ Officer William Wright

Billy Wright was still a very inexperienced young submariner, but with war raging at full pelt and Hitler's 'Unterseeboots', or U-boats, wreaking havoc across the oceans of the world, good officers were hard to come by. Billy and his submarine crew had sailed from Portsmouth harbour two weeks earlier on a routine hunter mission, looking for U-boats and protecting allied convoys from German destroyers. The captain had received the details of a new mission ten days into the voyage. The details of the new mission had been secured in the submarine's safe box upon departure and were only to be opened on command. They had been sealed in a brown manila envelope, and were only to be opened on the orders of the Admiral of the Fleet. Ten days into the voyage the order had come through that the captain was to replace his existing orders with the new ones in the safe box. The captain set new coordinates and the submarine began her new mission. No one but the captain knew where they were sailing toward. Billy had developed a good sense of direction, even beneath the waves. By his reckoning they had sailed south toward France and Spain, before navigating a wide 'U' turn which had put them on a course for the Irish Sea.

The atmosphere on board had been tense. The uncertainty of any secret missions led to rumours and the sceptics on board had a field day speculating about where they were headed and why. Billy had overheard some of the crew discussing that they were heading on a secret mission to kill Hitler himself. Who was actually going to carry out the alleged assassination was beyond his imagination, but if it kept the men occupied then so be it.

The air inside the submarine was dank and stale, a mixture of male sweat and diesel engine oil. Conditions were cramped, unhygienic, and privacy was nonexistent. This particular voyage had been made worse by an outbreak of food poisoning which in the confined space of a submarine was nothing short of a disaster. A rogue batch of pork pies which were meant to be a treat had been riddled with staphylococcus bacteria. The bacteria are carried by most people in their nasal fluids and are spread usually by poor hand washing procedures, or in this case by people sneezing into the pork mince as they prepared the pies. The effect of an outbreak of vomiting and diarrhoea in such confined quarters was devastating. No sooner had the submariners been laid up for forty eight hours or more as the bacteria passed through them, than they were re-infected by their shipmates as they contracted the virus too. The voyage was shambolic as men soiled their pants waiting in line for the toilets to become vacant. The smell inside the submarine was dreadful. The submarine commander had requested permission from the admiralty to put into port to seek medical attention and to disinfect the vessel, but permission was refused point blank. They could not deviate from their mission.

On December the 14th the commander was taken ill for the second time of asking. He was confined to his quarters where he was squirting bodily fluids from both ends simultaneously. He called for his junior officer to be sent to his cabin. Billy Wright was recovering from his first dose of poisoning, but he was in much better shape than his superior officer. He could hear the commander retching as he knocked on the cabin door.

"Enter," the commander moaned.

"You needed to see me sir," Billy said. He was holding his breath to avoid having to smell the sickening mixture of fresh vomit and excrement. His own stomach was still queasy from the illness.

"Come in and close the door William," the commander said.

"Yes sir."

"I need you to take command William, read through this set of orders and match the detail to the charts. Once you have plotted the new coordinates onto the charts you must destroy the old ones. There can be no record of this voyage. You will need to memorise the charts as they cannot leave this cabin, do you understand?"

"Yes sir," Billy answered, although he didn't really understand anything yet.

"The admiralty is concerned that there are leaks in the ranks and that important naval data is being fed to the Germans.....," the commander stopped mid sentence to vomit in the bucket which he had placed strategically next to his private toilet. That way he could vomit and excrete at the same time. His eyes streamed with tears at the effort and sticky globules of saliva dangled from the corner of his mouth.

"Forgive me. The admiralty has information that the German Navy is disguising merchant ships as British warships and using them to transport spies to the mainland under the cover of darkness." He retched again but this time nothing came up. "They are using Ireland as cover in daylight and then sailing into the Irish Sea at night."

Billy studied the charts and the set of orders. It all seemed to be perfectly legitimate. The information was concise but not so accurate that it was suspicious. Rogue ships were being spotted by fishing vessels at night, across a wide area of the Irish Sea, but particularly around the Bay of Liverpool. He nodded as he digested the orders.

"I am gauging that we are in or around the Bay of Liverpool now sir, is that correct?" Billy asked.

"Excuse me..," the commander vomited again. This time as he did so a loud farting noise came from his behind and Billy watched in horror as a brown stain began to spread across the commander's shorts.

"I have the instructions Commander, I'll get onto it straight away." Billy picked up the orders and left the charts on the commander's table. The sound of vomit splattering into the bucket followed him into the tight corridor. Billy went directly to his own cabin. He had a good memory, but it was short term. Billy was well aware of his ability to retain information, and he knew his weaknesses as well. He took his own set of charts from his desk and transferred the data that he had seen in the commander's cabin onto his own. It was the only way he could be sure to remember his orders. Once he was happy with the charts he hid them in his desk, just in case he might forget. He headed back into the bridge area with his new orders fixed in his mind. The submarine sailed its new course for two hours without incident.

"Take her up to periscope depth," Billy ordered.

"Eye, eye, sir," a midshipman gave the reply and then repeated the order to everyone who was within earshot in true naval fashion. The vessel groaned as the submarine blew ballast and it headed closer to the surface.

Billy Wright brought up the periscope and pressed his forehead against the sight mask. He scanned the horizon and turned the scope a full circle. If there were spy ships out there it was very unlikely that they would be burning any kind of lights at all. Seeking the hulk of a vessel in the darkness was a skill and Billy had learned never to allow his first glance to convince him that there was nothing there to see. He swung the scope around once more, but slowly this time as his eyes became accustomed to the darkness. There it was in the blackness, a dark hulk, darker than the night that surrounded it. There was no doubt that it was a warship at first glance. Billy could make out the bridge and the foredeck gun turret. It was the foredeck gun which made him look again.

"Pass me the identification chart," Billy ordered without taking his eyes from the scope. The chart was a poster which had the silhouettes of every type of naval vessel known to the Admiralty, and it was updated with new sheets every time a ship made port. Billy scanned the hulk in the scope and he matched it mentally with every ship he had seen. It looked similar to a frigate, but it wasn't a real frigate. The fore gun turret wasn't the correct shape. It looked more like the deck gun of a German U-boat. The information from the Admiralty was looking solid. The vessel in the scope was a merchant ship disguised to look like a warship.

"Number three, I need you to identify the vessel in the scope," Billy Wright followed procedure and gained a second opinion from his nearest ranking officer.

"Eye, eye sir."

"All ahead slow and maintain our course," Billy ordered as he checked the identification charts. He knew the silhouettes of every naval warship by heart but he checked them anyway. The midshipman echoed the order across the submarine.

"I can't identify her sir, She looks like a merchant ship to me with a deck gun welded to the foredeck sir."

"Excellent number three, my thoughts exactly. Load forward torpedo tubes one and two, and then rear tubes four and five" Billy had a rush of adrenalin as he gave the order. They had been sent on a search and destroy mission. They had found their prey and now they would move in for the kill.

"Number three I need you to relay the status to the commander and get his authorisation to fire," Billy watched his prey through the scope.

"Eye, eye sir." The officer turned and disappeared down the metal corridor.

"Torpedoes are ready sir."

"Thank you, hold her steady," Billy had the vessel dead centre of the sights. There was a ruffling down the corridor as the number three officer returned.

"The commander says that you have command of the ship sir."

"Thank you number three. Fire torpedoes," Billy Wright gave the order. The submarine shook as two huge torpedoes were launched from the forward torpedo room. Billy watched as they reached the surface and then ploughed through the waves toward their target. The disguised merchant vessel had no chance. It was a sitting duck. Two white wakes hurtled toward the stern of the ship, and a few seconds later the ship exploded into a huge fireball.

"Fire torpedo four," Billy ordered.

"Eye, eye sir. Firing torpedo number four."

Within minutes the holed vessel had tipped vertical as the holds below decks filled with sea water. It seemed to float for a moment before sliding quickly beneath the surface. The whole thing from impact to sinking was less than two minutes.

It was the first of three vessels that they sank that night. It was a memorable night for the crew and junior officers of the submarine. Each suspect area on the charts given to them by the Admiralty yielded another victim. Their information was spot on, almost too good, but the adrenalin rush created by the sinking of enemy shipping had wiped out any concerns the young submariner may have had. They had no idea that they were sending British sailors to the bottom of the ocean along with the biggest cargo of mustard gas shells ever manufactured. Billy Wright kept the charts which marked the coordinates of every attack in his personal belongings as a souvenir of his fantastic achievements that night. One day he would regret keeping them.

CHAPTER 7
Tank

Chen walked back into the meeting room with a stack of papers underneath his arm. Every resource that the intelligence agencies possessed was being applied to tracking down the whereabouts of the submarine commander that Geoff Evans had been stalking and bombarding with letters. They were working on the supposition that if Commander William Wright was still alive then he may have vital information that could lead the taskforce to the possible chemical weapon dump sites. The Terrorist Task Force were working on the speculative information gathering of one aggrieved man, who believed that his father had been killed during a government cover up. There seemed to be very little hard evidence to follow but there was some substance behind the theory. It was up to the taskforce to fill in the blanks and add the detail. Tank and Grace Farrington had left the headquarters a half an hour earlier to check out the aging submariner's last known address. Unfortunately when they arrived at the address the houses that once stood there had been demolished and modern apartments had been constructed in their place. It was a complete dead end.

"I have the latest electoral roll details here," Chen announced proudly patting the thick wad of papers that he was carrying.

"Do we have any possible locations?" Major Stanley Timms asked without looking up from his laptop screen.

"Yes we have one hundred and forty six men called William Wright in the Liverpool area. However if we consider the rest of the country then we have seventy thousand males named William Wright, and two thousand females christened Willamina

Wright," Chen beamed a toothy smile.

The Major rolled his eyes skywards behind the cover of his computer screen. It looked like Chen was going to do all his thinking out loud. He liked to do that to the annoyance of the rest of the team. Major Timms carried on his internet search in silence despite Chen's attention seeking.

"Of course if we discard the females and the men who are under eighty years of age then we are left with a much more manageable list of names. If we were to concentrate the search to Merseyside then we are investigating a total of six men, assuming that this information is correct," Chen frowned at the Major, who was taking absolutely no notice of his display of investigative prowess.

"Billy Wright lives at the Sunnyside Rest Home, Orford, Warrington. Tell Tank and Grace immediately," the Major said, looking over the top of his screen. He tapped the print button on the keyboard and stood up to retrieve the information from the printer. Chen looked confused.

"How did you narrow that down so quickly?" Chen asked flatly. He was obviously put out by the Major's success in finding out the information before he had.

"I logged onto the Royal Navy's benevolent fund. They pay the medical bills and accommodation for a retired submarine commander by the name of William Wright, aged eighty four at the Sunnyside Care Home. Technology at its cutting edge Chen my boy," the Major winked at his disgruntled agent as he handed him the details and Chen forced a smile.

"I'll check it out myself and make sure that he is still alive and well," Chen picked up the telephone and dialled the care home. The line crackled and then connected to the number. It rang twice and then it was answered by the grumpy receptionist. Her brief attempt at being polite had long since past.

"Hello Sunnyside, how may I help you?"

"Hello, I'm calling to enquire about the status of a beneficiary of ours, a retired submarine commander by the name of William Wright," Chen enquired charmingly. He smiled brightly as if the receptionist could see it.

"Are you really, and who is enquiring please?"

"I work for a government agency," Chen replied, parting with as little information as he could.

"Well our Billy Wright is quite the celebrity today isn't he? He is definitely a man in demand at the moment," the receptionist wittered sourly.

"Oh is he indeed?" Chen pursued. "I assume that he has received some other recent enquiries then."

"Yes he has, people have been calling for the last few days. He is being interviewed by the Royal Navy's journalists as we speak, and a photographer too, but I'm sure that you are aware of that anyway," the receptionist studied her manicure with a critical eye as she spoke.

Chen made a note on the pad in front of him. He ripped it off and handed it to the Major. The Major frowned. He picked up the phone on his desk and stabbed a speed dial number. The call was answered and the Major spoke quietly into handset.

"Get hold of the Naval Benevolent Fund and speak to the secretary. I want to know why Commander William Wright is being interviewed by naval reporters. I want the telephone records of every call that has been made to that nursing home for the last two weeks, and I need them quickly," the Major instructed.

"Yes sir. I'll do that straight away sir."

The Major switched his handset to another channel so that he could hear the conversation that Chen was having with the receptionist at the nursing home.

"How long have our naval journalists been with Commander Wright?" Chen asked politely.

"I checked their identification details fifteen minutes ago exactly," the receptionist replied as she checked her visitors' book. She was very proud of her rigorous attention to detail.

"I see, I didn't get your name," Chen said leaving the sentence unfinished to prompt a reply.

"Yvonne, my name is Yvonne," she answered.

"What a beautiful name, Yvonne was my mother's name," Chen lied. The Major raised an eyebrow as he listened to Chen trying to charm information from the gullible receptionist.

"Thank you," she blushed.

"I wonder if you saw which agency they were from, we have so many these days," Chen lied again.

"I didn't get the exact agency I'm afraid. It said Royal Navy on their cards. They had press cards though I'm sure of that. I've seen hundreds of press cards before so I can be certain of that. Is there a problem?" she became defensive as her procedures came under scrutiny and obvious failings were exposed.

"I'm sure you have Yvonne, don't worry there is no problem. Thanks for your help," Chen hung up the call.

"It could be nothing," the Major said.

"Then again it could be something," Chen speculated. "I don't believe in coincidence."

"How far away from Warrington are Grace and Tank?" the Major asked.

"Five minutes at the most. I'll redirect them immediately," Chen was reaching for the telephone as he spoke. "I think it would be prudent to investigate the commander and his journalist friends sooner rather than later."

"Absolutely," the Major concurred.

There was silence on the line for a second, and then a polyphonic ring tone followed.

"John Tankersley speaking," Tank's gruff voice appeared on the conference line.

"Tank we have an address for the commander," Chen said.

"Give it to us."

"Sunnyside Rest Home, Orford, Warrington, do you know the area?"

"Yes I know it, we're not far from there now. The snow is slowing things down but it's only minutes away," Grace interrupted.

"How recent is the information?" Tank asked. He indicated to the traffic behind him that he was turning right. The nursing home was less than two miles away from them.

"It's spot on. I've confirmed with the reception that he is there, and that he has a naval background."

Tank looked at Grace and they exchanged a glance that said neither of them was totally happy with the situation. There seemed to be something in Chen's tone that implied that there was more to the story than an address.

"Is there anything else that we need to know?" Tank asked.

Chen looked to the Major to reply. The Major nodded and

took the lead.

"When we contacted the nursing home they mentioned that the commander had been receiving several enquiries this week. He is also being interviewed today by someone from the Navy, a journalist accompanied by a photographer."

" When is his interview?"

"It started fifteen minutes ago."

"I have the feeling that you're not totally comfortable with something," Tank pressed.

"We are making some enquiries with the Navy into the nature of the interview, but I haven't had any details back yet," the Major explained. "I have a hunch that we're not the only ones looking for Commander Billy Wright. Wait a minute Tank, there is some new information here."

A blond haired agent walked to the Major's desk and handed him a printed page. She was dressed in an immaculate grey pinstripe suit, although the Major noticed that her hemline was a little too short. He studied the paper and his face darkened as he digested the information. The line remained silent as the taskforce agents waited for the major to speak.

"The Royal Navy haven't sent anyone to interview Billy Wright, journalist or otherwise, and as far as they are concerned there have been no enquiries made by them as to his current status. All their enquiries about beneficiaries are made formally on a quarterly basis, and that was completed last month. You had better hurry Tank, and I'll send backup immediately," the Major passed the printed information to Chen and he sprang into action to despatch armed backup.

"Roger that Major, we're nearly there. Two minutes at the most," Grace Farrington answered. She removed a set of keys and opened a lock box which was situated between the seats of their black Jeep. Inside were four Glock 9mm automatic pistols, the choice weapon of Special Forces the world over because of their accuracy and reliability. She slotted a magazine of seventeen soft nosed high velocity bullets into each pistol and holstered two pistols for herself. British counter terrorist units favour soft nosed bullets because they spread on impact with the skull causing the maximum damage to the brain of a suspect. Because the bullets are soft they remain inside the victim's skull which reduces the risk of collateral damage to bystanders from a 'through and through' round. Tank brought the Jeep to a screeching halt in the nursing home car park. He took the two remaining Glock automatics, holstered them and turned to Grace.

"You take the back of the building and I'll go in the front way, I've got a feeling this is going to turn nasty."

CHAPTER 8
Commander Billy Wright

Billy Wright woke up with a start. His face felt completely numb and he couldn't swallow. His last few conscious moments rushed back to him in a flash and he tried to move but he was tied fast. He swallowed hard and got the thick copper taste of his own blood sliding down the back of his throat. There was something in his mouth impeding his ability to swallow properly. He tried to call out but couldn't. As his senses returned to him he could hear running water, and then he felt the sensation of being in water, very cold water. Billy opened his eyes and he blinked hard as he tried to work out what was happening to him. He saw the clinical white tiles of his bathroom and he recognised the light fitting that he had fitted himself two months ago. Strong hands grabbed his thinning hair and pushed his head roughly beneath the water. He thrashed about but couldn't find any relief from the vice like grip of his attacker. Billy felt as if his lungs were about to burst when the strong hands pulled him clear of the water. He gasped and almost choked on the gag. He felt a big hand squeezing his broken jaw and salty tears filled his bleary eyes. The gag was pulled clear and he gulped fresh air deep into his lungs.

"This can be as quick and simple as you make it old man," a thick guttural voice rasped. Billy thought he could detect an Eastern European accent, probably Polish. He thought it was strange that even though he was more frightened than he had ever been, his brain was still processing information in a calm logical manner. Perhaps his brain was protecting him from complete panic. 'The man that is trying to drown you has a Polish accent'.

"You are Commander William Wright, correct?"

Billy nodded his head slowly. Even the slightest movement of his head made the pain in his broken face feel like hot knives were piercing his brain.

"Very good" the voice rasped. "You were the second officer on board a British submarine in forty three?"

Billy Wright nodded again. He squeezed his eyes tightly closed as a bolt of pain ripped through his nervous system.

"Well done Commander. Your submarine was sent to the Irish Sea to hunt for German spy vessels, is that correct?" the gravelly voice asked.

Billy opened his eyes wide and cast his memory back in time. His submarine had been sent to seek and destroy several suspected German merchant vessels which had been disguised as British war ships. Their mission was to find them, identify them as spy ships and destroy them. The Admiralty had informed the submarine fleet that the Germans were trying to land German spies on the mainland by sea and by parachute. Allegedly the German boats were sailing from the cover of southern Ireland at dusk, deploying their spies by rubber dinghy under the cover of darkness and then retreating back to their hideouts in the daylight hours. His memories disappeared as his head was forced back under the water. He gurgled and a rush of air bubbled from his mouth as he choked again.

"Yes or no old man, did your submarine receive orders to search and destroy German spy ships in the Irish Sea?" the gravelly voice sounded distorted from beneath the surface but Billy understood the question and he nodded. The man released the pressure on him and dragged him up for air again. Billy coughed and fluid flew from his nostrils. His confused brain raced through the possible scenarios, befuddled by pain and the lack of oxygen. He couldn't understand why these men were torturing him. Billy had been prepared to answer questions about his war service, but this wasn't what he had in mind when he agreed to meet reporters.

"We need to know the exact location of the ships that you torpedoed on that mission," the guttural accent rasped again.

"Please, it was so long ago, I have no idea....," Billy gasped as his head was pushed back beneath the water. This time he had no time to fill his lungs with air and he felt that he really would drown. What strength the octogenarian had was spent. Darkness filled his mind as his lung screamed for air.

"You're going to kill him," an unfamiliar voice spoke for the first time. Billy's brain identified it as English, probably public school educated. Funny that he was so close to death yet his hearing was still sharp. He remembered that he was once told that the last thing to fail when you die was your hearing. He felt cold air on his face as he was pulled free of the water. His lungs rattled as he drew breath and fresh air had never tasted so good.

"He has several ships' log books in here, some charts and hundreds of pictures," the English voice spoke again. This time it sounded like he had walked back into Billy's living room. Billy could hear him routing about through his precious belongings. There was a clatter as something was thrown across the room, and then Billy could hear the distinctive whirring of a camera phone. There were several flashes from the other room.

"Did you record the sinking of the German spy ships on any of those charts?"

"I don't think so, it was so long ago. I can't remember.....," Billy gasped the answer but was forced under the water again. He was too weak to struggle anymore and he welcomed death to come and take him, but it refused to end his torment just yet. The strong hands pulled his thinning hair and he was above the suffocating liquid once more.

"You had better remember quickly old man. Did you record the details of sinking the German spy ships, or not?"

"I may have a copy marked of an oceanic chart with the suspect sectors that we were given to search on one of our missions," Billy gasped for breath. His will to survive was far greater than his allegiance to protect a sixty year old chart.

"How can we identify it?"

"I would have to show you," Billy Wright gasped. Maybe he could get them to lift him out of the bath. Billy could see a glimmer of hope. The pain from his shattered cheek bone was becoming unbearable and his eye was swollen completely shut. Talking sent spasms of pain through his broken jaw and the nerve endings in his teeth were screaming. He knew that he was close to death. He also knew that the only reason he was still alive was because these men needed the whereabouts of an ancient sea chart.

"Just tell me how to identify it old man, or do you want to go back under the water permanently?"

"They all look the same unless you know what you're looking for," Billy's voice was becoming nothing more than a whisper.

"They do all look the same. Drag him out of there," the English voice spoke from the other room.

"For fuck's sake just bring the charts in here and let him show us in here. How many are marked with a year on them?" the Polish accent snarled.

"None of them have a year on them. Do you think I'm a fucking idiot?" the English voice retorted. "Now get him out of that fucking bath before I shoot you through the head."

Billy heard the venom in their voices and it gave him a lift up from the dark place that he was in. They were arguing with each other, and that could only be good. The fact that they had guns was not a good thing though, unless they shot each other of course. The man grabbed Billy by the feet and yanked him hard. Billy was pulled roughly beneath the water before being lifted clear of the bath completely. His back was scraped badly as he was hauled clear of the rim. The man continued to pull him and Billy's head struck the bathroom floor hard. The fracture in his jaw splintered sending a bolt of white hot pain through his body. This time Billy screamed louder than he had ever screamed before.

"Shut him up you bloody fool, do you want the world and his wife to hear him?"

"I told you that we should leave him in the bath. Don't talk to me as if I'm stupid or I'm warning you....," the guttural accent snarled.

"You're warning me what exactly?" the English accent growled back.

"Look let's just take all the fucking charts and get out of here. Everyone in the building must have heard him scream."

"I've photographed the charts on my camera phone. What about him?"

"Kill him. No one must know why we were here."

Billy Wright squeezed his eyes tightly and waited for a bullet to end his torment.

CHAPTER 9
Tank

Tank was less than fifty yards down the corridor when he heard a blood curdling scream. He was being accompanied by a female member of the nursing staff who had insisted that she must ask William Wright if his interview with the navy press reporter could be interrupted. She had tried his room phone but the line was dead, so she opted to escort the hunky new visitor herself. Life behind the reception desk was very mundane and the appearance a strange muscle bound male was always welcome, even if he was very frosty and disinterested in her. When they heard the scream she froze on the spot and pointed toward Billy's door with a shaking hand. Tank drew his Glock and waved her away.

"Get these rooms emptied now, and make sure no one comes down this corridor," Tank whispered to her sternly.

As he approached Billy's room Tank assessed the door and the frame with an expert eye in less than a second. There was no time to show caution. He was going through that door no matter what the outcome. Tank hit the door with his huge shoulder, running at full pelt. The wood frame cracked down the middle and the hinges were ripped from their fixing as the door disintegrated beneath the colossal force. The momentum carried Tank through the doorway and into Billy's apartment. He dipped his shoulder and rolled onto the floor. His eyes scanned the room and his brain calculated the situation that he was presented with before him.

There were three men. One of the men was old and badly beaten. His eye was swollen shut and his facial features were horribly distorted by purple bruising and ugly swelling around his mouth and jaw. He was being held up by the feet, his head and shoulders were on the floor supporting his body weight. Two men stood frozen for an instant, just long enough for Tank to identify the good guys and the bad guys, and to pick his first target. The man holding the old man had a long dark ponytail. His hands were occupied holding Billy Wright, which meant that he wasn't a threat for the moment. The second man had greying hair swept back from his face and jelled to his scalp. He looked like a Wall Street banker dressed in a sharp suit. As Tank weighed up the situation the banker reached inside his jacket. Reaching for his gun was the last decision that he ever made. Tank aimed his model 17 Glock automatic and squeezed the trigger three times. Classic Special Forces training is to shoot three times tap, tap, tap, two bullets to the chest and one to the head. The first bullet hit the sternum and flattened before ripping a path through the chest cavity and bursting his right lung. The second ripped a three inch rent through his heart before finally stopping in the liver. The third hit him square in the centre of his forehead. The bullet hole was a neat circle surrounded by ragged blackened skin. Once the high velocity soft nosed bullet was inside the skull it bounced around like a red hot pinball turning the brain matter into mush. He was dead before he hit the floor.

Ponytail dropped the old man and sprinted for the kitchen area. He grabbed a handful of maps as his colleague crumpled onto the carpet. Tank fired at the fleeing man and two bullets shattered into the wall showering the man with plaster shards. A third shot clipped his upper arm and he cried out in a language that Tank didn't understand. Ponytail ran headlong without showing any sign of stopping. He took a huge leap up onto a dining chair and then stepped onto the kitchen table kicking a crystal fruit bowl and its contents across the room. He covered his face with his hands and launched himself toward the window. Tank fired again and the bullet smashed into the fleeing man's shoulder. Ponytail hit the glass pane at speed and the window shattered into a thousand pieces as he crashed through it. Tank heard gun shots coming from outside and guessed that Grace was firing at the fugitive as he fled the building through the window. He reached the window and watched as ponytail sprinted across a grass lawn toward the car park. Grace was seventy yards to the left of his vision, and she was sprinting level to the fugitive, stopping every time she had a clear shot. She kneeled and fired again. The bullet ricocheted off the brick building spraying brick shards across the grass. There were civilians milling about and they hindered Grace taking aim. A black Mercedes screeched across the car park toward the running man, but Grace was in between them. She heard the gunning engine and turned toward the speeding vehicle. Grace had a split second to fire or jump out of the way, but she couldn't do both. She dived across the bonnet of a Ford Mondeo narrowly avoiding the Mercedes as it roared past her. Grace rolled off the other side and cracked her head on the front wing of a Transit van. The impact stunned her momentarily and she lost her grip on the Glock. It skidded across the layer of snow which had coated the tarmac.

Tank fired at the vehicle twice. The driver's window exploded into a million pieces. He could see the driver covering his eyes from the flying shards as he pulled the Mercedes to a screeching halt. Ponytail jumped over the bonnet of the car and the passenger door was thrown open as the driver leaned across the vehicle to allow him entry. The rear wheels went into a spin as the tyres tried to gain purchase on the tarmac. Ponytail flung the charts into the vehicle and made ready to climb in. Tank steadied his wrist and squeezed the trigger once more. The weapon recoiled and a second later a large red hole appeared on the centre of Ponytails forehead. His head jerked back as if he had been hit with an invisible sledgehammer, and he was tossed from the vehicle like a ragdoll. The Mercedes sped away toward the main road leaving ponytail dead on the car park. There were too many civilians milling about near the main road for Tank or Grace to fire again, and their vehicle was at the front of the building. By the time they reached it the Mercedes would be a mile away.

CHAPTER 10
Canning Place, Liverpool

"How is the old man," Tank asked as Grace Farrington walked into the bunker meeting room. The Canning Place police station was the nerve centre of the taskforce operation, and was also the government's secret communication centre. Three traffic tunnels had been built beneath the River Mersey in the sixties and seventies, and the British Government used the huge construction project to camouflage the building of a bunker network beneath the city. The idea was that in the event of war London would be destroyed. Liverpool offered a safer haven than the capital city, and could facilitate smuggling the cabinet ministers out of the country via submarine if an enemy invasion was imminent.

"He's not good at all. He has a compound fracture of the jaw, a depressed cheekbone and several broken ribs. At eighty four years old that's a lot to cope with," Grace walked to the table and placed her bag on the back of the chair before sitting down.

"Will he live?" Helen Walsh asked. Helen had been brought into the meeting to act as a medical advisor for the government. She was primarily a physiotherapist, but she had studied the effect of blister agents on the human body as part of her thesis at university. The interest had turned into a professional one as she collated information from all over the world about chemical weapons and their effects on the human condition, and the environment. Helen was a pretty woman, blond and lithe. She had turned at least a dozen heads when she entered the police headquarters above the government bunker.

"It's touch and go at the moment."

"How much information did he give to you," Major Stanley

Timms asked, cutting through the niceties and getting to the point of the meeting.

"Between the information from the commander and the evidence recovered from his apartment we have a reasonable idea about what's happening," Grace replied. She removed a note book from her bag which contained some prompts for her to refer to.

"Are we expecting any other departments?" Chen asked. He flicked on the digital screen and placed the remote on the table in front of him.

"No. We need to be one hundred percent certain of what we are dealing with before we bring in the other agencies," the Major replied.

"What about the Royal Navy? Surely we'll need them to monitor any possible dump sites," Helen Walsh asked naively.

Everyone turned to look at her and she blushed crimson.

"It would probably be a little too obvious to have a great big battleship sitting out in the Bay of Liverpool. The terrorists may think that we're onto them," Tank said sarcastically. Helen blushed again and played with her pen nervously.

The Major chuckled and patted her on the back patronisingly. He was trying to put her at ease, but it had the opposite effect. Helen felt patronised.

"As I said, we need to be certain of our facts before we start bringing in any other agencies at all," the Major looked at the faces around the table. "The twenty twelve Olympics is the biggest showpiece that our small nation has been honoured with since the World Cup of nineteen sixty six. We must avoid any potential disasters at all costs, and more importantly, we must never allow a sniff of any plot to leak into the press. It would be an international catastrophe of unprecedented proportions if this potential threat were to become public knowledge." The Major eyed everyone individually to reinforce the point that he was making.

"I am still not completely clear as to why Christopher Walsh would want to attack the games at all, what is the motive?" Chen asked.

"There doesn't seem to be any clear political benefit," Grace added.

"Maybe he has developed a new focus, an extremist cause to follow," Tank speculated.

"It is all pure speculation at the moment, all we have is the information found by the intelligence service which has led us this far," the Major said. "The attack on William Wright demonstrates that a determined enemy is planning something doesn't it?"

"It certainly supports what we suspected, but the motives are still unclear," Chen said. He shrugged his shoulders and turned the palms of his hands face up as if the answer may drop into them.

"If I may, I might have a reason for him to plan such an attack," all eyes turned back to Helen Walsh, and the blond blushed again. She coughed and regained her composure.

"Christopher Walsh is related to me, hence the same surname," she began. The Major's face darkened and he looked at Chen who was responsible for bringing advisors to the taskforce table.

"I didn't realise," Chen said shocked. "It never crossed my mind because it is such a common surname."

"He is a very distant relation. I am only aware of him because of our interest in science, chemistry especially. My parents used him as an example for me to emulate," Helen interrupted. "What I do know about him is that he is, or was, always highly motivated by money." She flipped through some textbooks that she had brought with her, looking for something specific.

"As you know I'm here because of my knowledge of blister agents, and their effects on the human condition," she waffled as she rummaged through book after book. "Please bear with me a moment, I'm sure I can shine some light on the issue."

"Perhaps you could give us some indication of your theory while you find what you're looking for Miss Walsh," the Major prompted her.

"Helen, please call me Helen. Christopher was often under a dark cloud at university, and then medical school," she nodded vigorously to emphasise her point, although it wasn't clear to anyone else in the room.

Tank rolled his eyes toward the ceiling and Grace threw him a scolding glance. Grace was empathetic to the dizzy young woman. Being thrust into the male dominated world of Special Forces and government agencies was a very daunting task.

"Do you mean that he was in trouble at university?" Grace tried to help her out.

"Oh my god yes, terrible, terrible trouble," Helen became excited as she spoke. She had found the text that she was looking for. "Here it is."

"Please share it with us before I explode with anticipation and excitement," Tank folded his thick arms across his chest. Helen glanced at him and thought about telling him that he was rude, but the look in his eyes warned her off the idea.

"What kind of trouble?" Grace prompted her again.

"I'm sorry, I'm being vague aren't I?"

"Almost nebulous," Tank muttered under his breath, which drew another withering glance from Grace.

"He used his interest in chemicals and his superior knowledge to make money at every opportunity," Helen smiled widely as if this snippet of information explained everything.

"Oh for god sake," Tank hissed.

"Let me explain."

"Explain please, before I lose the will to live."

"Well, he started off innocently. He would make fireworks for the students on bonfire night, and sell them of course. Then he was suspended for distilling moonshine, which almost led to him being arrested. Later it became more serious, ecstasy tablets, LSD; he even produced a rough form of ketamine. Then there were rumours that he had been involved in making explosives to blow up a mosque, although he was released without charge."

"I'm failing to see the link here," Chen said.

"He never did anything for nothing, there was always money involved. That made me think about this article he published," she held up a copy of the Lancet. It was a medical magazine which was read the world over. "He published this article about the use of sodium hypochlorite as a treatment for blister agent burns."

There were several confused glances exchanged and the team struggled to grasp her point. Helen blushed again realising that she hadn't been successful in communicating her point.

"He had experimented with normal household bleach as a base chemical to neutralise the use of sulphur mustard gas. The bleach counteracts the effects, restoring the ph balance. He took the research so far that he claimed to have developed a liquid treatment for blister agent burns."

"You think that he is trying to sell his formula?" Grace clicked on.

"Yes, it makes perfect sense."

"If a terrorist blister agent attack was carried out at an Olympic Games venue it would receive world-wide news coverage," Tank clicked on to the idea too.

"Whoever had a formula to counteract the chemical could sell the formula to every government on the planet," Chen said, catching up.

"Even the threat of its use would drive the price through the roof," Helen Walsh looked relieved that her theory had finally been understood, and it appeared to have been accepted.

Tank sat back in his chair and smiled widely at Helen. She wasn't sure if he was scarier when he smiled or when he didn't.

CHAPTER 11
Liverpool Bay 2009

The Mersey Dock and Harbour Board was the owner of the River Mersey's commercial facilities and also responsible for the maintenance of the Manchester Ship Canal. The ship canal connected middle England to the ocean and carried millions of tons of aggregate for use in industry. The Harbour Board was a going concern and collected the rents and licence fees which amounted to a substantial financial reward for running the port. Until 1973 they were also responsible for the safety of shipping in Liverpool Bay, which involved the manning and maintenance of four lightships. The lightships were anchored permanently off shore and had huge revolving reflectors and oil lamps which warned approaching ships of dangerous shallows. The lightships were decommissioned over a period of decades and replaced one at a time by solar powered beacons which were drilled into the seabed. One or two of them were used every now and again to service the beacons which had made them obsolete. Two of the lightships were placed into maritime museums for posterity while another two were sold to private collectors and turned into tourist attractions.

Christopher Walsh bought one of them in a poor state of repair. She was a heavy metal boat painted a dull red colour to distinguish her from other shipping and to increase her visibility to other ships. She was over one hundred yards long and stood sixty feet above the water line. The light tower was positioned in the centre of the mid-ships above the bridge. Its previous owners had converted it into a floating coffee shop which was anchored in the Albert Docks for a number of years, but Christopher had other ideas for her. Below decks were a series of small cabins and several larger watertight compartments which had been perfect for his chemical experiments. The lightship never had a name, she was always 'L 2', which was painted in huge white figures on her stern. L2 had undergone comprehensive repairs at a dry dock near Seaforth, which was to the north of the city. The repair work had given him time to plan, but now that she was seaworthy and back in the water they were ready to put her back at sea for a short while. In the meantime he could use the lightship to continue with his live research undetected by prying eyes.

Christopher was reading the weather reports for the Irish Sea when he heard a diesel engine outside on the dock. He put the forecasts down and headed for the bridge. It was dark outside but he could clearly see that his panel van had returned from its mission. The driver and his mate jumped down from their seats and headed to the back doors. He could hear their guttural accents drifting across the dock to him. Christopher Walsh was using eastern European immigrant muscle to do his dirty work. As long as they were paid well, and on time, they were very loyal. They were also ruthless in their pursuit of a task. There was a heavy padlock fitted to a clasp, and the driver struggled with a set of keys before opening it. His mate climbed inside the van and Christopher could hear him banging around in the back of it. The driver reached inside, hidden by the back doors and then both men appeared again carrying the body of a man. He could tell it was a man from the matted beard he wore. That was a nuisance because it meant that he would have to shave him.

"Good, another one," Christopher Walsh said to himself, and he rubbed his hands together in glee. He turned and ran down the metal stairs to the lower decks, humming a tuneless song as he went. All the time he held tightly to the metal handrails, falling down these steps could be fatal. His footsteps echoed through the metal craft. At the bottom of the steps he reached a thick metal door. It had been designed to act as part of the superstructure when it was closed, and it was also watertight. In the centre of the door was a four inch thick piece of polished quartz, which acted as a window into the cabin beyond. Quartz was used by shipyards at the time the lightships were built because it could withstand far more pressure than glass. He looked through the quartz into the cabin.

The homeless man inside the cabin was once called Seth, but that was before he had been abducted from a park bench to be used in a scientific experiment. Seth was sat on a small bunk bed naked, although it was difficult to make out any distinguishing features because his body had become a mass of huge water filled blisters. His hands and feet looked like four yellow balloons, and the fingers and toes were virtually invisible, enveloped in bags of stinking puss. The skin on his chest and torso had become toad-like. There were blisters growing between blisters and the skin was stretched so thin that you could see the red layer of epidermis beneath it. His face looked like he had been attacked by a bear. There were deep rents in the flesh of his cheeks as if massive claws had sliced into him. The deep gashes were self inflicted and were a result of the terrible itching caused by the blister agent that Christopher Walsh had sprayed onto his flesh. The itching had been followed by an intense thirst. Seth had drunk two gallons of water in less than twenty minutes. The water intake had supplied the blisters with fluid, and now the slightest movement from the homeless man would cause his paper thin skin to burst. When the previous subjects that had been treated with the blister agent reached a similar condition their swollen blisters had burst, and then they had died soon afterward. Christopher had been fascinated by how much water they would drink once the thirst claimed them. He had even given some of them buckets of sea water instead of fresh water to see what would happen. The thirst that overwhelmed them was caused by blistering in the oesophagus and the victims couldn't distinguish between them and had drunk the lot. The best experiment so far though had been when he placed two of them into one cabin together. They had literally torn each other to pieces to get the water. He couldn't decide what he enjoyed watching the most, the thirst, or the itching. Watching them burst was fun too, although the smell when they removed the bodies was terrible. Seth would burst soon and then he could experiment with the new one that they had brought him. Two things were certain though, his serum to treat the burns didn't work once the blisters appeared. The subject had to be treated with the counter measure before the blisters had formed, and the second conclusion that he had drawn was that the thirst was worse than the blisters.

CHAPTER 12
The Terrorist Task Force

"What information did we find at the scene of the shooting?" the Major asked.

"We have the body of Charles Barr, an ex-army veteran. He was last known to the police for being deported from the Congo where he had been fighting as a mercenary. He was allegedly involved in a diamond smuggling operation. They said he had committed atrocities, although there were never any charges made," Chen answered. The picture of the dead man appeared on the screen followed by his regimental photograph which had been taken many years earlier. "We have his mobile phone, which has several pictures of certain sea charts stored on it. The pictures were taken shortly before his death, and we connected them with Billy Wright's memento collection."

"How did he die?" Helen Walsh asked quietly as she looked at the image of the body. She was visibly shaken by the picture of the dead man with a bullet through his forehead.

"Tank shot him," Chen answered.

"Oh," she said looking at Tank in horror.

"Don't concern yourself with that Helen please, Tank shoots lots of people," Chen said matter of factly. Tank smiled behind his hand enjoying Chen's sarcastic sense of humour. He really didn't like the use of civilian experts, but he understood their value to the taskforce. What he couldn't stand was their innocence and the way they judged with their eyes. They didn't know the first thing about the type of monsters the taskforce had to eliminate for the good of society as a whole. The civilians wanted to live in a peaceful society where no one was shot through the head by the authorities, but unfortunately the real world had a dark underside. That is where Tank and the taskforce lived and breathed.

"These are blow up images of the pictures that we took from the memory card in his telephone," Chen carried on and the screen displayed a series of blue sea charts.

"They all look the same to me," the Major said reaching inside his jacket pocket for his glasses.

"They are all the same, except for these three markings here, here and here," Chen pointed to the marks.

"I asked Commander Wright if they were significant and he's confirmed that they are the positions of three German spy boats which were torpedoed on the evening of December the fourteenth, nineteen forty three. The locations were given to the submarine commander at the time as top secret information by the Admiralty," Grace added. The room remained silent as the implication of the Admiralty being responsible for torpedoing their own men sank in.

"So we could indeed be dealing with a chemical weapons dump at sea," the Major conceded in a grave voice.

"We could be dealing with three," Chen added.

"Christopher Walsh only needs to get to one of them," Tank said. "We need to eliminate the deeper water sites and concentrate on the most accessible wreck. If he is going to retrieve shells then he will go for the most accessible load."

"I would agree," Chen concurred with Tank's theory.

"Shouldn't we be watching all three, just in case?" Helen Walsh asked. All eyes turned to her again. It appeared that she didn't understand the protocol required from a visiting expert, which was shut up until someone asks you a question.

"We could use the Royal Air Force or we could ask the intelligence agencies to commission a predator spy drone. Failing that we could place an advert in the News of the World asking everyone to keep their eyes peeled for some blokes recovering chemical weapons from the sea. That would be chemical weapons that never existed. That would be chemical weapons which one of the country's greatest leaders dumped in the ocean along with a few dozen sailors," Tank had lost his patience with the newcomer.

"Although Agent Tankersley has the tact of gorilla with a machinegun, you must understand that we operate independently of any other organisation or agency until we know exactly what we are dealing with," Grace tried to smooth it over. "We cannot trust the internal grapevine of any other military organisation not to leak this information to the press. Do you understand?"

"Yes. I'm sorry if I annoyed you Agent Tankersley," Helen said curtly, blushing once more.

"Oh, he isn't annoyed. You should see him when he's really pissed off," Chen joked. There were a few muffled giggles around the room but the look on the Major's face soon quelled the mirth.

"If we could get back to business please ladies and gentleman. Who was the second man?" the Major steered the meeting back on track.

"We don't know yet I'm afraid," Chen said switching the screen image to the dead body of ponytail. His forehead had been mashed by the soft nosed bullet from Tank's Glock. "He has tattoos which would place him from an Eastern European gang, but beyond that we have no matches of him on the DNA database or COTIS."

Helen Walsh looked at the image on the screen and then looked at Tank. He caught her eye as she looked at him and she suddenly realised that he didn't care what she thought. He was like a machine. Thank God he is on my side she thought, but she didn't speak this time. She didn't need to ask who had shot the man, because she already knew the answer.

"What about the mobile? Was there anything useful on that?" the Major asked.

"No. All of the call memory had been deleted. We are having the chip analysed to see if the tech boys can recover anything. We can assume that the charts which were stolen are the same as the ones in our possession, which means they have the details of the wreck sites," Chen said.

"We need to agree what our priorities are for the next twenty four hours," the Major said.

"We must allocate satellite time to Liverpool Bay. It is the only way we can monitor the area without arousing suspicion," Tank spoke first. Everyone nodded in agreement, except Helen Walsh.

She just looked at him warily and tried not to catch his eye.

"We have two potential satellites which cover that area but unfortunately that would give us a blind spot of ten hours every day," Chen explained.

"There is no way a salvage operation could be carried out in that period of time, is there?" Grace asked.

"Not without the presence of alien shipping in the area. We can access the Harbour Board and their manifesto, and then cross check it with anything that sails into these vectors," Chen replied.

"Okay, we are all agreed on that. What else would they need to recover the mustard gas shells?" Grace asked.

"That would very much depend on whether they intend to transport any salvage by sea, or if they plan to land it first, and then move it by road," Chen answered.

"What condition will this chemical ordinance be in after all this time under water?" Grace asked looking at Helen Walsh for the answer.

She blushed again and cleared her throat before speaking. She tried very hard not to look at Tank but she couldn't help herself. His piercing blue eyes made her uncomfortable, but she wanted to impress him somehow. She had been invited into an alien world of espionage and violence, and if she was to succeed here then she needed the respect of people like John Tankersley.

"I'm not an expert in munitions, but my guess is that the shells would have been stored in holds below deck, and some would have been piled on pallets on deck," she began.

"That would be our assumption also. We are in possession of a photograph which shows munitions stored in rows above decks," Grace encouraged her.

"If I'm correct then the munitions exposed to the sea will have corroded by now, releasing any vapour stored within them. The corrosion would have happened over such an extended period of time that the condition of each shell would be unique to itself. We would not have noticed any significant environmental evidence, although indigenous sea life may have declined in the immediate proximity of the wreck," she sounded more confident as she explained a subject that she was expert in.

"There has been a significant reduction in fish stocks all over

Liverpool Bay for decades," the Major interrupted looking over the top of his spectacles. Sea fishing was his favourite pastime and the oceanic environment was close to his heart. The decline of fish stocks in the waters around Britain was always attributed to overfishing by giant Icelandic trawlers, but even when quotas were introduced the decline continued unabated.

"Well whether that is a coincidence or not I can't tell you, but I can tell you that any munitions stored inside water tight holds will be in reasonable condition," she said.

"What do you mean by reasonable condition?" Tank wasn't one hundred percent certain what she meant.

"Well, the brass shell casing will be oxidized, and will have turned green by now," she looked Tank in the eyes as she spoke. She was feeling much more confident now. "The blister agent inside should be in perfect condition, especially because the temperature down there on the ocean floor will keep everything refrigerated."

"They wouldn't be able to use the shells as artillery munitions then?" the Major asked.

"No. The explosive charges which fire the projectiles will be in a highly unstable state. I think that moving them or exposing them to a significant change in temperature could cause them to explode," Helen Walsh looked around the table and for the first time she felt as if she had contributed something of value to the investigation.

"That is not what I wanted to hear," Tank sat back in his chair and folded his huge hands behind his neck.

"That is definitely not good news," Chen added.

"I don't know if it is such bad news," Grace interrupted. "If they cannot be moved without exploding then surely that is a good thing."

"That would depend on where they explode," Helen Walsh replied confidently.

"What do you mean?" Chen asked.

"If they remained stable during the recovery, and the explosive begins to sweat and become critical, then it could be several hours before they exploded," Helen explained.

"Which means that they could be on the mainland when they exploded," Grace encouraged her.

"Exactly."

"What if they explode beneath the water?" Tank asked.

"I'm sure that if the shells are still dry and they should be, then one exploding shell could ignite the whole load," Helen used her hands to reinforce the point as she spoke.

"Would the sea water dilute the blister agent in the shells?" the Major asked.

"No, because it isn't technically a gas, it's a vapour which would make its way to the surface as bubbles. Once it was above the surface then it would cloud above the sea, but because it is heavier than air it wouldn't dissipate into the atmosphere for days," Helen answered.

"Like a fog?" Grace asked.

"Exactly like a fog, and just like a fog it would be at the mercy of the winds," Helen answered.

"So if there is an onshore wind the vapour could be blown toward the city?"

"Yes."

"Fucking hell," Tank said beneath his breath.

"My thought exactly," said the Major removing his glasses and rubbing his tired eyes.

"What is the worst case scenario of a vapour cloud drifting into the city?" Grace asked.

Helen Walsh picked up her pen and held it between two fingers. She flicked it quickly back and to as she contemplated the answer.

"The problem with a vapour such as this is that no one would know that they had been infected until the symptoms became apparent. By which time it would be too late to treat," Helen put the pen down and looked at the Major as she spoke. "It would be four to six hours before the first symptoms showed. First an intense thirst which is caused by burns appearing in the delicate tissues of the oesophagus, followed quickly by the blistering of any skin tissue which came into contact with the vapour. Any exposed skin including the eyes would be terribly burned, and if the burns are not treated quickly then the victims usually bleed to death. If they do not bleed to death then they drown in their own bodily fluids as blisters form in the tiny air sacks within the lungs."

"I can understand how the lungs would become damaged by the blister agent but I'm not sure I understand why victims would bleed to death too?" Grace asked.

"If you can imagine the epidermis beneath the blistered skin becomes similar to the texture of a piece of wet bread, and the victims cannot stop scratching the blisters. They literally tear their own skin off. The thirst and the itching causes a state of delirium, a madness like a rabid dog," Helen spoke clearly and without over dramatising the issue. The meeting remained silent.

"I have to ask the question, where does this detailed information of the effects of the blister agent come from?" Grace asked curiously.

"There have been several in-depth studies carried out. The earliest recorded experiments were carried out by the Germans, during the First World War, and then further experiments were completed at several of the death camps in the forties. Then there is detailed evidence from Iraq during the nineties, but most of the information comes from a paper written by Christopher Walsh," Helen replied. It was obvious to everyone in the room that human guinea pigs had been exposed to this terrible chemical and the results recorded. Another blinding example of man's inhumanity to man.

"If this stuff drifted into the city during a rush hour when commuting is at its peak then we would be dealing with a national disaster. Victims driving, sailing or flying out of the city wouldn't display any symptoms until they were hundreds of miles away, by which time they would have infected dozens of others," Chen clarified the scenario.

"We need to get to Christopher Walsh well before he gets to one of these wrecks. We must concentrate on stopping them reaching the shells in the first place, and then we don't have to worry about the blister agent being released at all," the Major said. There was little point in dwelling on the impact of a vapour cloud reaching the city. It would be virtually impossible to plan for such an incident.

"If they propose to land the salvage then they would need a functioning cargo dock, cranes, containers and the full works," Tank regained his composure and spoke.

"Correct, and we would have to assume that they would

try and land them nearby. We could alert the port authorities to a possible arms shipment and have them on alert," Chen suggested.

"I'm not so sure," Grace said. "If I were trying to land a cargo like that I would head for Ireland, transfer the salvage from one vessel to another and then I would sail it back, or alternatively I would move it via containers through the Irish ferry ports."

"We need to cover every eventuality. Grace I'll leave it to you to monitor cargo berths here and across the Irish Sea," the Major put his glasses back on and made notes as he spoke.

"Roger that sir," she replied. Helen Walsh chuckled at the use of military jargon by Grace. Grace looked at her sternly. She had redeemed herself by knowing her subject, but it wouldn't take much for her to lose the little respect that she had gained. Helen took the hint. She stopped giggling, and looked sheepishly at the screen.

"John, you and Chen could ask some of our European friends if they know who is working for Christopher Walsh, and apply a little pressure to some of the uniformed division's informers. The foreign communities are pretty tight and in a situation like this one someone out there must know something," the Major removed his glasses again and looked at Tank. Tank looked at Helen Walsh to see if she had understood the implication of the Major's orders. He didn't think that she had, and he didn't really care.

"Miss Walsh, I mean Helen, I need you to work with a crisis team. Put together a plan of action in the event of blister agent infecting a large group of civilians," the Major ordered.

"I'm not sure that I'm qualified to do that Major," she replied, taken aback by the order.

"We have crisis teams in place who already have a number of contingency plans set out in the event of a disaster Miss Walsh. They will come up with all the logistics based on the information that you give them. From there they can adjust their plans. What I need you to do is explain in detail the after effects of an infection. I also need you to pass on the details of the potential treatment that you mentioned to our chemists. They may be able to emulate the chemical that Christopher Walsh has patented," the Major was more insistent this time.

"Okay Major, I'll do my best," she blushed again and looked at Tank again. He nodded to her which she took as encouragement. He smiled and she relaxed a little taking the gesture as a huge compliment from the taskforce's lead agent.

"If we are to assume that Christopher Walsh is trying to benefit from his blister agent serum, then any publicity at all means that he has won. He will have achieved his objective. We don't have much time people, so let's do what we do best and take this bastard down," the Major stood up and walked out of the room. The time for talking was done.

CHAPTER 13
Lightship L2

Joe Hammond was coming round from a deep alcohol induced slumber. It was a sensation that he had experienced many times before over the last six years or so. His recent memory was somewhat blurred and he had the sensation of being carried from one place to the next, and of being transported by a vehicle. This feeling wasn't alien to him. He had lost count of the number of journeys he had endured in the back of a police van or an ambulance. At least the police usually put him into a warm dry cell where he could sleep it off, where as the ambulance rides resulted in some jumped up young doctor sticking a tube down his throat and pumping his stomach. Silly bastards, if he didn't want the whisky in his stomach then he wouldn't have drunk it in the first place. They didn't understand that he wanted the oblivion that whisky brought him, more than that, he needed the oblivion. It was his escape from this shithole of a world he had found himself in. He was too much of a coward to check out completely. Suicide frightened him because he thought that it would hurt. He had been raised as a catholic and somewhere in his pickled brain he knew that suicide was a bad thing. Joe wanted to die, but he didn't want to live in the world sober while he waited for his imminent death. The whisky was his solution.

Joe Hammond had been a successful recording artist in the nineties. He had a string of top ten hits followed by a brief career just being a celebrity. Every reality television show that you can name involved the pop star Joe Hammond. He hated every moment of it but it paid well, and his agent said it was imperative that he maintained his high profile as long as he could.

The problem was that Joe Hammond was thrust underneath the public's microscope. The real Joe Hammond was not a nice person to know. Beneath the pearly white grin was a nasty jealous man. Reality television gave the public, especially his young adoring fans a window into his soul, and the more they grew to know him the more unlikable he became. Over a period of time he had dropped from the 'A' list to the 'Z' list and his appearance work dried up. The less work he had the more bitter he became. As a last ditch attempt to revitalise his career he released a new album which he financed himself with the remnants of his fortune. It was a huge flop as his fan base of young fans had all grown up, and his bad reputation on reality television was off putting to new ones. His home was his only collateral and he was forced to sell it to pay a huge outstanding tax bill. Joe Hammond was left homeless and destitute. The army of friends and colleagues that he once adored to insult had long since turned their back on him. Many of them took great joy in watching his demise. Whisky became his mistress and only friend, and he sought solace with her as often as he could afford to.

The reassuring sound of a diesel engine from somewhere in his subconscious stopped. The sensation of being transported changed to one of being still. He registered these changes but was still unable to physically do anything about it. He would probably wake up in a warm prison cell soon. The sound of heavy boots in an empty metal void was his next conscious memory. He thought he could hear voices, but he couldn't recognise the language. Joe was suddenly aware of being lifted roughly by his feet and hands. He tried to open his eyes but he could only manage a blink. It was dark and he was in the back of a van, and then he was outside in the cold night air. The thick guttural accents continued to chatter as he was carried along. He was aware of the smell of the seaside, seaweed and salty air. A seagull squawked in the distance, first one and then it was joined by dozens more. The sound of the gulls took his drunken mind back in time to a much happier place. He was sat on a beach made from white powder sand looking at a turquoise sea. The sky was cloudless and the sunshine was intense. It was Clearwater, Florida and he was enjoying a picnic with a brunette bronzed beauty, but he couldn't remember her name. He did remember arguing with her because she didn't enjoy rough sex and he did, probably a little too much. She was nursing a thick lip and badly bruised thighs which she was covering up with a wraparound sarong. Then he remembered a fat seagull swooping down and stealing the sandwich from his hand as they argued. He had stood up and chased the bird down the beach, as if he could catch the winged food thief. When he realised that pursuit was futile he turned back to the picnic and to his horror there was a flock of seagulls swooping on it. The picnic was ruined within seconds by the feathered dive bombers. In his mind the memory faded as quickly as it had appeared, but he could still hear the seagulls.

Joe was rudely awakened by the smell of bleach. He could feel a harsh scraping at his face and neck and he opened his eyes momentarily. His head was banging. The cheap whisky was eating into his brain, and his vital organs were in the final stages of cirrhosis. Every nerve ending in his body screamed at his brain for more booze to quell the pain. He managed to open his eyes. He tried to move but couldn't, because he was bound to a chair. His head was forced backward sharply and the painful scraping carried on. His befuddled mind registered that someone was shaving his matted beard. His scalp felt cold and exposed as if it had already been shaved. The disposable blade nicked his throat and he groaned.

"He is waking up," a gruff voice spoke in a foreign accent.

"Hurry up and finish shaving him," an English voice spoke.

There was a distinct smell of bleach, not just in the air, but also on him. He was confused. He heard water being squeezed into a bucket, and then he felt something like a sponge being rubbed on his legs. There was a strange tingling sensation were the sponge touched him.

"What's in the bucket?" the foreign accent said.

"It is a mild acidic solution, not dissimilar to a dilute form of bleach, and it should protect the treated skin from the blister agent."

"Should do? Hey you don't sound too confident," the foreign man chuckled as he spoke.

"It is nearly perfected but you can't do enough testing. Trial and error is the only way forward in medicine."

"You know that you are a very sick man don't you Mister

Walsh, a very sick man indeed," the foreign man laughed and shook his head as he spoke.

Christopher Walsh stopped what he was doing and glared at the Estonian man. The man stopped laughing immediately and carried on shaving the homeless tramp. Christopher was not a physically frightening man by any stretch of the imagination. He was tall and lean with thick fair hair. His face was handsome and freckles covered his nose and cheeks which gave a youthful appearance. The Estonian man wasn't scared of Christopher, but he had seen the victims of his experiments, and that made him wary of causing him offense. The man was warped. Plus he paid well and the promise of a bonus running into six figures endeared him further. Uri had seen many acts of extreme violence in his homeland where he had worked as hired muscle for ruthless organised crime families. He had lost count of the number of men that he had killed with his own hands, but Christopher Walsh was a different kettle of fish all together. He was a complete genius, and that was obvious. He was also a complete psychopath, which was also obvious. Uri would take his money and do as he was bid, but he would have to watch his back while he did so.

"I'm not sick Uri, and you will not think I'm sick when we are millionaires," Christopher spoke sulkily like a grumpy teenager. Uri laughed again and shook his head.

"Whatever you say, you're the boss," Uri said.

"Yes, I am. You should remember that too," Christopher replied churlishly as he applied more liquid to the aging pop star. He studied the homeless man's face curiously. "I recognise you, now where do I know you from?"

Joe Hammond stared at the fresh faced man. He was sponging his legs with a clear liquid, while another man shaved his head and face. It registered in his fuddled mind that he had spoken to him, and that it would be good to offer a reply. Although his mind was numbed by whisky, he sensed that he was in danger. This place was neither a prison cell or a hospital, and something in the young man's eyes frightened him.

"I'm Joe Hammond," he croaked. Talking had disturbed the phlegm in his lungs and he coughed. It had been weeks since he had spoken to anyone.

"Who?"

"Joe Hammond," he repeated and spluttered again.

"Joe Hammond, Joe Hammond, now why does that name ring a bell?"

"I'm a singer, well I was a singer, I've been having a hard time recently," he spluttered again. This time he managed to clear the phlegm in his throat and a globule of green fluid dribbled down his chin.

"No. I've never heard of you, and that is disgusting by the way," Christopher sneered.

"Why am I here?" Joe managed to say. His words were slurred by the booze.

"What did you do with the other one?" Christopher turned to Uri ignoring the drunk.

"What other one?" Uri replied.

"The other body you fool."

"Oh, you mean your last experiment," Uri chuckled again as he finished shaving the tramp. He had emphasised the word 'experiment', mocking his young employer.

"You know very well what I mean," Christopher became a petulant child again.

"He's fish food, just like the others."

"There is no way they could be washed up, or found floating somewhere?"

"We turn them into bite size chunks before we dump them Mr Walsh, there's no need to be concerned," Uri enjoyed teasing his strange employer.

"Good, and I'm not concerned. I pay you to be concerned. He is ready to be sprayed. See to it Uri," Christopher Walsh stood up and removed his rubber gloves. He held Joe Hammond by the chin and turned his face to the left, and then to the right, studying him. "No, I don't recognise you at all. Make sure you spray his head and face well. If he was to be found I don't want anyone recognising him. Handcuff him to the bulkhead and put the water out of his reach."

"You really are a sick man," Uri laughed again. He left the cabin and closed the door behind him. Joe was alone and confused. He was more frightened than he had ever been. His brain was fuddled but the snippets of conversation that he had heard terrified him and he was sobering up quickly. He heard the word body, and experiment. The words that stuck in his mind the most were 'fish food'. It reminded him of black and white gangster movies, or a scene from the Godfather. He struggled against the bonds that tied him but there was no give in them. The door opened again and Uri stepped back into the cabin. He fastened a steel handcuff around Joe's left hand and dragged the chair over to the bulkhead. He then fastened the empty cuff to a steel pipe which was fastened to the superstructure. Joe looked at the pipe and followed it up to the ceiling. It led to a showerhead the size of a large dinner plate. Joe didn't have a clue what to think. He was frozen with fear. Uri placed a box cutter blade on the floor next to Joe and then lifted a two gallon water container onto the table, which was on the opposite side of the room. Joe was really confused when Uri cut the rope that fastened him to the chair. Uri smiled an evil smile as he left the cabin and closed the watertight door behind him.

"Wait please, I'm Joe Hammond, why am I here?"

Joe Hammond heard the pipes rattle and he heard a hissing sound coming from the showerhead above him. A vapour poured from the showerhead and fell on to him. He felt a dampness touching his skin and instinctively he tried to get away from it, but the handcuff held him tight. There was nothing he could to avoid the vapour. Maybe it was some kind of fumigation, but he doubted it. There was an odour of garlic in the vapour and he breathed it deep into his lungs through his nose as he tried desperately to identify it. He felt a wave of nausea engulf him and he sat down on the chair again. The effects of the whisky returned with a vengeance and unconsciousness tugged at his mind. Joe wished that he had some alcohol, but he didn't. There was only water in the room and that was out of his reach. He rested his weary head on his hand and leaned it against the bulkhead. The metal was cool against his skin. It soothed him as he dropped off into a troubled slumber.

Upstairs in the bridge of the lightship Uri and Christopher Walsh watched the footage from a close circuit television camera which was fixed on Joe Hammond. The ruined pop star had been sleeping for nearly two hours when the first signs of the blister agent started to appear. The skin on his head, face and torso had started to redden. His legs and feet however showed no signs of being burned. Christopher Walsh looked at his wrist watch and made some notes in a scruffy note book. He seemed to be excited by his observations. Uri looked out of the window onto the dock as a Mercedes pulled up behind the panel van. He tapped his boss on the shoulder and pointed out of the window to the newly arrived vehicle.

"Gari is back, but he is on his own," Uri said matter of factly.

"Fucking hell, where are the others," Christopher ran across the bridge and pressed his face against the glass to cut out the glaring reflection from the lights. He could see the driver climbing out of the vehicle clutching something under his arm.

"Maybe they had trouble. The vehicle looks damaged," Uri shrugged as he spoke.

"Well then, go and find out," Christopher pointed to the door as if he were sending a naughty dog out of the room for making a bad smell. Uri looked at his boss and smiled crookedly.

"I will deal with it, don't worry," he said.

"There can be no room for mistakes Uri, none whatsoever," Christopher was still pointing to the door. Uri looked his boss in the eye and then looked at his outstretched arm. Christopher blushed slightly and dropped the offending limb sheepishly. He realised that he was talking to Uri as if he were an infant. Uri smirked and left the bridge. Cold night air drifted into the lightship and Christopher heard the seagulls calling in the distance. The heavy metal door swung closed again shutting out the noise from the docks.

He watched the big Estonian man as he climbed from the bridge down eight metal steps onto the foredeck, and from there he crossed a metal gangplank which had rope handrails onto the dockside. Uri was talking to Gari as he walked around the Mercedes and began pointing at the vehicle as he moved around it. Christopher could see that he was becoming agitated and angry. Gari was following him and talking back in an animated fashion. The two men were arguing. Gari was waving a roll of papers and gesticulating wildly with his hands. Uri stopped circling the car and walked toward Gari quickly. Gari stepped back instinctively and pulled a small knife from his belt buckle. The blade glinted in the darkness. The two men stood looking angrily into each other's eyes. They were too close to each other for comfort, and it was obvious that neither of them was about to back down. Gari had drawn a blade, which in Eastern Europe was unforgivable, and now he would have to use it or back down.

Christopher looked at the Mercedes again. He could see that the driver's window wasn't there but he thought it had been lowered at first. Then he saw shattered glass glinting all over the seats and in the foot wells. It didn't bode well. Gari had been sent with two other mobsters to speak to an aging submarine commander and to press him for information. The man would have been in his eighties and probably stunk of his own piss. How difficult could it be for three ruthless gangsters to interrogate him?

Uri snarled at Gari and poked a big finger into his chest. Gari made to push Uri with the flat of his hand but Uri was much quicker and he still had the box cutter blade that he had used to release the tramp in his pocket. He swung his right hand in a wide arc too fast for Gari to react. The razor sharp blade sliced through one side of his throat, and out of the other side before he had even felt it strike. A plume of warm blood jetted from his jugular vein and he grasped at the gaping wound with both hands trying to stem the flow. There was a strange hissing sound from his severed windpipe. His legs buckled as his life force sprayed across the dock. Uri looked around the deserted quay to make sure that no one had inadvertently witnessed the confrontation. He grabbed Gari by the belt at the back of his jeans and carried him like a folded suit carrier to the back of the Mercedes. The bleeding man twitched gently but could not offer more of a struggle. There was a thick trail of blood around the vehicle. Uri popped the trunk and heaved the dying man inside. He looked up at the bridge of the lightship and saw that his employer had watched the whole episode. Uri thought that it was probably a good thing that he had. Christopher Walsh wasn't the only cold blooded killer on the planet. Uri looked at him again and waved toward the vehicle. He picked up the rolls of paper and headed back up the gangplank.

Christopher opened the heavy steel door and met him on the metal steps. He remained silent and waited for Uri to explain.

"They encountered the police while they interrogated the old man, Gari was driving and he said the other two were dead," Uri said gruffly. Christopher nodded understandingly, and waited for him to expand.

"I told him that he should not have brought the vehicle back to this place and that he should have disposed of it. I told him that he would not be paid for this job, and that he had fucked it up!" Uri was annoyed. "Gari said that if he was not paid he would tell the police where we are and what we are doing here himself, and that is unforgivable. I will deal with the disposal of the vehicle and his body now." Uri handed the charts to Christopher and he took them without saying a word to the big Estonian man. Uri turned and headed back down the steps toward the gangplank in silence. He reached the dock and climbed into the Mercedes. Uri needed to dispose of both the car and its bloody luggage.

Christopher Walsh was impressed with his foreman. Uri was a dangerous man who didn't suffer fools gladly. He smiled as the Mercedes pulled of the quayside and he walked back onto the bridge. He opened the charts and laughed out loud as he studied the details on them. The charts reinforced his theories and he was a step closer to his treasure. There was movement on the camera monitor which caught his eye and looked closer to see what stage the experiment had reached. He smiled again as he was just in time to see Joe Hammond trying to chew through his own wrist to get to the water that was out of his reach. His body had become unrecognisable as huge fluid filled blisters had formed all over his head and torso. His legs and feet showed no sign of burns, which was the whole point of this particular experiment. Joe Hammond was gnawing at his wrist bone furiously, desperately trying to escape the handcuffs and get to the water. Obviously the thirst had kicked in. It was to be his last performance in front of a camera, reality television gone mad.

CHAPTER 14
Tank

John Tankersley sat in the driver's seat of a black pick-up truck. It was a Japanese copy of the huge American gas guzzlers that are popular in the United States. The cab was fitted with all the bells and whistles that you would expect in a top of the range modern vehicle, plus a few others that you wouldn't expect. Tank was looking at a computer screen which had been fitted where the satellite navigation would be, but instead of an aerial map it showed the picture and details of his target. The man he was waiting for was a Polish immigrant who called himself Victor Brastz. The information on the computer had been compiled by the intelligence agencies, and contained a mixture of drug related arrests, fire arms offences and serious crime unit reports. The uniformed police divisions had been watching Brastz for years. Eventually he had been implicated in a protection racket and under the threat serious charges being brought against him, which would have resulted in a lengthy prison sentence he had turned informer.

Informers, or snitches, as the police called them, are owned by one particular officer who becomes their handler. Only the designated officer is allowed to contact an informer, which helps to protect their anonymity. Victor Brastz was handled by an officer from the serious crime unit, and Tank had hacked into their confidential files to find an Eastern European mobster that was already on the payroll of the police. It had taken less than five minutes to find an informer that they could use. Of course no one but Tank and the taskforce knew that he was waiting for the snitch. Normally the taskforce would have to go through Victor's handler before they could speak to him however there wasn't time for that now. The Serious Crime Unit would be up in arms if they had found out what Tank was about to do, not that it would matter if they did. The Terrorist Task Force didn't need permission to interrogate a suspect, no matter who they were protected by.

Victor Brastz was working out in a scruffy body building gymnasium in the Speke area of the city. It was close to the John Lennon Airport and a passenger jet flew low overhead on its way to land. The area was renowned for drugs and prostitution rackets, and several high profile gang members had been gunned down outside of this gymnasium. Anyone who was anyone in the underworld trained at this gym. It was odd that rival mobsters would train yards away from their arch enemies, and yet there was never any violent conflict in the gymnasium, outside was a totally different ballgame.

Tank was familiarising himself with Victor's criminal record. It read like a successful organised crime member's record should do, drug smuggling, people trafficking, bank robbery, kidnapping, hijacking and a not guilty verdict in a triple murder case, which was very impressive for a reasonably young, thirty five year old gangster. Brastz had status and integrity amongst the local crime families, although he had no allegiance to any one in particular. He was one of the many European freelance mobsters that had flooded into the country when the European borders were merged. As far as the local uniformed divisions were concerned he was invaluable as a resource. Tank was going to use the inside knowledge that Victor possessed to find out who was working with Christopher Walsh. If Tank could find out who was on the scientists payroll, then they could take the whole operation down before they could get anywhere near the munitions on the wrecks.

Victor Brastz stepped out of the narrow stone stairwell which led from the first floor gymnasium situated above a row of shops. He was accompanied by two other men. All three men were wearing sweat stained tracksuits and hooded jackets, and all three men were obviously injecting nandrelone into their buttocks every day. Victor was a heavy set man, pumped up by steroids and looked to weigh about fifteen stones. His face was red and heavy around the jowls, and his neck was covered in acne which was a classic sign of steroid abuse. The two men with him were slightly smaller, but they displayed the same tell tale signs. Approaching Brastz while he was in their company would only end in a violent conclusion. Tank needed Victor alive and able to talk, shooting him and his friends was not an option at this stage. He watched them walking toward a row of car parking bays at the front of the shops. Tank flicked a switch on the dash and a listening device crackled into life. He focused it on the three men as they reached their vehicles. Victor Brastz leaned against the boot of a sleek Bentley Continental, and the indicator lights flashed as he opened the vehicle by remote.

"And they say that crime doesn't pay," Tank said to himself as he admired the Bentley. It would cost more than Tank earned in a year. He tweaked the listening device, and focused it on the men.

"What do you need, tabs or needles?" Victor's voice had come through the pick-up's speakers. He was completing a steroid deal.

"What have you got?"

"Both, but it depends what results you are looking for," Victor said rummaging around in the boot of the Bentley.

"I just want to get bigger. I can't seem to put on anymore muscle," the younger of the two men spoke with a heavy scouse accent. They were obviously local men attached to one of the organised crime families. Most of the young gang members started off as hired muscle, earning their stripes as bouncers on nightclubs, before moving onto enforcement work and the more lucrative drugs and prostitution rackets. Reputations were made and broken working in the door security world. Cowards were soon exposed, and those with a talent for violence floated to the top of the pile. A few extra kilos of hard defined muscle didn't go amiss in the security industry.

"You will need to stack the drugs by combining needles and tablets together. A tub of one hundred dianabol tablets will cost you fifty notes, and decca-durabolin jabs are eight pound for each needle. You need one two mil needle a day for six weeks, which is two hundred and eighty eight quid plus fifty for the tabs, is three hundred and thirty eight of your crisp English pound notes my friend," Victor was an excellent sales man. Tank could see why these young hoodlums looked up to him. He was big and he was convincing.

"Sound, can I pay you for the steroids tomorrow mate?" the young man tried his hand.

"Yes you can, as long as you don't want the gear until tomorrow my young friend. I don't do credit," Victor slammed the boot closed and glared at the two men.

"Alright mate, calm down," the younger man reached into his sports bag and produced a bundle of notes.

"You're a cheeky bastard," Victor said shaking his head as he opened the boot again to get the steroids.

"Yes, and you're a fucking no mark Polish gobshite," the young man pulled a small metal cosh from the holdall while Victor had his back turned. He swung the truncheon and hit Victor at the base of the skull. The big Pole dropped to his knees, stunned by the force of the blow. He maintained his grip on the boot of the Bentley which kept him upright. The second man grabbed the boot lid and slammed it closed on the back of Victor's head. Victor fell backward onto the road and cracked his head on the tarmac. The first man reached into the Bentley and lifted out a holdall full of steroids. He looked inside and was impressed with the size of his haul. The young thug stamped on Victor's genitals and he twisted over onto his front to protect himself as the two men started to kick him viciously. The whole thing had happened so fast that Tank was frozen still in the pick-up. He had to make a decision quickly, help his target or leave him to the mercy of the younger thugs. Tank needed him alive and able to speak. He opened the door and jumped out of the pick-up. The two men saw Tank coming toward them, and there was a look of confusion on their faces. Tank was a big man, much bigger than them, but they didn't recognise him from the gymnasium. The smaller man stopped kicking Victor and turned to face Tank.

"If you have got any sense you'll get back into your truck mate, and don't get involved."

Tank was less than three yards away from the man as he issued the warning and the colour drained from the man's face when he realised that Tank wasn't about to stop. The man took a wild swing with his right hand. Tank raised his left forearm and parried the blow without stopping for breath. A left hook was blocked with similar ease. The man had left his face wide open and Tank lunged forward with his head. The butt connected with sickening force and the soft flesh around the nose and top lip were split wide open. Tank grabbed him by the testicles and squeezed hard whilst lifting him up to shoulder height at the same time. He twisted his upper body and slammed the man head first into the pavement. The man crumpled like a bag of dirty washing and Tank turned to face the second man.

The second man watched mesmerised as Tank tossed his friend aside as if he wasn't there. There was fear in his eyes and mentally he was already beaten bar the fighting. Tank saw that Victor, who was still on the floor, was moving again. The Pole swung his legs at his attacker, catching him on the back of the knees. The man dropped onto his back and cracked his head on the tarmac. Victor moved like lightening. He lifted his right foot high into the air and slammed it down heel first into his attacker's face. The force of the blow smashed the back of his head against the floor hard and knocked him unconscious. Victor used the bumper of his car to help him get up off the floor. He rubbed the back of his skull and tried to clear his head, while keeping a wary eye on Tank. A small crowd of onlookers had gathered to watch the fight. Another group of men from the gymnasium were also gathering at the bottom of the stairwell.

"Thanks for your help," Victor nodded to Tank and picked up the sports bag full of steroids. He swung a kick into his attacker's head as an afterthought. The man groaned and rolled over.

Tank nodded back to him silently and walked back toward his pick-up. He couldn't risk any further exposure here and there were too many people about. The men from the gym were talking angrily and one of them ran toward the two unconscious locals on the floor. Victor slammed the Bentley into reverse and the tyres screeched as he pulled away from the melee. A big man in a vest and baggy tracksuit bottoms threw a bottle of water at the Bentley as it drove past him at speed. The plastic bottle clipped the windscreen and bounced off. It rattled across the tarmac and landed at Tank's feet. He crushed it as he climbed into the pick-up. He started the engine and followed Victor Brastz from a distance.

CHAPTER 15
Uri

Uri pulled the Mercedes away from the dock. He looked up into the bridge of the lightship and he could see his employer Christopher Walsh staring at the camera monitor and smiling. Uri shook his head and wondered how he had ended up working for an eccentric English business man who was like some type of mad professor and conducted terrible chemical weapon experiments on homeless people. On top of that he had plans to threaten the 2012 Olympics. At first Uri thought the plan was to highlight a right wing agenda that his boss was loosely connected to, but as time went by the fascist, racist connections became more tenuous every day. Uri was convinced that the plot was about money and not any political motive. Uri had to admit that he didn't really care as long as he was paid. He had introduced most of the hired guns that were required for the operation, and the majority of them were from Russia and the Eastern Block. There were more people involved, divers, undersea welders and the like; although Christopher had been introduced to them by Uri, the Estonian man had no further dealings with any of them. Christopher dealt with all the technical personnel himself. It wasn't good for security but Uri had no say in the matter. He would have to deal with people like Gari whenever they stepped out of line, and trust that Christopher knew what he was doing with the other side of the operation.

Uri had been in the country for ten years now. He had joined the Estonian mafia at the age of nineteen. He was from a small town called Voru, which was on the borders of Latvia and the Russian federation. Uri was naturally a big man, and he was also as tough as nails. He began driving vehicles which were stolen to order from Britain and Western Europe into Lithuania, across neighbouring Latvia, through his home Estonia, to be sold in Russia. His employers noted that he had a talent for crime, and they lured him to the West to work in their businesses in the United Kingdom. It was working in these businesses where he made many contacts from his homeland and other countries in the East. His role within the Estonians' organisation had fizzled out as the people that hired him moved on, and several of the senior members were jailed for people trafficking. It was then that he branched out on his own and became a Mr Fix-it. If anyone needed muscle then he could supply it. If they needed a safe cracker or a cat burglar then he could supply them also. Uri used his connections to become an agency for organised crime personnel. The system worked well and the risk to his liberty was low. Uri rarely became involved in the criminal activity that he facilitated, and it became a very lucrative business. However safe and sound his business had been, it was not as lucrative as the position Christopher Walsh had offered him, and so unusually he had become personally involved in this operation.

Uri needed to remove the Mercedes and Gari's body from the dockside. He drove through a series of roads which serviced the quaysides and reached the dock road unhindered. There was no sign of the port authority police. He edged the Mercedes into the traffic and took the main road north out of the city centre. To the north of Liverpool was a Victorian seaside resort called Southport, once the jewel in the crown of the North West's tourist industry. It was once the home of the rich and wealthy merchants who worked in the port of Liverpool and it was also the holiday destination of millions of tourists every year, but it had fallen into decline decades ago. Now it was a mishmash of rundown boarding houses and derelict businesses. The centre piece of the resort was a huge kidney shaped boating lake around which a miniature steam engine would pull day trippers. The waters were now green with algae and littered with shopping trolleys. The majority of the ornate three storey hotels on the promenade, once thriving, were now converted into bedsits and were full of Polish immigrants who worked for peanuts in the dying tourist industry. Uri had a large pool of criminal contacts that lived and worked in the town. He gunned the engine and pushed the Mercedes faster as he reached a wide dual carriageway which connected the revitalised city of Liverpool to its smaller decaying neighbour. Uri made a call on his cell phone.

"Hello."

"It's Uri."

"Hello my friend, it's been a long time," a Russian voice said sarcastically.

"It has indeed, at least a week. How's business?"

"You know how it is Uri, we duck and we dive. It is getting harder all the time to export our products out of this god forsaken country," the man laughed as he spoke but it sounded forced. There was suspicion in his voice.

"Exports always were tricky my friend, that is the reason for the call, I need a Mercedes to disappear," Uri said.

"I didn't think that you were calling to enquire about my health Uri," the man laughed gruffly. "What model is it?"

"It's a black CL500 on a two thousand and eight plate. There is damage to the driver's window and luggage in the trunk," Uri explained his problem without alerting any unwelcome listeners that may have been listening. He had to be careful with every phone call that he made, just in case he or his associates were being bugged by the serious crime units.

"What kind of luggage Uri? It is hard enough moving vehicles as it is, especially Mercedes," the man became irritated.

"It's another load of meat," Uri answered, referring to the dead body in the boot.

"Another one, Jesus Christ Uri what have you got yourself into?"

"It's a one off contract and it is nearly completed, I need it gone tonight," Uri remained vague.

"Okay, but what about the car?"

"You can keep it. I just need it to disappear," Uri kept his cool. He knew that the Mercedes would bring a hefty price in the Russia, especially since the collapse of the Soviet Union. Western decadence had overtaken communist ideals a long time ago. Disposing of one dead body was chicken feed in comparison to the return that they would make on the prestige vehicle.

"You have a deal," the voice remained gruff and unfriendly.

"Where should I deliver it to?"

"When do you need to get rid of it?"

"I need it taking immediately, I'm on my way now."

"Okay, take it to the chop shop at the old funfair. Someone will meet you there."

"I'll be ten minutes," Uri cut the call off and pressed harder on the accelerator.

Uri reached the coast road and headed toward the beach where the old Pleasure Beach funfair stood rotting next to the ocean. A massive wooden rollercoaster, which once had carriages thundering up and down a series of precipitous inclines, was now a derelict relic of greater days. Its cracked white paint glowed and made it loom out of the darkness from about a mile away down the deserted promenade. It was now a pile of firewood waiting to be demolished. Uri drove slowly along the beach road. To his right were the twinkling lights of the town across the stagnant boating lake, and to his left was the Irish Sea, which was hidden by the darkness of the night. It was a black void. The Southport coastline is wide and flat. When the tide retreats it leaves miles and miles of wet sand exposed. At its furthest ebb when the tide turns it is not visible with the human eye from the coast road. Far out at sea tiny lights flickered in the pitch darkness. There were four gas drilling platforms operating in Liverpool Bay and one of the largest ocean wind farms was also just offshore. These industries required a small armada of boats to maintain and supply them. That was what Uri's boss Christopher was hoping to use as a smoke screen for his salvage operation. Uri was glad that he would be keeping his feet on dry land during this operation.

Uri approached the entrance gates of the old fairground. There was a tall wooden archway with metal gates hanging from it. The once vivid paintings of cartoon characters on the arch had long since faded and the coloured wood had cracked and warped. The thick metal gates were blistered with rust and were secured with a padlock and chain which looked out of place as it was relatively new. There was a sign hanging at a lopsided angle warning people to keep out, and that trespassers would be prosecuted. He pulled the Mercedes in front of the gates and waited. The beach road was deserted but for a few cars parked randomly, probably containing courting couples with more urgent things on their minds than the black Mercedes near the Pleasure Beach. Uri saw a narrow beam of torchlight approaching the gate from the opposite side.

A figure emerged from the gloomy fairground and he reached through the rusted bars and jiggled the padlock around to his side, so that he could unlock it. The chain dropped free, and the gates swung open with a tortured squeal. Uri engaged first gear and drove the Mercedes through the gates into the Pleasure Beach. The caretaker stayed silent and locked the metal gates behind him. He walked in front of the car and waved to Uri to follow him. Uri looked around the derelict fairground and a shiver ran down his spine. Uri thought that there was something eerie about the funfair at night, but even more so when it was deserted and decaying. The building to his left had a weathered sign identifying it as the 'River Caves'. Tall weeds and grass now grew were the river boats once floated in fluorescent blue waters. The imitation caves were once filled with life sized plastic dinosaurs which had long since been sold on to fairgrounds elsewhere. To the right hand side of the caves was the 'Hall of Mirrors'. The caretaker waved Uri toward the alleyway between them. There was a set of double doors and he pulled them open one at a time, revealing a busy chop shop within. Inside the shell of the derelict fairground attraction were a dozen vehicles. Each vehicle was undergoing a makeover before it would begin its journey to the East. There was a small army of men and machines, cutting, grinding and re-spraying the stolen prestige cars. A radio played an Oasis track somewhere at the back of the building. The noise inside was dampened by thick strips of carpet and cardboard which was nailed to the doors and walls, making it impossible to hear the men and machines from outside.

Uri pulled the Mercedes into the unit. He turned off the engine and released the boot catch before climbing out. Four men wearing white paper suits which were covered in engine oil and grease opened the trunk and removed the body. None of the men that were cutting and grinding paid any attention to the others as they struggled between the cars with the dead weight. Uri watched as they carried the limp corpse across the workshop to a wooden bench. The bench incorporated a large band saw, and had been draped with a polythene sheet to minimise the mess. The electric saw sprang to life and the body of Gari was pushed through it half a dozen times in different directions. Within five minutes the corpse had been expertly dismembered ready for disposal at sea. Uri had seen it done many times before but it never failed to fascinate him just how quickly a man can be wiped from existence.

"There's a fire exit at the back of the unit which will take you back onto the beach road," the man that had opened the gates said gruffly. "Unless there is anything else, do you need a lift anywhere?"

"No thank you. I'll walk, I could do with some fresh air," Uri took one last look as the men scraped Gari's intestines into a bucket. He was a hardened criminal but he wasn't sure how much more of this business he could stomach. He headed for the exit and decided to have a few beers before getting one of his men to pick him up and drive him back to Liverpool. He had an unhealthy craving for vodka after drinking beer especially after completing a cleanup job. Uri stepped outside and the sea breeze cleared his head. The fire exit door closed shut and the noise of the chop shop inside was silenced. Out in the bay he could see small deck lights flashing as the gas industry continued to search for vital fossil fuels. His thoughts were disturbed when his mobile phone vibrated and he cursed under his breath as he removed it from his pocket. He squinted in the darkness and then looked at the screen. The handset's caller identity told him that Victor Brastz was on the line, and he never called unless there was trouble.

CHAPTER 16
The Lightship

Christopher Walsh scanned the oceanographic charts in detail, and he compared them with some of the surveys that his divers had already undertaken on his behalf.

"Are you absolutely sure that this is the site where you made a contact on the seabed?"

He was very excited because the charts confirmed something that he had suspected for a while. There were three areas marked on the maps that they had retrieved from the old submarine commander, which were allegedly the exact sites of torpedo attacks on suspected German spy ships in 1943. The issue Christopher was contemplating was purely a matter of physics. He knew from the study of dozens of wrecks that a sinking ship never travels vertically to the seabed. They usually travel at a steep angle from the surface which can take them hundreds of metres away from the actual point of conflict when they finally hit the ocean floor. Millions of dollars had been invested and ultimately lost all over the planet by treasure hunters looking for wreck sites. Pinpointing the exact resting place of any ship was a science more akin to winning the lottery. Christopher had invested time and money into finding the whereabouts of these particular wrecks even though he couldn't be certain if they were there at all, or if they contained blister agents. He only suspected that the wrecks held caches of mustard gas shells. It wasn't until he had sent his men to interrogate the submarine commander in his sheltered accommodation that he began to feel more confident that he wasn't on a wild goose chase. His men had encountered armed police, who had killed two of them as they tried to escape with the charts. Armed policemen are a rarity in the United Kingdom and they certainly don't patrol retirement villages at random. They must have been there for the same reason he had sent his men. Now he was absolutely convinced that the authorities believed the same thing that he did. There were wrecks containing blister agents on the seabed.

If he was correct in his assumptions then the authorities would be monitoring the Bay of Liverpool area, and searching for him. The good news was that his divers and their salvage teams had made a Sonar contact about a mile from one of the sites which had been marked on the charts by the junior submarine commander in 1943. Christopher was hoping that it was one of the alleged spy ships.

"This is it here," the charts also showed a steep slope running along the seabed from the suspected site to the Sonar contact. "You can see how close the contours are here. If a wreck hit the seabed here it would roll down the slope and come to rest somewhere near here, which is where we made a contact."

Christopher clapped his hands together with glee like a child at Christmas. That meant that the ship could have been torpedoed and then sunk, and then simply rolled down the trench at the bottom of the sea for nearly a mile before coming to its final resting place. There was no way that the authorities could have known that, even if they had the charts in their possession, unless they had also surveyed the geography of the seabed. They would be looking in a completely different part of the bay. He had to get the salvage operation underway immediately, before they realised their mistake.

"Okay, we start diving tonight, I must be sure that it is my wreck. We can investigate and remove a selection of samples for analysis," Christopher clapped his hands with delight.

"We can't dive tonight. To attempt to penetrate a wreck at night with such limited visibility would be an act of madness," the dive master retorted.

"We will start the salvage operation tonight or I'll find divers that will step into your shoes. What is it to be?" Christopher Walsh sniped.

"I don't understand what the rush is, and why do we need to dive at night? You said that you have the salvage rights which would give you unlimited access to the wreck."

"I lied about the salvage rights," Christopher admitted. "I'm sorry about that." He smiled and turned away from the diver to camouflage his mirth. He hadn't told the dive team the true goal of his salvage operation. They were criminals but even so he couldn't risk them knowing what he was planning to retrieve.

"Now you have decided to tell the truth I would like to know everything before my team enters the water. I know the law well and we can get around the legal problems by claiming rights on the wreck tomorrow and then we will have no problem diving in daylight. What exactly are you trying to recover?"

"Shells," he said. Christopher looked out of the bridge at the sea. There was a stiff breeze picking up and the boat was swaying gently against the swell.

"Shells?" the dive master asked confused.

"Yes. Brass shells."

"Brass shells?" the diver was becoming impatient. There was certain amount confusion caused by the language barrier but Christopher's vagueness was frustrating him.

"Yes. The ship was loaded with tens of thousands of artillery shells. It was torpedoed with the loss of all hands. Each shell has a brass casing which is worth over ten pounds as scrap metal," Christopher sounded convincing.

"I don't see the problem with diving in the daylight," the dive master shrugged his shoulders.

"It's simple, all hands were lost on that ship which means it is a war grave," Christopher explained. "We would never get legal permission to dive on the wreck. What difference does it make if it is daylight anyway? Surely it will be dark at that depth."

"The diving is not the problem Mr Walsh. It will be dark and the visibility will be limited, but if you require salvage to be recovered from the wreck then we cannot bring it up to the surface safely at night," the diver was being pedantic. The more problems he raised the higher the final bill would be.

"I see." Christopher turned away from the diver. His face was flushed with anger. A huge oil tanker was cruising past on the other side of the river. "I was under the impression from Uri that you were the best."

"We are the best Mr Walsh. The sea is an unforgiving place

to work in. Diving at night was never discussed, and neither was working with munitions."

"If you cannot dive at night, remove the shells and bring them up to the surface then there is no salvage job for you," Christopher stared at the diver as he spoke. He realised that they were embroiled in a mental wrestling match. The winner would take a greater slice of the financial rewards.

"I did not say that we couldn't dive at night," the diver back peddled. "Technically it is much more difficult and we would need some very expensive equipment to recover the salvage."

"Go on," Christopher baited the trap.

"We would need to hire submersibles. That way we could load sledges with salvage and use the subs to bring them up safely. The divers would need cutting gear which we can run from the subs power source. It is the only way to do it safely at night and not attract unwanted attention," the diver explained. He was pleased with his pitch so far. He guessed that his new employer would have absolutely no idea what he was talking about. He could pick a figure out of the air and double it.

Christopher reached into a pile of papers and retrieved a file containing some pictures and a diving magazine. He placed them on the table at the rear of the lightship bridge. The dive master walked toward them with a curious look on his face.

"I have two submersibles in the water ready to go. They are fitted with oxyacetylene torches and cargo sledges. My lightship is a familiar vessel in the bay, and so she will act as your support vessel, unless, you have any more objections that is?" Christopher pushed home his advantage and watched as the dive master's lip quivered.

"The equipment is fine Mr Walsh, but we still have the issue of handling munitions. We will need more money," the diver tried to recover his position.

"Of course you will. Ten thousand pounds sterling for every sledge you recover?" Christopher said matter of factly. He held out a sweaty hand and the deal was cemented.

CHAPTER 17
Victor Brastz

Victor glanced in the wing mirror of the Bentley and spotted the dark pick-up truck again. It was six or seven cars back but he was convinced that the driver was the same guy that had helped him out earlier on that day. It was dark now and he couldn't see the driver anymore but it was the same vehicle. He was sure of it. The police hadn't followed him for a long time, ever since he had turned informer. He was confused as to why someone would be tailing him, especially someone as dangerous as the man who stepped in and stopped him being kicked to death. The man was built like a battleship and he had walked through his attacker as if he wasn't there. He wasn't a conventional law enforcement officer of that he was certain. Victor clocked the registration plate of the truck and scribbled down the first three letters. He had to wait until the line of traffic behind him navigated a sharp left hand bend to get a clear look at the last digits. He scribbled them down and then stabbed a fat finger onto his car phone. The system cut off the stereo and filtered the telephone call through the speakers.

"Hello Victor," a voice answered. The man was Victor's handler from the Serious Crime Squad. He wasn't supposed to talk to anyone but him.

"I'm being followed by someone and I want to know what the fuck is going on," Victor growled down the line.

"Calm down Victor," the officer said irritated by his tone. "I haven't put a tail on you. What type of vehicle is it?"

"It's a black or dark blue Nissan pick-up truck," Victor replied.

"We don't use them. As far as I'm aware only military units use that type of vehicle," the officer sounded curious as he spoke.

"What types of military unit are you talking about and why is he following me?"

"I'm not sure, some of the counter terrorist agencies have used trucks in the past, but I'm not certain. You said why is 'he' following me," the officer emphasised the singular.

"Yes, he is a man. Are you stupid?" Victor missed the point completely.

"I understand that Victor, what I mean is that he is alone in the vehicle," the officer spoke slowly to try to help Victor to understand.

"Yes he is alone. Why does that matter?"

"It is significant because police and law enforcement agencies forbid officers to work alone at anytime," the officer explained. "Are you sure he isn't working for one of your associates?"

"No I can't be sure of that, but I am sure that I don't know him. I have the registration plate of the pickup. You can find out who it belongs to, right?" Victor read out his scribbled registration plate. There was a brief silence on the other end of the line.

"I'm not supposed to run vehicle checks on the whim of a paid informant," the officer said angrily.

"Look you might not have an informant if this guy is here to kill me," Victor snarled.

"What, are you scared Victor? That's not like you at all, is it?" the officer laughed as he mocked him.

"I'm glad you think that it's funny, just find out who the pick-up belongs to, you idiot," Victor was getting frustrated.

"I have the details on my screen Victor, and you're not going to like what I'm looking at," the officer's voice tailed off as if he was preoccupied.

"Go on then, I'm waiting."

"It's a government vehicle, registered to the ministry of defence."

"What does that mean?"

"It means that you have obviously attracted the attention of some very serious people Victor. What have you been up to?" the officer was intrigued by the fact that his informant was being tagged by a government agency. He was also pissed off that they were muscling in on his patch.

"Well do something about it then," Victor shouted at the

hands free kit.

"Victor even the divisional commander doesn't have jurisdiction over these guys. I'm afraid that you will have to deal with this on your own, however I'll make a few calls and see if I can shed some light on it."

"Thanks a fucking bundle, how is that supposed to help me now?"

"It's the best I can do under the circumstances. All I can suggest is that you keep out of trouble while they are following you."

"Brilliant. Why didn't I think of that?" Victor snapped.

"One thing I can tell you though Victor," the officer sounded cheery as he spoke.

"What?"

"If they wanted you dead then you would already be in a box. Stay calm while I make some calls and don't do anything stupid," the officer ended the call and the system fed the local radio station back through the vehicle's speakers.

Victor punched the ceiling of the Bentley twice, scuffing the skin from his heavily scarred knuckles. Things hadn't been going to plan recently, and now to top it all he had a government agent tailing him. He had been building a bank of cash up for the last six months. Victor was planning to flee back to the East away from the clutches of the police and his informer lifestyle. It was only a matter of time before the underworld realised that he was feeding information to the serious crime departments, and when they did he would end up being pushed through a band saw and fed to the fishes. That was not going to happen. The police had left him alone to a certain degree; as long as he fed titbits of information to his handler he was free to operate as normal. He had his fingers in lots of pies and his nest egg was growing nicely. Now that he was being tailed it would be far more difficult to disappear. Victor had to get rid of the man. There was only one person he could trust to help him out of this situation. He stabbed at the speed dial again and pulled up the number he needed. The name on the flashing screen was Uri.

CHAPTER 18
The Task Force

Grace Farrington hung up the telephone and sat staring at it for a moment before she finally stood up and moved away from the desk. She joined Major Timms and Chen at the digital screen which they were studying. The image on the screen was a satellite photograph of the Irish Sea. There was a zoom shot of the bay. The clarity was excellent. It showed the ocean wind farm which was situated off the North Wales coast near the tourist town of Rhyl. Across the bay there were three gas drilling rigs. The picture showed amazing detail and the rig workers could be seen on the platform. Their yellow hard hats were unmistakable against the metal structures.

"Is there anything unusual so far?" Grace asked as she joined the huddle.

"Not really," the major said. "It's a busy stretch of water. Supply ships and maintenance vessels are operating twenty four hours a day."

"I've finished speaking to all the ports that could feasibly handle unloading heavy cargo and there are no new or unusual vessels expected by any of them," Grace said.

"What about the possibility of smuggling salvage ashore somewhere and hiring the plant machines that would be needed to move it?" Chen asked.

"You can stick a pin in the map anywhere around the coast of Ireland where the bays and coves have been be used to unload contraband for centuries," Grace swept her hand along the southern coast of the emerald isle on the satellite picture. "We have alerted the coastguard and the local uniformed police divisions that there is the possibility of salvaged munitions being smuggled ashore. They're on red alert and watching all the possible landing sites, but it's like looking for a needle in a haystack."

"We are still looking for the wrecks," the Major turned to Grace as he spoke. "The Commander's oceanographic charts were marked here, here, and here. The satellite pictures have picked up six possible soundings, but we know that the bay is full of wrecks of every size and description therefore we cannot take it for granted that any of them are our wrecks. We have requested a Royal Navy submarine to make a pass through the area to survey the possible wreck sites, but they don't have a vessel close enough for a week."

"We daren't make too much noise on the subject of why we urgently need a submarine in the bay or the navy might become suspicious," Chen added.

"We have acquired full use of the NASA satellite as it passes over the Irish Sea. All we can do now is monitor the bay and look for anything unusual going on," the Major pointed to an aerial photograph of an area of the Bay of Liverpool, which was North West of the city. "The Navy are sending a mine sweeper to search this area here. It is the proposed site for an extension of the ocean wind farm which is sited there." The Major indicated a sector of the bay which was already the site of an experimental wind farm. The development of off shore green electricity production had been given the go ahead by the current government who were eager to boost their flagging ratings.

"We have requested a full sweep of the seabed prior to expansion the wind farm in this area here." The Major pointed out the proposed sites that he had identified.

It was perfectly normal for the Navy to search areas of the sea when a wind farm was to be built, especially in Liverpool Bay. The city was heavily bombed during the Second World War and there are hundreds of tons of unexploded ordinance offshore. Finding bombs when drilling the seabed is not advisable, hence the Royal Navy minesweepers are always sent in before any drilling work commences. It was the ideal ruse to get the Navy in the area without arousing suspicion.

"When will they have a ship available?" Grace asked.

"The day after tomorrow, the Major answered."

"Will they report anything going on beneath the surface, I assume there is drilling going on out there?" Grace was worried that the area wasn't being monitored twenty four hours a day.

"They will if we ask them to. When they arrive we'll ask for detailed reporting from the area."

"How did we get on tracing the submersibles that MI5 had information about? You had model numbers and pictures during our first briefing on the issue?" Grace asked Chen.

"MI5 were alerted by the purchase of the two subs. They investigated the purchase and discovered that they were acquired by a company registered in the Cayman Isles which they then investigated. The submersibles were shipped to Rotterdam in freight containers, and the intelligence agencies tracked them as far as Dubai. When the containers landed they were impounded and placed into a bonded customs warehouse and opened by a Dutch police unit which had followed them from Rotterdam. When they opened the containers there were no sign of the submersibles," Chen shrugged and clicked the image on the screen to the one that he had used in the earlier briefing. "When they opened them the containers were full of BMW motorbikes. Somewhere along the voyage there had been a switch."

"What about the company that bought them?" Grace asked. She frowned and her forehead wrinkled.

"We have found nothing at all, no offices, no business address, just a virtual company and a website. The directors don't exist and there are no bank records or any trace of any transactions in their name, apart from the purchase of the submersibles," Chen explained.

"I assume that we don't know where they are then?" Grace mused.

"Correct, we don't even know who bought them. MI5 haven't got a clue," the Major said.

"So potentially they could be operating below the surface without us knowing."

"They need a support vessel. A surface ship to provide power and air, and to land the salvage and that's what we have to look for, the support vessel," Chen explained.

Helen Walsh entered the office and headed toward the Major

and his agents. She was being closely followed by the robust figure of David Bell, who was affectionately nicknamed the fat controller. David Bell was the communication link between the taskforce and the other law enforcement agencies and intelligence units. He was an expert in most things and made sure that everyone was aware of that.

"We are having something of a disagreement," Helen snapped as she approached the throng. Her face was crimson and she looked flustered and annoyed. Her pretty blond features had darkened considerably with her mood.

"What is the problem?" the Major smirked. The fat controller looked red faced as if he had been in an altercation and he'd met his match.

"We cannot quarantine an entire city Major, it's absolute nonsense!" the fat controller removed his glasses and began to clean them with his tie. It was a routine action that had become a bad habit. He placed the spectacles back onto his nose and took a deep breath. He seemed to calm down a little before he spoke again. "There are nearly one and a half million people in this city centre at any one time. You simply cannot pen them in like rabid dogs, there would be absolute mayhem."

"On the contrary, if you allowed infected people to leave unhindered then the entire region could be contaminated within hours. He does not understand the nature of this chemical. He is comparing it with measles or a nasty cold, the man is a buffoon!" Helen countered bringing a wry smile to Grace's lips. Chen sniggered behind his hand

"I think that you should both calm down and explain what the contentious issue is. Please, let's all sit down and discuss this rationally," the Major gestured to the long meeting table and ushered them toward it. He looked at Grace and shook his head as if he were dealing with naughty children. Grace smiled back at him. It suddenly occurred to her that Tank had been gone all day and no one had heard from him. A shiver ran down her spine as if someone had walked over her grave. Her fear was probably unfounded because Tank could obviously look after himself, but still the thought lingered. "He would have called in if there was trouble, wouldn't he?" she thought.

"Now then, what is the sticking point?" the Major prompted

them as everyone sat down. He noticed the look of concern on Grace's face, and she glanced at her watch and then at the clock on the wall. Instinct told him that she was worried about Tank and the hairs on the back of his neck stood on end. He too had a strange feeling that he was in trouble.

"I'm concerned that my explanation of the effects of blister agents on infected people are not being taken seriously. Mr Bell used the analogy of rabid dogs, and he isn't far from the truth. According to several papers that I have studied infected victims suffer a period of total delirium when the thirst strikes them. You will in effect have a city full of rabid dogs if you do not evacuate. He has no idea how easy it is to infect anyone and anything that comes into contact with this chemical. Simply touching their clothes will pass the infection on for months," Helen Walsh kept her mouth hanging open even when she had made her point. It added to the impact of the words she had said.

"I am completely aware of the impact of a blister agent incident Miss Walsh," the fat controller removed his glasses again for effect.

"Helen."

"What."

"My name is Helen," she blustered.

"I'm aware of that, Helen, I'm sorry, but your proposals are completely impractical," David Bell tried to calm himself. He had to make his point clear to the Major without appearing to be unreasonable.

The Major stood up and walked to the coffee machine. Everyone remained silent as he pressed a button and the machine whirred into life. It delivered a hot brown liquid which was described as hot chocolate but rarely tasted anything like it.

"Perhaps it would be best if you explain what your counter measures would involve Helen, and then we can discuss the pros and cons as a team," the Major said as he sat back down at the table.

"The first thing to realise is that none of the people who have been exposed to the blister agent will know that they have been infected until the symptoms become apparent, by which time they could have infected dozens of others," Helen spoke clearly and precisely. She looked directly at the Major to reinforce her position. "You would have to treat everyone as if they have been infected until it is proven otherwise or until they have been thoroughly decontaminated."

"How would you propose that we quarantine an entire city for heaven's sake," the fat controller butted in.

"Please let Helen make her point," the Major said quietly without even looking at David Bell. He smiled and nodded at Helen. "Carry on."

"Working on the assumption that a chemical release was to happen either off shore or in the city limits, then you would have to make plans to seal off all the exit roads," Helen stood up and walked to the screen. The satellite picture of the bay and the surrounding coastal areas was still displayed. "The city has obvious boundaries. Some of them are geographic and others manmade."

Helen pointed to the coastline and the river estuary, and then followed the grey outline of the city's motorway system which could be seen clearly encircling the metropolis on the satellite image.

"The river is the natural boundary to the West, and the M53, and M56 motorways are the manmade perimeters to the south and east. The M57 motorway is the boundary to the north. They form a complete border encircling the entire city," she looked back to the group and tried to gauge their response. Chen, Grace and the Major were nodding in agreement but David Bell was staring at the ceiling as if he had no interest in her theory.

"If we used all the emergency services, police, firemen and ambulance services in the first instance, assuming that they all have access to protective clothing and respirators, then they could set up a cordon around the city. In phase two we would need assistance from the regular military and the Territorial Army to maintain crowd control at each checkpoint. We would set up decontamination showers and medical assistance centres at each intersection. Then we would have to filter the people through as quickly as the decontamination process will allow," she looked at each member of the team for a response.

"The whole idea is preposterous, absolutely impossible to administer and still leaves us with huge issues within the city centre," the fat controller could remain silent no longer.

"It seems perfectly plausible to me," Grace said. She looked to the Major and he nodded in agreement.

"Oh for god's sake don't tell me that you agree with this nonsense," David Bell stood and joined Helen next to the satellite image. "What about all the hospitals? What about the three high security prisons within the perimeter? What about the thousands of people at John Lennon airport or using the tube network? How would we get them to your decontamination showers Miss Walsh?" He was animated as he tried to express his opinion, and globules of spittle sprayed as he spoke. It wasn't one of his finer qualities.

"Helen," Grace said.

"What?" the fat controller glared at her and wiped spit from the corner of his mouth as he realised that he was becoming irate.

"Her name is Helen," Grace was winding him up.

"I'm well aware of that, I'm sorry, I don't mean to be rude," he took his glasses off again as he tried to regain his composure. "Look here, in the unlikely event that this scenario was to take place how the bloody hell would you keep all these people calm at a checkpoint? How would you get the emergency services to coordinate this and keep the actual facts from the wider public? The country would be in panic," he tried to slow down his delivery so that he could speak without spitting.

"There has to be a contingency plan in place. We cannot just sit back and hope nothing happens," Chen shrugged.

"I take your point about the airport and institutions being isolated but that would be the case anyway," the Major added.

"If we leave the city inhabited then the situation would be compounded later on as the blister agent's symptoms started to manifest themselves and people sought medical help. We would have to evacuate the city. Helen's perimeter plan is a sound one," Grace backed her up.

"What about the emergency services? The whole plan revolves around having a coordinated response from every service, how on earth can you ensure that and maintain a complete news blackout?" David Bell asked exasperated.

The Major was silent and he thought deeply about the scenario. He stood and walked back to the vending machine. He pressed the hot chocolate button again, completely forgetting that he hadn't touched the first one that he had poured just five minutes ago. The machine whirred into life once more and dispensed a murky brown liquid.

"We need to get the Ministry of Defence behind the evacuation scenario and implement a fake dress rehearsal," the Major turned to face the group. "We will tell the Minister of Defence that this is our worst case scenario, and to have the emergency services on standby for a dry run preparation exercise for a serious terrorist incident. That way we can keep a lid on things and still have complete control over what happens in the city."

"Brilliant," Chen said. "That way there will be no panic because no one would be aware that they may have been infected until they have already been decontaminated."

"Correct, and we can have all the services on standby without arousing too much interest from the public or the press," the Major walked back to the table. "Helen I need you to work with David on the action plan details please." Helen took a deep breath and smiled. She was relieved that the team had taken her advice. The fat controller had a face like thunder.

"David I need you to coordinate this joint response please. Communicate with the police commissioners and fire chiefs. Explain that we are going to implement a unique plan that will be a coordinated response for every major city in the British Isles, starting with Liverpool," the Major didn't expect any aggravation from the fat controller once his decision had been made, and he didn't receive any. "Get moving straight away."

The telephone rang and Chen picked up the handset and walked away from the table to take the call. Grace looked at his face to see if his expression gave anything away. It could have been her female curiosity but she didn't think so. There was something eating away at her, a gnawing niggling sensation in her mind that all wasn't well. She was hoping that the call was from Tank. Grace hoped that he was calling to tell them that he had gleaned some important information from the informer which he had gone to interrogate off the record. Chen's face darkened and he covered the mouth piece with his hand and signalled to the others that he had important news.

"It's our satellite monitoring people calling," he said. "There is an extreme weather warning being issued now by the BBC World

Service. A cold front from the Russian continent has passed over France dropping the heaviest snowfall for the last eighteen years, and it's heading straight for us." The group waited anxiously as he finished his call, but the news didn't get any better. "They are telling me that the cloud cover over the entire UK will be so thick that we will not get any useful surface pictures for the next seventy two hours at best."

The fat controller digested the information quickly and his razor sharp brain was already working on the problems that the heavy snow would create. Apart from the obvious problem of covering up the Irish Sea with thick cloud and blocking their satellite surveillance, the United Kingdom is renowned for grinding to a complete standstill when more than a few inches of snowfall occur. Every mode of public transport ceases to function when bad weather strikes our small island. Buses, trains, and taxis generally cease to operate. While motorways are a priority for the gritting crews and snowploughs, access roads to them are rarely passable when a snowstorm hits, which makes keeping them clear a farce as traffic can't reach them in the first place. The country simply grinds to a halt until the snow thaws.

"I'll include the highways department in the communications Major. If the main roads were to become impassable then Miss Walsh's, sorry I mean Helen's perimeter plans will be rendered worthless." There was no malice in his tone, just a factual observation of the new slant on the situation.

"Do that please David and let's get the gritting crews out on the main roads tonight. Use whatever leverage you have to get one step ahead of the game," the Major hadn't considered the weather as an important factor in their planning. He walked to the window and looked out across the River Mersey toward the Irish Sea and the Bay of Liverpool. The sky was masked by thick cloud already, and it had the curious luminous glow to it that signals a snowstorm is imminent. The first flakes started to drift down past the window. The lights of the city twinkled in the darkness from the streets below as the snow fall quickened and more flakes hurtled past the window. There were big fluffy flakes of new snow floating innocently down to the city's roads and pavements. "Dear god I hope we are blowing this whole thing out of proportion, because if we aren't then we are in deep trouble."

CHAPTER 19
Beneath the Waves

Christopher Walsh scanned the dark waters of Liverpool Bay with his binoculars. He had purchased them from a military accessory website for less than the price of a pair of designer shoes. They were far more useful than shoes. He could see for hundreds of yards through the darkness and the night vision binoculars cast everything with a green hue. Humans appeared as bright green blobs and the glasses highlighted body heat as well as form. The aft and stern lights of rig support ships that were working in the gas fields appeared as a bright lime green colour through the lenses. They hadn't encountered any problems on their journey from the estuary out into the bay. They had past a River Police launch near the mouth of the estuary but the officers didn't pay the lightship a second glance. The big red lightships were part of the port's maritime history. Two weeks prior he had anchored the two submersibles to an automated beacon close to the wreck site. They were safe there and had been less than three meters beneath the surface resting on a sandbank. The automated lightship beacon warned passing shipping of the sandbank's existence, forcing them to steer clear of the area, which made it the ideal place to operate from unnoticed.

The initial dive had gone well and the wreck had been positively identified as a ship built in the forties. There were rusted shell casings on the sandbank around her which must have spilled from a huge rent in the hull. The forward holds looked to be secured and the divers had begun to cut through the hull with torches. The first penetration of the wreck had yielded plenty of salvage. A sledge had been loaded with over one hundred blister agent shells and had been successfully transferred to the L2. They were about to set sail and return the salvage to the quayside, which meant that the submersibles would continue to operate on the wreck using their integrated batteries while the support vessel was away. The plan was to unload the first batch under Christopher's supervision and then the dive master would return for the second bigger sledge load with the lightship, recharge the submersibles with power and air and repeat the process. At least that was the plan. The dive master wasn't at all happy leaving his team below the surface while the support ship returned to shore. He said it was too risky. Christopher on the other hand said that they were being paid for the risk that they were taking, but the two men were still at loggerheads.

"The subs can work down there unaided for six hours, and that is just a guideline," Christopher pointed to the information sheet that he was quoting from.

"Exactly it is a guideline to be used when everything is fine and the divers don't encounter any problems," the dive master countered.

"They haven't encountered any problems."

"They haven't encountered any problems yet. They are using the wrong cutting torches. I told you that we couldn't use any old system where munitions are concerned," the dive master had specified that acetylene could not be used at all deeper than ten metres because the gas becomes unstable at depth.

"I had acetylene torches and you said it was too deep to use them. You specified hydrogen torches and that is what I supplied. They are state of the art," Christopher crossed his arms sulkily.

"No Christopher, you have supplied oxy-hydrogen torches which are far hotter. It is madness to cut the ship open with them when we don't know what is behind each panel that we cut."

"There is only eight hundred degrees centigrade difference you idiot. Hydrogen torches cut at two thousand degrees centigrade which is hardly a huge leap at those extremes. Your men would have to be ultra careful using those cutters anyway. If you are trying to push the price of the job up again then forget it. I'm taking the first sledge back now as we initially agreed. We will unload it and you can be back to your team within the allotted time," Christopher was adamant.

"Why are you remaining on shore?" the dive master snapped. He was resigned to the fact that he didn't have a great deal of say in proceedings.

"The shells are in varying stages of decay. I need to assess the load and then plan their shipment accordingly. I need them landed and moved tonight."

The dive master looked away from his employer without speaking and opened the door of the bridge. The weather had closed in and snowflakes were tumbling down onto the old red ship. The snow was starting to stick, coating the metal decks and the handrails with crisp white powder. The engine roared and the water at the rear of the lightship turned into white foam as the propellers began to churn up the waves. The boat moved forward slowly at first but soon it was cutting a sway through the dark waters back toward the twinkling lights of the port and the city beyond.

Beneath the waves Ivan Rostock was trying to copy his colleague. Ivan had spent most of his life lying and cheating for a living. His only true attempt at being an honest working man had been a two year spell working as a guide for a scuba diving company in Kenya. He attained his open water diving certificate whilst on holiday in Egypt and from there applied for the position of scuba guide in Africa using forged documents which identified him as an advanced diving instructor. Ivan was given the job and by diving with groups of tourists twice a day he soon became a competent diver. The warm clear waters of the Indian Ocean were a pleasure to work in. He earned a modest salary which was usually trebled every month with tips from grateful tourists. Being a guide around the reefs meant that knowing where all the best sea life hangs out would pay a dividend. Each section of the coral masses is a unique ecosystem consisting of different marine life, some common but others far rarer. Knowing where the rare creatures lived could double your tips for the day as the divers captured unusual photographs and a highly prized entry for their dive logs. Seeing rare species would give them the bragging rights at their local dive centre when they returned to their respective countries.

The job finished when Kenya tore itself apart in a bloody civil war following shambolic rigged elections in 2007. The elections disintegrated into terrible ethnic cleansing as neighbouring tribes turned on each other. Tourists were told not to risk visiting the African country and foreign workers were advised to leave the country until the violence subsided. Ivan decided to try and ride out the political storm but the foreign visitors heeded the advice and stopped coming. Within weeks he was out of work and broke. Ivan headed for the United Kingdom and drifted from one bad job to the next. Soon he had fallen into cahoots with the Eastern European crime families, and when the word went out one day that experienced undersea salvage workers were required for a one off operation he lied his way into the dive team. The diving bit wasn't too difficult for him, although it was much deeper than he was used to, and the visibility was appalling. Once he had become used to a technical diving rig instead of a standard aqualung, then the basics were the same.

All they had to do was cut through the hull of a wrecked navy vessel with gas burning torches to allow the submersibles access with their grabs. The subs would then move onto the wreck to remove salvage. In theory it should have been a simple operation. The problem was that he had never used a cutting torch above the waves never mind below them. There was very little light from the cutting torches as they burned which was deceiving as they were cutting at two thousand eight hundred degrees Celsius. Ivan watched his colleague as he carved a ragged line down the hull of the ship. His torch seemed to be making light work of slicing the thick metal open where as Ivan was struggling to make any headway. He held the torch closer to the hull and squeezed the oxygen trigger tighter. The effect was to boost the cutting temperature to its highest possible limit. Ivan didn't realise that the hull was thicker where he was cutting, hence his progress was slower.

The reinforced section of hull was harder to cut which forced Ivan to leave the cutting torch focused on one section for longer. Although he managed to penetrate the metal it was causing the surrounding hull to reach a much higher temperature, and so were the shells behind it. His colleague waved a gloved hand toward him. At depth in the murky waters of the bay it was barely noticeable. He was trying to warn Ivan not to burn the torch so close to the metal. Ivan caught the movement in the corner of his eye and pulled the torch away from the hull. His colleague opened his finger and thumb apart to indicate a six inch gap was needed between the cutter and the hull. Ivan nodded and made an okay sign before beginning to cut again. He noticed a dull red glow coming from inside the ragged hole that he had cut. It looked like the tip of long cigarette was burning inside the ship. In actual fact Ivan had burned clean through the hull and ignited the tip of a Bangalore torpedo, which is sometimes called a Bangalore Blade. They are an explosive charge attached to the end of a hollow metal tube and are used by soldiers to clear barbed wire, mines and other booby traps. The charge fuse had been ignited by the heat from Ivan's cutting torch. The burning fuse would reach the main explosive in less than two minutes.

CHAPTER 20
John Tankersley

Tank followed the Bentley Continental out of the city. It was heading north toward the seaside resort of Southport. The Bentley was half a dozen vehicles in front of him as they approached a section of dual carriageway, and as the road widened, the prestige vehicle accelerated like a rocket. The massive engine took the car from sixty to over a hundred in seconds. Tank was trapped in by other cars and could only watch as the vehicle's tail lights faded into the distance. He had been following the vehicle for most of the day now, waiting for the right moment to get the occupant Victor Brastz alone. In hind sight it would have been easier to snatch him off the street and put him in custody for interrogation, but that would have alerted the serious crime units as soon as he had been released. There was nothing for it now but to wait and see where he was going.

Tank floored the accelerator pedal and the pickup roared after the speeding Bentley. A small two door hatchback in front of him pulled out into the overtaking lane and blocked Tank's progress. He had to slam on the brakes to avoid running into the back of it. Tank slammed a huge fist onto the horn and flashed the main beam headlights. A hand appeared from the driver's window and the middle finger was raised prominently in a gesture of defiance. The gesture angered Tank further and he pushed the pickup to within inches of the obstinate driver's rear bumper. He flicked the main beam again but this time he left it on. The light was blinding the driver in front and the dazzling reflection from his rear view mirrors became too much to tolerate. The driver indicated to move over and swerved into the slower lane, he offered Tank his middle finger again as the pickup truck roared level with him.

Tank floored the accelerator once more and the truck lurched forward again gathering pace. The tail lights of the Bentley disappeared in the distance as the vehicle took a wide bend in the road ahead. Tank guessed that it was at least half a mile in front already. He had to catch it before they reached the maze of one way streets that dissected the town ahead. Tank knew the resort well but the Bentley could easily lose him if he didn't close the gap. The pickup was flat out and the speedometer was passing one hundred and ten. He approached the bend where he'd lost sight of the vehicle at full pelt, and as he turned through it, he could see a line of traffic up ahead which was stopped at a red light. The Bentley was five hundred yards ahead of him stuck behind an articulated lorry and a convoy of a dozen other cars. Tank eased off the gas and brought the pickup to a reasonable speed as he joined the queue behind the lorry. He was three vehicles away from Victor's Bentley and two miles away from the Victorian resort's centre.

The next two miles were uneventful as they passed through a series of traffic lights and pedestrian crossings. The articulated lorry hogged the road and there was no room to pass it. They approached the junction of Lord St and the promenade as they entered the town centre. Lord St was the main shopping area and lined with high class fashion outlets and grand hotels. It was the only remaining section of the town to be kept in decent order as the resort around it fell into varying states of dereliction. The Bentley took the left hand filter which headed onto the beach road. Tank indicated left and followed it. The beach road forked about two hundred yards further on; one road led to the promenade area which encircled the old boating lake and a decaying marina, while the other headed for the beach road and the old funfair. The Bentley reached the fork in the road and stopped. There was no other traffic around and Tank was only fifty yards behind the vehicle. Tank gritted his teeth and swore under his breath. If the Bentley didn't move quickly then Victor would see him in his rear view mirror. The game would be up before it had started. Suddenly the Bentley's engine roared and the vehicle screeched away toward the beach road leaving a cloud of burning rubber smoking behind it. Although the beach road was miles long it was essentially a dead end. The beach itself was miles wide and literally ten miles long. There were long sections of the beach that ran up to acres and acres of undulating sand dunes. If Tank followed him then he would have to confront him there and then. There could be no more cat and mouse. Tank cursed again and steered the dark pickup onto the beach road.

The diesel engine in Tank's truck sounded louder than usual as he crawled toward the dark shadows of the derelict fairground. The remaining wooden skeleton of the rollercoaster was looming in the darkness. Tank noted that a few flakes of snow had started to fall. He looked at the sky. It was heavy with thick grey snow clouds waiting to dump their loads. He stared into the darkness looking for any sign of the Bentley but there was nothing to be seen. Tank turned off the headlights and pulled the truck over to the side of the road. He needed to allow his eyes to become accustomed to the darkness. The car phone bleeped and the screen displayed a withheld number. The text on the display was specific to only one number, and he knew from experience that it was someone on the taskforce network calling.

"Hello," he answered.

"What's happening?" Grace kept the conversation sharp and brief in case there were other people listening.

"I'm secure Grace," he said indicating that he was alone and could talk freely.

"We're checking in with you, have you had any joy tracking your informant?"

"Not yet but I'm about to confront him, he's driven down a dead end and I'm following. Once I've located him I'll break cover and take measures to retrieve any information that he may have."

"Does he know your tailing him?"

"I don't think so, but we'll soon find out."

"Be careful," Grace lowered her voice. Grace Farrington the agent had gone for a second and was replaced by Grace his lover.

"What's the matter Grace?"

"Nothing, I've got a bad feeling about this one, that's all."

"Woman's intuition working in overdrive then is it?" Tank tried to lighten the tone but it didn't work. His eyes were becoming used to the pitch darkness and he could distinguish the shapes of several vehicles parked randomly on the wide sands of the beach about half a mile away, although none of them was a Bentley.

"We have lost the use of the satellite to monitor the bay," Grace changed the subject.

"Why?" Tank asked, and he watched snowflakes sticking to his windscreen. He instantly knew the answer.

"There's a huge snowstorm on the way," she answered.

"That's all we need. Can we get the navy out there any faster?"

"There's a minesweeper en route."

The contoured silhouette of the Bentley moved out of the shadows a few hundred yards up ahead. The vehicle had been obscured from his view by the funfair. It had no headlights on as it drove down an access ramp onto the dark sands of the beach.

"My target is on the move Grace I need to go," Tank didn't wait for a reply. He disconnected the call and pushed the gearshift into first. The black pickup purred loudly as it moved slowly toward the fairground and the beach beyond it. The Bentley's headlights came on and pierced the darkness with two wide beams of light. The vehicle accelerated quickly leaving deep tyre tracks in the hard sand. Within seconds it was out of sight behind the sand dunes which separated the road from the beach. Tank drove the truck past the fairground and then down the access ramp onto the beach. The rear end of the truck fishtailed as the tyres tried to find purchase in the sand. Tank flicked the pickup into four wheel drive and the vehicle instantly began to grip the surface. Once he was on the sand he could see the rear lights of the Bentley in the distance. The car was travelling at speed and would soon be out of sight again if he didn't act now. He kept his own lights switched off and accelerated across the wide open sand in pursuit of Victor Brastz.

Tank edged the pickup up to sixty miles an hour when the back end started to fishtail again. He eased of the gas and regained control. The Bentley wasn't any closer but it wasn't any further away. A car loomed out of the darkness to his left. The windows were steamed up by the heat generated from the courting couple within. The roof and bonnet were already covered in a fine coating of white powder. The snow was starting to stick. Tank turned his attention back to Victor Brastz but the red taillights had disappeared completely, and so had the headlights.

"Shit!" Tank shouted, and he punched the steering wheel. He leaned closer to the windscreen and peered hard into the darkness but he couldn't see further than about fifty yards across the sand. It was total blackness. The dull glow of artificial lights from the nearby resort was screened out by the tall undulating sand hills. He had no choice but to switch on his headlights. The powerful beams revealed nothing but miles of sand as far as the eye could see. Tank steered the truck to the right to aim the beam that way. There was nothing. He steered the truck to the left and repeated the process, and still there was nothing.

"Shit! Where are you Victor?" Tank hissed. He steered the pickup hard left and headed toward the sand dunes. The hills were tall and steep like a miniature mountain range. The more established dunes were bound together by thick sharp grasses. Wide paths had been trampled through the grasses by the armies of tourists that crawled over them every weekend.

"You can't just disappear," Tank said slapping the steering wheel again.

There was a glint of light five hundred yards away from the bottom a large sand hill. The grasses were thick there. Tank aimed the truck in that direction and he could clearly see the rear wheel arch of the Bentley. He steered the truck toward it.

"What are you doing out here Victor?" Tank whispered in the darkness of the truck cab. The glow from the dashboard instruments accentuated the muscles in his jaw. They twitched with tension as he approached the sand dunes.

Tank flicked the headlights onto full beam as he neared the vehicle. He steered the pickup to come directly behind the Bentley, effectively blocking it in against the base of the dunes. As he straightened the truck he could clearly see through the rear window and had a good view of both sides of the Bentley. There was no one in the driver's seat, but the driver's door was open. Victor Brastz was lying on his back. His arms were splayed above his head and his legs were still in the foot well of the car. His head was turned sideways away from Tank. The engine was still running and exhaust fumes were blowing from the tailpipe.

Tank smelled a rat straight away. This had the word trap

written all over it. He took out his nine millimetre Glock and opened the driver's window. Tank steered the pickup toward the Bentley and the prone man. When the front of the truck drew level with the rear of the Bentley Tank reached out of the window, pointed the Glock and fired twice. The first bullet crashed into the driver's door and shattered the panel into three jagged pieces. The second smashed the driver's window into smithereens of glass. Shards of the material sprayed Victor Brastz but he didn't move. Tank gritted his teeth and drove the truck forward. He aimed and fired two more rounds into the sand near Victor's head. The bullets crashed into the compact sand spraying huge fans into the air and covering Victor's head and face, but still he didn't move.

"Either you're very brave or you're very dead," Tank whispered to himself.

He aimed the off side tyre onto Victor's extended hand. The body twitched slightly as the heavy pickup crushed the exposed digits to pulp, but even then didn't move. Tank opened the door of the truck and climbed out onto the sand. There was a fine coating of snow on the ground and it crunched in the silence as he scoured the floor for give away footprints but there was nothing unusual. He took a few steps toward Victor and leaned over him. Victor's body was illuminated by the headlights from the pickup and Tank could see a dark trickle of blood which ran from the centre of his forehead into his right eye. There was no telltale black ragged bullet hole there though. Maybe Victor Brastz wouldn't be parting with any information after all. He looked like he had been hit very hard or shot with a small calibre handgun. Tank lowered the Glock and checked Victor's pockets for his wallet and any other information that he might have on him.

There was a rustling in the grasses on the far side of the Bentley. Tank looked over the bonnet and noticed that four boot prints had been left behind on the vehicle itself by whoever had hit Victor. That was how they had left the scene without leaving any prints on the ground. Unfortunately Tank had noticed the clues too late. A shape exploded from the grass and leaped across the bonnet of the Bentley, touching it only once. Tank stood to face the attacker and he raised the Glock ready to fire, but the man was too fast and had the drop on him.

Uri launched himself off the bonnet of the Bentley and hit

Tank with the force of a steam roller, before he could raise his gun and fire. The Glock span out of Tank's hand and landed in the sand underneath the Bentley. The two men hit the front of the pickup truck with a loud clang. Tank connected against the front grill of the truck with the side of his head. He took most of the impact below the temple which stunned him momentarily. Instinctively the men grappled as they fell and then bounced onto the sand. Each man was trying to get a decisive grip on the other. Tank was incredibly strong but the head trauma had weakened him considerably. It was all he could do to hold onto his attacker. Uri freed his right hand and swung it in a wide arc. The right hook hit Tank in the temple, the same one that he had injured in the fall and a blinding flash of pain seared through his brain. Tank tensed his neck muscles and his forehead shot forward and connected with Uri's mouth. The head butt cracked one of Uri's front teeth and smashed his bottom teeth against his lips. The fragile tissue of his lower lip split wide open and he cried out in pain. Uri released his bear like grip for a second and Tank shrugged free of him.

Tank was on his feet in a flash and although his legs were unsteady he pounced on his attacker. As he lunged at Uri he was hit hard from behind by an unseen fist. The punch caught him below the left ear and bruised the soft nerve centre there. A blinding flash went off in his head and he turned to face the fresh onslaught. Victor was crouched in a wrestling stance ready to attack. Tank was confused and looked at his crushed hand. The fingers were twisted into unnatural shapes but they didn't look real. Victor smiled and tapped the forearm below his wrist. It made a hollow plastic noise. The limb was prosthetic and Tank hadn't noticed it, nor had he read it in his file. Victor wiped the trickle of blood from his forehead and Tank realised that there was no wound there at all. He had been set up. Victor grinned and then flew at him.

Tank anticipated the rush and stepped sideways out of harm's way. As Victor came into range Tank swung his right shin using all the power in his body by twisting from the hip and it crashed into Victor like a baseball bat. Tank's shin bone was conditioned by years of training on heavy pads and sandbags. The blow cracked three of Victor's ribs as he careered past him. Tank followed up with a heavy elbow strike to the back of his head. Victor crumpled like a concertina onto the sand. Tank turned to see that Uri was rising quickly and he moved like lightening to initiate the first decisive attack. Tank launched a powerful left hook, right cross combination. The hook was parried by a skilful block but the cross hit the target and Uri buckled as the giant fist connected with his jaw. He hit the Bentley as he stumbled which stopped him falling on his back, but Tank wasn't about to let up the attack and he was already throwing the next set of blows at Uri. A vicious knee strike caught Uri straight in the centre of his face. His nose cracked and blood flowed freely from both nostrils. Uri was blinded as his eyes watered with pain. The blow was so powerful that his head bounced off the wing of the Bentley leaving a melon shaped dent in the vehicle. Tank threw a low roundhouse kick which struck Uri below the knee. It swept his feet from underneath him and he crashed onto the sand again. Uri was losing badly. The big government agent was just too powerful. Tank was on him like a flash and he forced a muscular forearm around his throat. The powerful limb squeezed his windpipe closed and consciousness began to fade. Uri reached a shaking hand into the lining of his jacket. He wrapped his fingers around a small aerosol canister of Mace and aimed it over his shoulder. He depressed the button and the incapacitating spray hit Tank full in the face.

Tank didn't see the aerosol spray coming. The gas hit him square in the eyes which blinded him instantly. The chemical constricts the airways of the nose and throat making it difficult to breath, and he released the choke hold that he had on Uri. Uri scrambled away from him and sat gasping for air on the sand. Tank collapsed to his knees. He was holding his hands to his eyes as the pain and discomfort increased. Victor was up and he kicked Tank in the ribs hard. The blow winded him badly as he was already struggling to breathe. Tank knew that he had to try and get away from his attackers before Uri recovered from the choke hold. He was totally defenceless, only his survival instinct was driving him onward.

Uri caught his breath and a dull glint of metal turned his attention beneath the car. Tank's Glock was inches away from his face. He grabbed it and stood up on shaking legs. Tank was trying to crawl away on his knees, but every time he made a yard of progress Victor threw a brutal series of kicks into his midriff. He was coughing and spluttering as the chemical constricted his breathing and the kicking began to take a terrible toll. Uri walked behind him and raised the Glock above his head. He was holding it by the barrel like a hammer. Uri brought the gun down in a wicked arc and it hit Tank on the first vertebrate at the base of the skull. The big agent groaned and shook his head. Tank knew that he was nearing unconsciousness and that he had been hurt. Uri lifted the gun a second time and brought it down with force again. Tank dropped face down in the sand for a second, but then he coughed and spluttered and tried to stand. Victor punched him hard in the face knocking his head backward and exposing his chin. Uri hammered the butt of the pistol across Tank's jaw, which twisted his head violently and sent the nerves in his spine into shock. Tank fell face down into the sand and became still.

CHAPTER 21
The Mersey Estuary

Constable Danny Lee had been an officer in the River Police division for nearly a decade. He thought that he had seen everything that there was to see on the River Mersey, drug smugglers, people traffickers, modern day pirates, arms smugglers, diamond smugglers, illegal immigrants and the odd Irish terrorist or two. The port handled millions of tons of freight every month, which was carried by container vessels from all over the globe. Despite the impressive list of arrests that he had made, his working day was usually trouble free. The small police cruiser he piloted was comfortable enough and was big enough to carry two police officers and half a dozen handcuffed passengers if necessary. They generally cruised inland up the estuary toward the many petrochemical plants that lined the riverbanks at Runcorn, and then navigated across the river at its widest point to the huge oil storage depot at Stanlow. It was one of the county's biggest storage facilities and had been the target of Islamic Extremists and the Irish Republican Army several times. Access to the oil tanks from the river was easy and so the River Police division monitored it hourly. From the oil depot they traversed the river again to pass by the John Lennon Airport which was also situated on the riverbank, and was another possible target for terrorists. Dropping a fully loaded passenger jet full of tourists would be relatively easy for a competent combatant with rocket propelled grenade training and a boat.

Constable Lee was half way through his nightshift when they were alerted to a suspected arms smuggling shipment that could possibly be sailing into Liverpool. The information was scant and they were ordered to be on the lookout for any unusual activity on the river. He was annoyed by the lack of specific details because he was a stickler for procedure. Being told that there could be arms being smuggled into the port was like being told that it might rain, but then again it might not. To cap it all he had also been told that there was an extreme weather warning being issued across the entire country. Heavy snowfall was expected. Constable Lee lived twenty five miles from the port in a green belt area which was serviced by narrow country lanes that were only wide enough for one vehicle at a time. When it snowed they became impassable and that would mean that he would have to walk home from the main road again for the third time in three months. The journey on foot would be a two and a half mile trek through the snow following a twelve hour night shift.

"Fucking hell, that's all we need," Danny said to his fellow officer.

"What's up Danny?"

"Severe weather warning apparently, there's a bloody snowstorm on the way," Danny Lee grumbled. He picked up his binoculars and scanned the mouth of the estuary. Snowflakes began to spiral down and they landed on the lenses where they melted and distorted his vision.

"You're in for a long walk home after the shift then eh?" his colleague scoffed. He reached into the cabin and retrieved a stainless steel thermos flask and two mugs. He twisted the top and steam drifted from inside. "Here get your mouth around this it'll warm you up."

"Thanks Darren, you're a star," Danny said as he took a steaming mug of strong coffee from him. He sipped it and although it burnt his lips it tasted good. Darren always brought good strong coffee and fresh meat pastries on board.

"Do you want a pastry?" Darren asked, even though he already knew the answer.

"What flavour are we on today then?" Danny asked, as he took another big sip of the coffee. Darren's wife was of Indian origin and she loved to cook for him and his workmates. Every day she prepared and baked different meats laced with oriental spices wrapped and baked in pastry.

"Lamb Tikka," Darren answered proudly handing one of

them to his partner. He held a second pastry underneath his nose and inhaled deeply enjoying the spicy aromas.

"I don't know where you found that woman but I'm glad you did," Danny joked. He put down the binoculars and bit into his pastry. "That's really nice," he added spraying pastry flakes from his mouth as he spoke. He brushed them off his dark police uniform with the back of his hand.

Darren picked up the field glasses and looked through them. Thick flakes of snow were tumbling with more vigour now. He took a large bite of his Tikka parcel as he scanned the estuary. "That is my favourite," he said with his mouth full. He was about to take another bite when he became still and stopped chewing. Danny noticed the look on his partner's face and followed his gaze to see what he was looking at. In the distance he could just make out the aft and stern lights of a vessel through the flurrying snow.

"What is it?" Danny asked his colleague.

"It's one of the lightships," Darren answered displaying the contents of his mouth as he chewed.

"What direction is she headed?" Danny was confused by Darren's concern. His eyebrows lifted and he screwed his face up accentuating the wrinkles around his eyes.

"She's headed toward the docks at Seaforth I think," Darren said. He took another bite of his pastry and washed it down with a mouthful of coffee.

"Which one is it?" Danny asked, still frowning. It wasn't unusual to see lightships in the estuary even though had been replaced by remote ships. They were still used occasionally to service the port authority's beacons. Some of them had been sold off to collectors and others were in maritime museums.

"L2," Darren said frowning. He put down his food and his coffee and looked at the ship again through the binoculars. He turned to his fellow officer with a look of concern on his face.

"L2?" Danny said. He reached for the shift manifest and checked all the sanctioned movements of port authority vessels for that day. "She isn't on our list for today."

"She isn't likely to be. She was decommissioned years ago."

"Are you sure?" Danny turned to look at his partner. He picked up the radio microphone and tried to make contact with headquarters. There was nothing but static. The storm clouds were beginning to effect radio communications.

"Of course I'm sure, she was used as a restaurant at the Albert Docks for a while, remember? We went there once with the girls," Darren said. He was referring to a day out shopping they had with their wives a few years earlier.

"Oh yes I do, it was defiantly the L2 that we had dinner on. What the bloody hell would she be doing out in the estuary?" Constable Danny Lee tried to call into headquarters again but he was met with nothing but static.

"I think we should check her out," Darren said.

"I agree but if we're sailing to a potential arms smuggling operation then we need to break out the weapons," Danny said. In the event that officers felt that they needed to be armed then they needed authorisation from senior firearms officers ashore, however if communications were broken then the unanimous agreement of the officers on board would suffice. "Are we agreed?"

"Agreed," Darren consented. Constable Lee took a keychain from his tunic and climbed down the step into the cabin where the weapon's lockbox was situated. His partner followed him and removed his own set of keys. The two policemen inserted their keys at the same time into the corresponding locks and turned them. The lockbox clicked open and they removed two model 14 Glock nine millimetre automatic pistols. The model 14 was smaller than the model used by Tank and his team, and as the number indicates it holds only fourteen rounds in the clip as opposed to the seventeen rounds held by its big brother the model 17. Both men placed Kevlar helmets on and then checked each other's equipment for combat readiness.

"I'll try headquarters again," Constable Lee said as they climbed back into the bridge. "Set a course to intercept her."

"We're all set on course, estimated time of interception is seven minutes," Darren said. "Is there any joy with the radio?"

"Nothing but static, I'm going to start signalling the L2," Constable Lee said. He climbed onto the bulkhead above the cabin and switched on an Aldis signal lamp which communicated to other vessels by sending Morse code via a series light pulses. He began to click the lamp on and off requesting the lightship to hold its progress and stop the engines. The river policeman signalled them to state the purpose of its voyage, and its destination. He repeated the message three times without receiving any response from the crew of the L2. "They're not responding to us, I've got a really bad feeling about this," Constable Danny Lee said shaking his head. Thick flakes of snow fell from his helmet. The river policeman didn't know how right he was. He thought he'd seen it all but he was about to learn that he hadn't at all.

CHAPTER 22
'On Board the L2'

Petre Gustav was becoming seriously concerned about the situation that he'd found himself in. He was originally from Poland and had travelled to the United Kingdom to look for work along with hundreds of thousands of his countrymen. When he arrived in the country the prospects of employment were very positive. The economy was at its peak and the future looked bright. The wages in the UK were worth ten times what he could earn at home in Poland. Twelve months later the world economy had crashed and things couldn't be any worse. Petre had worked in the gas drilling industry as a diver and welder based on the drilling rigs in Liverpool Bay. When the credit crunch arrived it wasn't long before the British workforce turned on their foreign workmates demanding that jobs were given to indigenous British workers before foreigners were considered for vacancies. There was a series of wildcat strikes which brought the petrochemical industry to a standstill forcing the government's hand. Petre and many of his countrymen were given their papers and made redundant.

Petre knew that Uri was a Mr Fix-it and he asked him to keep his ear to the ground for any diving work that he heard of, even if it was unlicensed or illegal. Eight months later Uri had come back to him with the proposition of leading a salvage team employed by a man called Walsh. Uri had explained that he was an eccentric character, but that he was an incredibly wealthy man. The price for the contract was ludicrous, almost two years salary for a what would equate to a few week's work. Petre couldn't refuse the opportunity. He pieced together a ragtag salvage team of Eastern Europeans and shook hands on the deal.

Now he was sailing back to shore with his dubious employer having left his team below the waves cutting up a warship full of ancient ordinance in order to recover the brass shells for salvage. It didn't add up. The price of scrap metals had spiralled upwards recently as the economies of China and India boomed and their capacity to manufacture goods was being limited by the amount of ores that they could purchase. Even so, ten wrecked ships full of brass wouldn't cover the cost of the wages that Christopher Walsh was offering. There had to be more to this operation than first met the eye. He had raised his concerns with Uri but he wouldn't expand on the details any further, and he wasn't the type of man that he wanted to anger. Uri made people lots of money but he also made people disappear. The only reason Petre was still here was the money. This was to be his last hope of securing his future in Britain. His hopes were dashed and his fears realised when he saw Christopher Walsh began to panic as a river police launch set a course to intercept them. The river police began to signal them.

"Fucking hell do something will you! Don't just stand there," Christopher Walsh shouted at Petre. Petre didn't understand why he was panicking.

"What would you like me to do?" he asked looking out of the bridge into the darkness. He cupped his hand over his eyes to stop the interior lights reflecting on the glass. The sky was dark and the snow was falling heavily now. It reminded him of his home, Poland. The police cruiser was cutting across the estuary at an angle, and was making a beeline to intercept them.

"We cannot let them see the sledge. Cover up the shells quickly," Christopher said. He was biting his lower lip and looked like a teenager in trouble.

"They are covered," Petre answered him without looking at him.

"Well check them for god's sake!"

Petre looked at his employer and headed down the stairs to the lower decks. The sledge loaded with the first batch of shells was slung at the rear of the ship where a life raft would normally hang. He walked along the narrow corridor toward the stern. The corridor opened out into a large open area which had been used as a restaurant when the ship was a tourist attraction in the port's refurbished dock area. The ship's hull was fitted with a series of portholes every few metres. Petre crossed the open space and looked through a porthole which was the size of a large dinner plate. The sledge was swinging gently with the ships motion and the shells were secured and covered with a thick green tarpaulin. Petre turned and headed back along the corridor. He walked past the metal stairs which led down into the cabin areas. Petre felt the urge to explore them. Curiosity got the better of him. He hadn't been down there before and he thought that he might be able to find something which would explain the predicament that he was in. None of Christopher Walsh's rhetoric made any sense at all. The lack of salvage rights was one thing, diving at night was another, and then using the wrong equipment in the proximity of munitions was the straw that broke the camel's back.

He descended the narrow steps and found himself in a dark corridor. There were cabin doors on either side, and each one was fitted with a round porthole. He peered into each cabin as he walked the length of the corridor. Most of the cabins were stripped to the shell but others were fitted with bunk beds and small foldaway tables. The cabins were not remarkable until he looked into the last one.

At first Petre didn't realise what it was that he was looking at. As the realisation hit him he felt his stomach twisting and his lower bowel loosening. His eyes widened and bile began to rise in is throat. On the floor was a bloated bloody body which was once Joe Hammond. The head, face and torso were blistered with huge yellow swellings which were stretched wafer thin as if they might burst at any second. In comparison the legs and feet appeared almost normal in their dimensions which amplified the condition of the upper body. One of the hands was severed at the wrist. The wound was jagged and pieces of bone and ripped arterial tissue hung from the stump. The hand itself was on the opposite side of the room hanging from a metal pipe. There was a silver handcuff fixed around. It looked to Petre as if the hand had been ripped from the arm, and blood was splattered across the walls and ceilings. He looked at the inhuman face and felt tears welling in his eyes. The eyelids were hideously swollen but between the tiny slits he could see the eyeballs moving. The abomination on the cabin floor was still alive. Petre tried to open the cabin door instinctively as the first tears ran down his cheek. He was fighting nausea with every breath and it was a huge effort to keep the rising bile down in his stomach. The door wouldn't budge it had obviously been locked. Petre began to back away from the cabin door still transfixed by the hideous being within, when a heavy monkey wrench struck him on top of the skull. It crushed the skull cap and cleaved a wide gash in the skin. Petre crumpled to the floor in a heap.

"Nosey bastard," Christopher Walsh spat as he watched the Polish diver twitching on the metal floor.

CHAPTER 23
Tank

John Tankersley started to come around but he remained absolutely still. He knew from his training and experience that as soon as he moved his attackers would be on him. He remained completely still as he ran through a series of mental checks. Tank assessed the pain that he was in and tried to analyse his injuries. The back of his skull was throbbing and felt swollen but he still had feelings in his torso and legs. That was a good sign and meant that his neck wasn't broken. His breathing was hindered which he didn't think was due to the pepper spray. The effects of that were easing and his eyes had stopped stinging, although his throat felt like he had swallowed razor blades. Tank could feel stabbing pains in his ribcage as he breathed in. There were at least three or four ribs cracked by his best guesstimate, and that was hampering his breathing. It would also seriously handicap him if he needed to fight his way out of whatever situation he was in.

Tank could hear a machine whirring at high speed and a grinding noise coming from somewhere close by. The sound was metal on metal. He could also hear compressed air hissing and diesel generators running. He was either in a garage of some type, a factory or a vehicle body repair shop. The chances were that he was in an illegal chop shop. Victor Brastz was known to have links with car ringers across the United Kingdom. Tank had read that in his file. He wished that he had paid as much attention to the rest of his file then he would have known that Victor had a prosthetic limb and he wouldn't have been caught out on the beach. Tank knew that now was not the time to highlight his mistakes though. If you made a mistake in the world of counter terrorism then someone died, today it would probably be Tank. He was in terrible danger he could sense that. Tank could also feel that he was bound tightly to a post of some type. There was no blindfold though and no gag, which wasn't a good sign at all. Whoever had him didn't care if he saw their faces, nor were they worried that he might start screaming for help. That meant that he was being held somewhere remote where his screams for help couldn't be heard, and that his captors planned to kill him once he had been interrogated so it didn't matter that he could identify them.

Tank listened intently to his surroundings to pick up any information that might help him out of this predicament. Apart from the machine noises there wasn't much to go on. There was a heavy odour of engine oil and spray paint. He could also smell thinners or turpentine. Tank was almost certain that he was in a chop shop, which wasn't good because it would almost certainly have Eastern European crime family connections. The Eastern Mafioso did not tolerate any threat to their business interests. Trouble was annihilated without mercy. He steeled his resolve mentally before opening his eyes. Tank spotted three things in the first few seconds.

The first thing that he noticed was a bad thing. The two men who had beaten him unconscious were sitting in a glass walled office about twenty yards away. They were talking to another man who was wearing oily overalls. His hands and face were smeared with engine grease. They spotted that he had awoken immediately.

The second thing that he noticed was a good thing. His black pickup truck was parked near to a set of double doors twenty yards to the right of the office. That was good thing because it was fitted with a GPS tracker, as are all government vehicles. If and when the taskforce realised that he was in trouble then the first thing that they would do is to check the tracker for its location.

The third thing that he noticed was a very good thing indeed. His model 17 Glock was on a workbench five yards away from him next to his wallet and his keys. The Glock was registered to the Ministry of Defence, and then sub registered to a counter terrorist unit with the highest security clearance. British law does not allow an armed officer to draw his weapon without clearance from a senior member of the hierarchy. This law caused a problem for the intelligence units and counter terrorist officers as the world they work in does not grant them the time to seek permission to use a weapon. To get around the red tape the taskforce and units similar to them, have their weapons chipped. As soon as a weapon is removed from its lockbox or holster a sensor reports it and the time and place are registered on the taskforce computer. The chip also feeds information from the weapon itself. If it is discharged another signal is sent. The technology is designed to alert high command that an agent has been compromised and could need backup. The icing on the cake is that every pistol is married to its user. If the weapon is used and then contact between the handle grip and the agent's hand is broken for more than ten seconds then an alarm is sent that the officer is either incapacitated, has been disarmed by an enemy or is dead. Tank didn't know how long he had been unconscious but he did know that the taskforce would already have a reaction team on route. The chips in the gun and the truck would lead them straight to him. All he had to do now was to stay alive until they arrived.

The three men in the glass walled office spotted that he was awake. Victor and his partner left the office and headed toward him. The grease monkey headed in the opposite direction toward the machine shop noises. He had to weave between a dozen or so prestige vehicles, some were covered in paint splattered tarpaulins others were painted in grey primer ready to be sprayed a different colour. There was a wide wooden sliding door which partitioned this section of the shop from the one where the machines were working. The grease monkey slipped between the door and the wall and was gone. The two men that had jumped Tank headed toward him. Tank noticed with some glee that Victor and his friend were banged up around the face. They didn't look very happy as they approached. Tank met them with a wide toothy grin.

"That lip looks sore Victor," Tank sneered as they approached. Victor's bottom lip was swollen to twice its original size and there were tooth marks etched deep into the pink flesh.

"I'm glad that you have a sense of humour," Victor growled. He swung his right hand in a clubbing motion and smashed Tank in the mouth. The punch numbed Tank's face and sent pain shooting upwards from the nerve endings in his teeth through his brain.

"To be fair I think my mother hits harder than that," Tank smiled and revealed blood smeared teeth. He spat a blob of blood and phlegm which landed on Victor's foot. Victor flushed crimson with anger but Uri pulled him back from hitting him again.

"He is trying to wind you up Victor," Uri said calmly.

Tank eyed Uri coolly. This man had been trained by the military at some point. Tank was trying to provoke Victor in order to avoid the imminent interrogation. It was standard Special Forces procedure if captured. The longer a direct line of questioning could be avoided the less information the enemy could glean. Everyone had a breaking point. The longer the captive would spend under torture the more information he would part with. Tank was playing the game but Uri knew the rules too.

"Let's stop fucking about shall we? Why were you following Victor?" Uri asked. He picked up a claw hammer as he spoke.

"I'm investigating a stolen car ring and we received information that Victor was involved. It looks like I've found the chop shop, thanks for that," Tank answered flippantly.

"You are not a policeman. Policemen investigate stolen cars not military units." Uri walked toward Tank and placed the head of the claw hammer against his cheek. Tank felt the cold tungsten steel against his flesh. "I'll ask you once more, why are you following Victor?"

"We know that Victor is an informer for the Serious Crime Squad. He passes information to one of their officers mostly about his European connections," Tank fed Uri a partially true line. He was playing the game again by trying to split the opposition. Uri looked at Victor and frowned. Victor blushed again and despite shaking his head he looked as guilty as sin.

"That is bullshit!" Victor punched Tank in the mouth again. Tank tensed his jaw against the blow to stop his jawbone from breaking. He could still fight and function normally with broken teeth and split lips, but a broken jaw was a totally different kettle of fish. Tank twisted his head and spat blood into Victor's face. Victor raised his hand again but Uri pulled him away again.

"Victor is a fucking grass, he turned informer to avoid a jail sentence and deportation. The Serious Crime Squad has him on their payroll. I needed some information about an Eastern European operation, so Victor was the first obvious person to milk for it," Tank added fuel to the flames. Uri was nodding his head and looking at Victor.

"I believe you," Uri said looking back at Tank. "What operation were you investigating?"

"What do you mean you believe him?" Victor was open mouthed as he turned on Uri. The two men faced each other, Victor was snarling but Uri was calm.

"There have been rumours about you for a long time Victor," Uri shrugged his shoulders. He turned back to Tank. "What operation were you investigating?"

"What are you talking about Uri, what do you mean rumours?" Victor protested vehemently. The more he protested the guiltier he looked.

"Shut up Victor," Uri said quietly. "Answer the question, what operations are you investigating?"

"We are investigating money which is being laundered in this country. It is then sent to Chechnya to purchase arms and aid to help the Islamic extremists who are fighting the Russians," Tank lied. Uri showed no signs of emotion in his expression. Tank couldn't read him so he decided to continue, but this time he was telling the truth. "Victor has a slush fund in an Icelandic bank that he intends to use to escape the country. I work for a military counter terrorist unit and we believe that his associates are using the same company to launder their money. I needed to question Victor about his Chechen associates here."

Uri stared at Tank as he spoke but he gave no indication whether or not he believed. Tank could not read his expressionless face.

"How do you know about Victor's bank account?" Uri was looking for threads of truth in the story that Tank was telling. The devil is always in the details. Concentrate on the details and the truth soon unravels.

"The account that he has is a fabricated one manufactured by the intelligence agencies. It is a virtual account created by the computer boffins in the serious crime units. They drip feed him small amounts of cash every time he spills his guts to the police. As soon as he tries to leave the country or withdraw a large sum of money it will be dissolved. There isn't really any account there," Tank explained. It was in fact the truth. Victor's face darkened again.

"Bullshit! Kill him now he's lying," Victor ran at Tank and punched him again. Uri tried to stop the blow and it glanced harmlessly off the side of Tank's head. Tank smiled again to annoy Victor even more. "I think my sister hits harder than that Victor. When you get to prison they'll love a little fairy like you."

"I'm not going to prison you bastard," Victor was purple in the face with anger.

"You're nothing but the crime squad's bitch Victor, and the best of it is that you're too stupid to realise that you're being fucked up the ass," Tank laughed and spat at him again, blood and phlegm trickled down his forehead and he smeared it away with his sleeve. His eyes had become dark and were full of hatred. Victor was the weak link and Tank had to keep the pressure on him. It was a diversionary tactic taught to Special Forces personnel all over the globe, 'the interrogated manipulating the interrogator'.

"He's a fucking liar," Victor lunged at Tank again but Uri grabbed him by the collar. "Uri I bought my Bentley with cash two weeks ago. Pound notes you fucking dog."

Tank laughed again which had the desired effect on Victor. Uri shook him violently to calm him down but he was having little success.

"They let you buy the Bentley because it has got more bugs fitted in it than the jam tent at the ugly bugs ball," Tank didn't know that but he was improvising and making a convincing job of it too. "Now they can listen to everything you say and do all day long. You're nothing but a puppet."

"It sounds like genuine secret service tactics to me," Uri said holding Victor by the scruff of the neck. "They catch a stool pigeon like you and pay them to sing, except the money never actually exists. Oh you can take a few hundred out here and there but the bulk of the balance that you see is an electronic mirage, virtual money. As soon as you try to run it will never materialise Victor my friend." Uri released Victor and he staggered backward a few steps.

"I'm not a stool pigeon Uri," Victor was beginning to lose his composure. "I've been stringing them along and feeding them bullshit to keep them off my back." Victor lunged at Tank again and kicked him hard in his left knee. It was painful but hardly an incapacitating blow. Tank spat in his face again. It was the ultimate provocation. All the time they were talking about Victor and his indiscretions the taskforce were getting closer, and Uri was getting nothing from Tank except trumped up accusations about Victor. He had to keep playing for time.

Victor wiped the blood and phlegm from his cheek and ran at Tank flailing his arms like a windmill in a hurricane. The blows were weak and ineffective. Tank closed his eyes and tensed his body to absorb the pain. Eventually Victor became tired and Uri once again pulled him away. He pulled a stool away from beneath a work bench and pushed Victor onto it. Uri placed his hands on Victor's shoulders and pressed down hard. Victor wouldn't stop glaring at Tank until Uri grabbed his chin between his fingers and thumb. He turned his head toward him and spoke very calmly.

"Victor, this man is a government agent and he is a good one too. He has been trained to impede any enemy interrogation by using a number of simple tactics. So far he has succeeded in deflecting my question about which operation he is investigating by provoking you, and because you are as thick as pig shit, you're allowing him to play for time. Now if you don't shut up and sit down I'll slit your throat. Do you understand me?" Victor seemed to understand that Uri was deadly serious. He nodded weakly and looked down at the oily garage floor. Uri waited until he was certain that Victor was calm before turning to face Tank.

"What Eastern European operation were you investigating?" Uri stepped closer to Tank. Without waiting for an answer he swung the claw hammer above his head and then pulled it downward at a sharp angle. The hammer smashed into Tank's cheek ripping the flesh from the bone and shattering one of his molars. The pain in Tank's head was blinding. He prayed to a god that he didn't believe in as Uri raised the hammer again.

CHAPTER 24
Grace Farrington

When Tank cut of their telephone call earlier he had said that he was about to confront his target. He had also said that he was heading into a dead end. Grace had replaced the handset and then sat looking at it for long seconds before making her mind up what to do next. Chen was on the other line at a desk across the room. Grace saw him frowning and he summoned everyone over to him with a wave of his hand. She really didn't have time for this.

"That was the port authority's night shift manger. The river police unit has set a course to intercept a decommissioned lightship vessel which is heading toward Seaforth docks. Most of the docks there are derelict. They have signalled her to stop her engines, but she hasn't answered," Chen said as he put the phone down.

"What the bloody hell are they playing at? We specifically told them not to engage anybody until we had been informed," the Major had a face like thunder.

"Apparently their radio is playing up because of the snowstorm. It is causing stratospheric propagation. They couldn't get a response via their radio and they eventually requested permission to engage by using a mobile phone. By that time they were almost on top of the lightship. They are estimating a three minute interception time," Chen shrugged. There wasn't a great deal that could be done about the situation.

"Get back onto the port authority and tell them to instruct the river police to stand down. They must shadow the lightship but they are not to engage her under any circumstances," Major

Timms said. Chen nodded and picked up the receiver. The Major turned to Grace and the team. "Get kitted up and meet that boat at the docks. Use all necessary force to see what is on board that ship."

"Major I want Chen to lead the team, I'm going to back Tank up. He was about to confront his target and I have a hunch that he'll need backup," Grace swallowed hard as she spoke. She knew that it didn't make sense, but she also knew that something was wrong.

"If John Tankersley needed back up then he would have requested it Grace, now get your team together and intercept that ship. That is an order," the Major growled. His face darkened as he spoke. Tank and Grace should not have been allowed to work in the same unit together. Their relationship was always headed for a train crash as far as professionalism was concerned. Grace was putting her concern for her lover over the welfare of a potentially crucial investigation. Everything that they had on the job so far was conjecture, but he couldn't risk being wrong about this one.

"I have a really bad feeling about this Major," Grace offered. She glanced at the clock on the wall. It had been twenty minutes since Tank hung up the call.

"If you're so concerned Grace then call him, and then get your arse over to that dockside and investigate that lightship. We need to discuss this situation between you and John in depth when you return," the Major couldn't tolerate it any longer. He had allowed it to go on far too long.

"Yes sir," Grace turned to walk away and she knew that her days as a taskforce agent were numbered. If the Major wouldn't tolerate their relationship any longer then it would be her that would be transferred. There was no doubt that Tank was the best operative in the best unit, in the best armed force on the planet. Suddenly a shout went across the office.

"We have an agent compromised!" a voice shouted from the monitoring section. An electronic signal had been received by the intelligence agencies listening posts, and then relayed to the taskforce. Grace felt her heart stop beating for a second and the noise in the office seemed to stop. All she could hear was the blood pounding through her veins and the words, 'We have an agent compromised', echoed through her mind. She looked at the Major and he looked back at her. He didn't say a word but she got the message from the expression on his face. There was a silent communication from him to her and Grace turned and headed for the elevators.

"You two are with me," she shouted to two taskforce agents that were close to her. The two men moved like lightening without questioning her orders for a second. The Major watched the elevator doors sliding closed and he could see the fear in Grace Farrington's eyes as she met his gaze. They hadn't confirmed that it was Tank that had been compromised yet, but they both knew that it was.

"What have we got?" the Major said as he turned and walked into the monitoring section.

"Approximately five minutes ago two shots were discharged from Agent Tankersley's Glock 17. Possession of the gun was lost shortly after that. The gun and his truck are currently on the move at these coordinates. We cannot get any response from him," the agent read the information from a computer screen. In the top right hand corner was a passport size photograph of Tank from his army days. The Major stared at the wide forehead and the angled jaw. He had a face like stone. Major Timms hoped that if he was still alive that he could live long enough for Grace to get to him. If he wasn't alive then God help whoever had killed him because Grace Farrington was a force to be reckoned with.

"Send that information and those coordinates to Grace Farrington. Keep updating her as the coordinates change," the Major turned to Chen. "Get your team ready and intercept that lightship at the docks."

"Roger that," Chen stopped. "Has Grace gone to back up Tank?"

The Major didn't answer he just nodded once and walked away. Chen could see that he was very worried. He was just about to head off when the monitoring section sprang to life again.

"Major you had better come and see this," the monitor shouted. All the agents stopped what they were doing and listened to what was happening.

"What have you got?" the Major asked.

"We have automatic gunfire reported from a container vessel

in the estuary. The location is where the river police and the lightship are," the monitor looked shocked as she spoke.

"Jesus, I told you to order them not to engage that lightship," the Major turned on Chen as he approached.

"I passed on your orders to the port authority Major. Maybe they couldn't get a hold of the officers on the launch," Chen answered.

"That's not all I'm afraid Major," the monitor interrupted their conversation.

"What else do you have?" the Major's voice was stern.

"We have picked up a number of underwater explosions in this sector here," she pointed to an area of the bay not far from a line of treacherous sandbanks. It was nowhere near the wreck sites that they had earmarked but it still didn't bode well.

"That's about a mile from any of the sites we're monitoring," Chen said.

"It's too much of a coincidence for it not to be connected Chen," the Major was struggling to understand how they could have got it so wrong.

"I'll check the geography between the explosion and the sector that we are monitoring Major. Only a strong undercurrent or a marine trench could explain how the wreck would travel so far away underwater," Chen answered embarrassed by the situation. "Is there any way that this explosion could have been caused by the gas rigs hitting an unexploded Second World War bomb or some other ordinance?"

"How big was the explosion?" the Major asked the monitor shaking his head.

"There was one major explosion followed by a series of large blasts. There was a considerable shockwave created by an explosion, and its epicentre was the seabed here."

"We need information from every vessel and drilling rig in the bay immediately," the Major ordered.

"What type of information Major?"

"We need visual reports from anything that is in that sector. Specifically relating to any flotsam on the surface and any unusual clouds or fogbanks."

"Fogbanks sir?"

"Yes, fogbanks, and do it now. Chen get your men to the docks and get them suited in protective equipment and respirators. Get the fat controller down here immediately," the Major headed to his office.

"Yes sir, anything else sir?"

"Yes, get a red alert to the police chiefs, and an all points bulletin to the relevant government departments. I need the Minister of Defence on the telephone now. We have to evacuate the city."

"Major," Chen shouted to him before he reached his office.

"What?"

"What about Grace, she's already out there without any protection?" the two men looked at each other for the answer but there was none forthcoming.

CHAPTER 25
The River Police

Constable Danny Lee continued to signal the lightship until they were in earshot of the vessel. He switched on the megaphone and hailed the pilot of the ship. The lights inside the bridge were on but he couldn't see anyone in there.

"L2 we need you to stop all engines immediately, and prepare for boarding," he wiped snow from his brow. There was a thick layer of white crystals covering the decks and rails now. He waited a moment for a response but none came.

"L2 please respond immediately," he tried again and got the same response.

"There's nothing doing Danny. They've got something on board that they don't want us to see," Darren said over the noise of the engines as he steered the boat closer to the lightship. They were just fifty yards to the starboard of her when they noticed movement inside the bridge.

Christopher Walsh dragged the unconscious body of Petre Gustav up the metal stairs into the bridge. He could hear the river police hailing them, but he had no intentions of acknowledging them. He had to buy enough time to get the lightship to its remote birth and unload its deadly cargo. Unloading would take twenty minutes or so. Once the shells were on land he had a truck ready to move them to a private airfield situated between Liverpool and the seaside resort of Southport. From there he could move them to any number of locations well out of reach of the authorities. With the shells safely stored somewhere he planned to release the details of the blister agent plot to the press himself. The authorities would deny that the shells had ever existed of course but then he could produce some of them. One to the BBC, another to Sky news, the New York Times and the rest could be distributed to a selection of foreign press contacts and organisations as solid proof that the plot existed. The news would spread around the world like a wild fire that the 2012 Olympics had been targeted by terrorists who were in possession of a blister agent. The resulting news furore would make his chemical counter measure treatment priceless. All he had to do now was lose the police launch.

Petre began to groan as he started to come round. Blood from his head wound had run down his forehead into his eyes and mouth. He licked the blood from his lips as he regained consciousness. Christopher ran back down the stairs and then reappeared a few seconds later with a jerry can full of paraffin. He flicked open the cap and began pouring the oily liquid all over the injured dive master. Despite being groggy, Petre could smell the flammable liquid and a stark realisation sent him into a panic.

"What are you doing, you lunatic?" he spluttered. He tried to stand and grabbed at the bridge rail to help him up. The dive master was groggy and his feet slipped from underneath him and he thrashed around on the metal decking. He tried to rise again to find the door and escape but his vision was blurred. Petre wiped congealing blood away from his eyes with his sleeve. Christopher stalked him as he moved toward the bridge door like a cat playing with a mouse, poised to strike.

"Get away from me, you crazy bastard," Petre shouted. He summoned as much courage as he could but the sight of the blistered man in the cabin below had shocked him to the core. His voice was cracked and shaky.

"Get off my boat, you piece of shit," Christopher pointed to the bridge door. Petre grasped the handle and opened the door. The cold air rushed in and a flurry of snowflakes drifted through the opening. Petre turned his back on Christopher and stepped out into the night. Christopher lit a match and threw it onto the dive master's shirt. There was a loud whooshing sound as he was transformed into a walking inferno. Petre tried to scream but as he inhaled, flames rushed down the trachea and frazzled his vocal cords. He could feel his lungs and throat crackling as they withered under the intense heat. Christopher grabbed the bridge handrail and lunged at the burning man with a powerful front kick. His foot struck the burning man in the small of the back and catapulted him over the guardrail and into the Mersey Estuary.

"Oh my god, did you see that?" Constable Lee shouted to his partner.

"I'm changing course now," Darren answered and he swung the boat starboard away from the lightship toward the burning man in the water. The flames had been doused slightly by the seawater but his hair and face were still burning fiercely. The engines of the lightship roared as the vessel accelerated away from them in the opposite direction.

"Jesus Christ, they'll get away," Danny Lee said. He took up a solid shooting stance and raised his weapon. He squeezed the trigger three times. The bullets smashed into the bridge of the lightship but he couldn't see if he had hit anyone or what effect they'd had. The L2 disappeared into the snow as the police launch reached the burning man.

"Get him out of the water," Darren shouted.

Constable Lee stepped off the bow of the boat and edged along the side ledge whilst holding onto the roof rails with one hand. There was a narrow ledge which allowed access to the stern. He leaned over precariously and reached into the water. He held tightly to the launch and grabbed the man by the back of the neck. The rise and fall of the waves made it difficult to maintain any grip on him.

"He's already dead," Constable Lee said. He was looking at the man's blackened face. The skin was peeling away from the bones of his face. One of his eyeballs had burst leaving a blackened ragged hole which was full of seawater in its place. "I can't lift him, you'll have to help me."

Darren brought the vessel to a stop and put the engines on idle. He stepped onto the ledge and joined his colleague. They reached into the water again and tried to grab hold of the body. The swell was worsening as the wake from the lightship started to buffet the launch. They waited for the body to rise with the swell and then grabbed at it again. It was then that they heard the sound of diesel engines approaching at speed. They looked around but couldn't make sense of anything in the snowstorm. Suddenly the bridge lights on board of the lightship came into view less than fifty yards away.

"What the fuck is that?" Danny Lee asked incredulously. He couldn't turn around without losing his grip on the body. Darren turned and his jaw fell open.

"Oh shit," he said calmly without any panic in his voice.

The river policemen released their grip on the dead man and watched helplessly as the L2 bore down on them at full throttle. There was a man stood on the bow of the deck aiming a machinegun at them. The muzzle flashed as a hail of nine millimetre bullets ripped into the launch. Two high velocity rounds hit Darren in the face ripping the left hand side of his skull away from his head. Danny Lee was splattered with his partner's brains and he wiped them away with his fingers. The L2 was three times the size of the polycarbonate police launch and was made from steel plate. It hit the police boat amidships ripping it in half. The launch exploded into a thousand splinters as the fuel tanks ignited. Constable Danny Lee was completely aware when the burning fuel engulfed him, and he had the sensation of weightlessness as the explosion tossed him high into the air. The initial pain as his skin burnt seemed to pass quite quickly and darkness overwhelmed him. He was dead before he hit the water.

Christopher Walsh steered the L2 full circle and headed toward the docks again. He was more than happy with the way things were going until a series of huge explosions a mile or so behind him rocked the lightship dangerously. He looked out to sea and watched a fireball spiral up toward the snow clouds forming a huge mushroom shape as it climbed.

"You were right about those cutting torches being too hot," he said to no one. He pushed the throttle of the L2 as far as it would go and the boat surged toward the docks. Christopher reached for his cell phone and dialled Uri.

CHAPTER 26
The Old Funfair

As Uri raised the claw hammer for the second time two things happened. Firstly there was a deep rumbling which sounded like thunder but louder. The sound proofing in the chop shop dulled the noise but it didn't stop the vibration that travelled with it. The second thing to happen was his mobile telephone began to vibrate and a shrill polyphonic ring tone echoed through the old fairground building. His eyes had glazed over and they cleared slightly as if the tone had snapped him out of a hypnotic state. The stoic expression on his face seemed to change and he lowered the hammer. Tank relaxed his muscles and breathed deeply. He was grateful for the temporary respite. The deep rent in his cheek was agonisingly painful and blood ran down his cheek and neck. It soaked into the neckline of his tee shirt, but it appeared that the onslaught had paused for the moment. Uri reached inside his jacket and removed his mobile. He looked at the screen to identify the caller and shook his head in disbelief when he recognised who it was.

"What are you doing using your mobile to call me?" Uri snarled at the caller.

"The radio isn't working. I think it's the snowstorm interfering with the signal. Anyway, where are you?" Christopher Walsh moaned.

"I'm busy clearing up your mess, and I'm keeping the authorities off your back Christopher. You shouldn't be using an open line to call me," Uri turned away from Tank and headed through the maze of vehicles toward the glass walled office.

"Shut up Uri, I need you at the docks now," Christopher

sounded panicked.

"What is the matter?" Uri asked.

"The river police were following us, and I caught Petre snooping about down stairs," Christopher answered.

"Did you go and see what he was doing Christopher, and did he see your experiment? You'll have to take care of him if he did," Uri ordered. "What are you doing on the river anyway?" Uri was confused and he fired one question after the other.

"They started diving tonight. I didn't know where you where so we began," Christopher sounded wounded.

"Jesus, have you recovered anything?"

"Yes, I have the first sledge on board now and the divers were still working on the wreck when we left the site," Christopher explained.

"What do you mean they were still working?" Uri became seriously concerned by his employer's demeanour and his use of the past tense.

"I think the wreck has just blown up," Christopher blurted.

"Shit, I've heard a lot of rumbling noises, were they coming from the wreck?"

"I'm not sure, I think so, there was a series of explosions and a fireball somewhere near the dive site."

"Where is Petre now?"

"He's dead, I had to get rid of him because the police were very close," Christopher was frustratingly vague. "He said that the cutting torches they were using were burning too hot."

"Okay, so where are the police?" Uri tried to bring him back on track.

"I scuppered their boat. They're gone now and I'm heading back to the docks, but I need help to unload the salvage," Christopher sounded like a lost child.

"The place will be crawling with police."

"No they will not find the berth, they'll be looking for cargo facilities and somewhere with cranes," Christopher was adamant that he was cleverer than the police.

"You might be right. I'll meet you at the dock in an hour," Uri cut off the phone call and placed the mobile in his pocket. He kicked an oil drum and it clattered across the floor. "The man is a fucking idiot!" he shouted and kicked the oil drum again. It catapulted off the ceiling and then bounced off the roof of a Jaguar hitting Victor on the head on its travels. Victor looked aggrieved but he daren't move from his stool. Uri weaved his way through the cars again toward Tank. He stopped at the workbench where Tank's gun was and picked it up. Uri switched the safety into firing position and chambered a bullet.

"This is your last chance to answer the question. What operation were you investigating?" Uri placed the cold metal against Tank's windpipe.

"You're going to pull that trigger no matter what I say," Tank said smiling. His face was distorted by the ugly swelling on his cheek. "So why don't you go and fuck yourself, pull the trigger and then look forward to spending the rest of your life in a cell next to Victor."

"We need to move Victor, get your car started," Uri ordered as he pressed the gun barrel hard into Tank's flesh.

"Victor will be pleased if you're his cell mate, at least he'll have someone to look after him in the showers," Tank goaded.

"Why don't you start the car and let me shoot the bastard?" Victor sneered as he approached them. He held out his hand to take the Glock from Uri.

"Yes, give him the gun, he's a useless prick," Tank said nodding toward Victor. "The chances are he'll miss and shoot me in the ear."

"Shut your mouth!" Victor screamed at the top of his voice. Once again Tank had riled him to the point of madness and avoided Uri's questioning.

Just for a split second Tank thought he had seen a green laser spot on Uri's chest but he couldn't be certain, it could just have been wishful thinking. Uri's attention flickered for a moment too, and he stared into Tank's eyes looking for confirmation of something. Tank didn't think that he'd given any indication that he'd seen anything, but then he couldn't be sure if he'd seen anything in the first place. Uri moved backward a step.

"Fuck it! The operation has turned into shit anyway," Uri said and he handed the gun to Victor with a sly grin on his face. "You have two minutes Victor, I'll be waiting in your car." Uri looked at Tank and smiled, and then for the second time that evening he turned and walked away toward the fire exit at the back of the chop shop, but this time he moved much quicker.

"What do you have to say now then, big mouth?" Victor sneered into Tank's face, revealing tobacco stained teeth. Tank could smell cigars on his breath.

"You should try a mouth wash every now and again, your breath reminds me of my dog's arse," Tank laughed as he spoke. The pain in his face was terrible but it was better than a nine millimetre bullet through the head would feel. He knew that these were the last few minutes of his life unless the taskforce arrived to save him, but somehow he felt it was too late. Victor raised the gun and smashed it backhanded into the wound on Tank's cheek. Tank grimaced and tried to suppress a cry of pain. He didn't want to give Victor the satisfaction of knowing how much it had hurt. His eyes filled with tears as the pain in his head reached an unbearable level.

"What's the matter, big mouth? Did that hurt?" Victor pouted like a woman applying lipstick. "Is your face sore? Have you got nothing insulting to say before I blow your fat bald head all over the workshop?"

"Please," Tank whispered. His eyes flickered closed and his lips moved silently.

"Please? Is that all that the big tough guy can manage?" Victor squeezed Tank's face in one hand while he held the gun to his throat with the other. His finger nails dug into the vicious wound on Tank's cheek and the pressure amplified the pain to white hot level.

"Please I want to..." Tank's whisper was almost inaudible. His eyes flickered slightly once more and his head lolled like a puppet with its strings cut.

"Oh dear, what do you want tough guy?" Victor goaded and mockingly turned his face so that his ear was closer to Tank. Tank's head flopped to the side as the strength in his body ebbed away.

"Please..." Tank mouthed silently but no words came out.

"Don't die on me, big mouth, I haven't shot you yet. What are you trying to say?" Victor laughed and turned his face some more.

Tank's eyes snapped open and he lunged his head forward like a King Cobra snake biting its prey. His teeth latched onto the meat and gristle of Victor's left ear and he bit down as hard as he could. Victor was so shocked by the sudden attack and the pain in his ear that he dropped the gun. He tried desperately to prise himself away from the gnawing teeth. He roared in pain and cried for help but Uri had exited five minutes ago and the mechanics couldn't hear over the noise of their machinery. Victor flailed wildly at Tank but the more he struggled the greater the pain became. Victor's blood poured from the corner of Tank's mouth. It mixed with his own saliva and ran down his neck. It was like a scene from a hard core vampire movie. Tank kept his head very still to stop the ear from tearing off completely but maintained the pressure of the fierce bite. He couldn't allow Victor to rip the ear free from his grip. If he did, Tank was dead. The pain in his cheek bone was sending flashes of white hot pain through his brain as he bit down hard, but he had to maintain the pressure despite it.

"I'm going to kill you, let go of me, you bastard," Victor screeched like a banshee.

Tank grimaced through the pain and bit down harder. Victor squealed like a pig. "I'll kill you! I'll kill you!"

"Let go of him, I think you're hurting him," a voice whispered from behind him. Even with his peripheral vision he couldn't see where the voice had come from because of the post that Tank was tied to. Tank could feel his bonds being cut by someone, but the voice was distorted as if they were wearing a mask of some sort.

"Where are the others?" the voice whispered as they cut through the ropes. Another taskforce agent with a respirator on his face moved swiftly in front of him. He took a black combat spike which looks like a square screwdriver and stabbed it through Victor's temple in one swift movement. The combat spike is designed to penetrate the human skull with a modicum of force thus killing the enemy quickly, and more importantly, in silence. Tank felt Victor's body sag as he died and he released the pressure in his bite. The body fell almost silently to the floor. Grace swooped around from behind him into his line of vision. She too was wearing a respirator.

"Where are the others?" She asked in a whisper. She removed a small satchel from her belt and flicked it open. From it she removed a spray anaesthetic and a gauze adhesive pad. She applied a field dressing to Tank's face in seconds. Tank pointed to the screen separator silently, indicating that the other men were behind it. Grace waved her gloved hand toward the screen and her two man squad threaded their way silently between the prestige stolen cars. Tank watched them check out the enemy's situation on the other side of the screen before they disappeared from site. Grace looked at his wounded face and his blood soaked clothes. She looked concerned as she removed a syringe and attached a needle to it. There were three small vials of amber liquid in the pouch and she removed one of them and extracted the liquid into the syringe. Tank felt a slight scratching pain as she injected it into his upper arm.

"Are you hurt anywhere else?"

"Three or four broken ribs I think. All of them on the left hand side."

"Pull up your tee shirt," she ordered as she rummaged through her field kit.

"You're so romantic," Tank joked as he lifted up his clothes. He winced with pain as he moved.

"Shut up Tank, this isn't funny," Grace never cracked a smile as she applied a pain relieving freeze spray to his ribcage before wrapping him up with a roll of thick splint tape to give him some support when he moved.

"I'm sorry, I was joking," Tank offered an apology. He began to feel the drug affecting him immediately as it coursed through his brain.

"Save it for the Major," she replied sharply. She looked away from him as the sound of suppressed automatic machinegun fire drifted from behind the screen. There were three bursts of fire and then her team returned. They ran their fingers across their throats to indicate that all the mobsters were eliminated. Tank noticed that the grinding machines had fallen silent. His brain felt like sponge but the pain was ebbing away.

"What's with the respirators?" Tank asked, his speech slightly slurred. Modern films depict Special Forces as always wearing gasmasks but it isn't always the case. They are only worn when the use of incapacitating gas is considered likely.

"There has been an explosion in the bay and a river police launch has been fired on," Grace explained. She turned to her men, "we don't know if it involves the blister agent yet but we can't take any chances. Help me with Tank." Tank winced in pain as the two men stood either side of him to give him support. They moved him toward the door.

"Wait, one of them left through the rear fire exit. He's the one that we need to follow, I'm sure of it," Tank gasped. "He was questioning me about an Eastern European operation and he was very concerned about it. If anyone knows anything, it's him."

"Okay let's move out and see exactly where he is headed," Grace ordered. She left her men to support Tank and weaved her way through the cars to the fire exit.

"Grace, wait!" Tank gasped. He was struggling with the pain from his broken ribs and the drug was affecting his thought process.

Grace turned and took up a defensive firing position before looking at Tank to see what the problem was.

"He was military trained, I'm sure of it. I think he knew that you had arrived too," Tank was piecing together the way Uri had left shortly after the laser dot had flickered on him. A normal untrained man would not have noticed it all until the high velocity round smashed through his breast bone and ripped his internal organs to shreds.

Grace made an okay sign with her finger and thumb and approached the fire exit. It had been left slightly ajar. She turned and fired two shots at the ceiling. The bank of fluorescent tubes disintegrated into white powder and the chop shop was plunged into darkness. Grace switched on a laser sight and scanned the crack between the door and the frame. She was looking for a tripwire or metal filament that could trigger a booby trap but there was nothing to be seen. She moved swiftly and kicked open the fire exit. The beach road was deserted and the snow was six inches thick at least. There was a wide fresh set of tyre marks in the snow which headed from the beach road down onto the sand.

"It looks like our x-ray is headed along the beach," Grace turned to Tank and his supporters. X-ray was the term sometimes used for an unknown enemy. "Is the pain any easier?"

"Yes, the drugs are starting to kick in now," Tank replied in a garbled drawl. Field dressings are laced with various pain killing drugs of various strengths. Their use is dependent on how serious the wounds are. Faz had given him a morphine based dressing because of the severity of the injury. She had also injected him with a double shot of the drug itself. Tank wasn't aware that the side of his face had been caved in by the last hammer blow which Victor had dealt him. He had a depressed fracture of the cheek bone which needed urgent medical attention.

"We need to get you out of the city to the perimeter as quickly as possible. The evacuation will be underway already," Grace signalled for her men to move toward their vehicle.

"I'll be fine, Grace," his speech was slurred and he sounded drunk.

"You're not fine, you're a liability to the team," she replied without looking at him. "One of my men will take you out of the city. The other will come with me in pursuit of the x-ray."

"Bollocks," Tank spat the word. "We'll go as a unit or not at all."

"You have a depressed fracture of the cheek bone, at least three broken ribs and a suspected broken jaw. Just how much use do you think you'll be in a fire fight?" Grace grabbed his arm and looked hard into his eyes. "The weather is closing in and we suspect that a blister agent is about to drift ashore which will turn anyone left in the city into violent rabid animals. You're going to hospital right now."

"I'm in charge of this unit and I give the orders. We are going to follow those track marks and find that man because I think he will lead us to Christopher Walsh," Tank tried to remain calm and in control but he was fast losing the power of speech. "What did you inject me with?"

"It was a big jab of common sense because I knew you'd be a stubborn pain in the ass," Grace said as Tank passed out. "Put him into his pickup and get him to the nearest check point. Here put this respirator on him." The three taskforce agents lifted their broken leader and carried him back into the chop shop. They placed him into the passenger seat and reclined it fully before strapping him in with the safety belt. Grace looked at his swollen features and felt a pang of guilt for injecting him but she couldn't assess exactly how bad the damage was beneath the swelling visually, he needed hospital treatment. If the suspect x-ray stayed on the beach then he was heading toward the Seaforth docks area of the city and that was where the rogue lightship had been sailing. Chen and his team were heading there too. She took one last look at Tank before she closed the door of the pickup.

"You look after him and get him to a doctor," she turned to her remaining operative. "Let's follow those tracks," she said as she climbed into her vehicle. The snow started to become a blizzard as an onshore wind picked up. Grace looked toward the city across the bay and swallowed hard as what looked like a fogbank about a mile across obscured the twinkling lights.

CHAPTER 27
The Explorer

Big Gordon Morris was the platform captain of a semi-submersible gas exploration rig called the Explorer. The Explorer was a huge floating mobile structure used to drill for oil and natural gas in offshore environments. The superstructure was supported by columns sitting on hollow hulls or pontoons which are ballasted below the water surface. They provide excellent stability in rough, deep seas. Big Gordon had worked on the rigs since being an apprentice engineer at the age of seventeen. He worked three weeks on shift followed by three weeks leave which suited him down to the ground. Gordon was married at a young age and twenty years on he had two beautiful grownup daughters and a long suffering wife who all worshiped the ground that he walked on. Big Gordon was a big man. His shoulders were as wide as a salon car. He was also a big drinker. He loved nothing more than a few beers and a game of cards with the boys. His favourite tipple was Southern Comfort, which he drank by the litre bottle. Many a foolish man had tried to keep up with Big Gordon round for round, and none had succeeded. The shift pattern that he worked allowed him to have plenty of time away from home where he could drink and play cards to his heart's content. Then with a pocket full of money he would spend three weeks at home in the bosom of his family. Life at home in his three bedroom house with three women could sometimes become hormonal and so by the end of his three weeks leave he was ready to get back to the male dominated world of the gas drilling rig.

This particular shift pattern was almost at an end. He had two nights left to work before the helicopter came to relieve his crew and take them back to the mainland. Everything was hunky dory until the deafening sound of an explosion rocked the Explorer to its core. The massive hollow pontoons on which it floated boomed like huge kettle drums as the shock wave hit the rig. Gordon and the majority of his crew had downed tools hours before and were in the relative safety of the crew module. The crew module was a purpose built survival pod as well a fully functional living space. It was made from fireproof polycarbonate and was designed to withstand gas fires and explosions. The modules were designed as a safe haven for the crewmen in the event of a disaster, and somewhere they could take refuge and survive until help arrived from the mainland. Everything that a full complement of men needed to live was inside the crew module, accommodation, medication, food and of course, water.

When the shock wave hit the rig there were three men above deck on safety watch. Their role was to monitor clocks and dials, pressure gauges and thermometers to ensure that the automated drilling process was running smoothly. The cost of fossil fuel exploration ran into the billions and any kind of down time on the rigs because of maintenance issues had to be avoided at all costs. The rig was hit by a concussion wave first, which was followed quickly by a deafening wall of sound. All three men on the maintenance shift turned and looked in the direction of the explosion. The initial blast was followed by a succession of smaller ones. Across the Bay in the distance towers of orange flame erupted from the blackness of the ocean. One of the men caught some of the smaller plumes on his camera phone.

"What's over there?" an electrician shouted to his colleague across the metal stanchions. He was pointing toward the towers of flame in the distance.

"I don't know, but there's no rigs over there."

"Might be a ship?"

"That wasn't a ship, maybe an unexploded bomb though."

"No way, there were too many blasts. It has to be a gas explosion," the speculation continued.

"Get Big Gordon on the blower. We'd better check in with him," the engineer headed to a communication booth fixed into the bulkhead of the superstructure. Before he could pick up the hand set it rang.

"What's going on?" Gordon asked.

"Couple of big bangs about a mile due west of our position," the engineer explained.

"Big bangs? I nearly spilt my beer," Gordon joked nervously. The first thought when an explosion is heard on a gas rig is that it is the rig itself. "There is nothing but sea a mile due west of us."

"We can't see anything up here, the weather is too bad. There were three or four explosions and then nothing. It could have been an unexploded bomb," the engineer was sticking to his theory.

"I don't think so, there were too many blasts," Gordon repeated what his workmate had said word for word. The engineer frowned in disappointment.

"You guys need to belt up, it could get choppy," the engineer said. "I'll report anything unusual immediately." Experience told him that there would be large waves headed in their direction although the chances of them affecting the huge rig were very slim indeed. If a crew member dropped a spanner on the floor then everyone was told to belt up, it was a standing joke on the rigs.

"Don't you worry about us we'll hold on tight," Big Gordon laughed again. "I'll report the blast to the port authorities."

Gordon replaced the handset and picked up a thick glass tumbler which was half full of amber liquid. He sniffed the fluid and savoured its powerful aromas. The Southern Comfort disappeared down his throat in one gulp. He smiled and rubbed his huge belly as the liquid burned inside him. On his desk was his PC and he logged onto the company website using his code and password. He clicked on the tab which was labelled 'Incident reporting', and filed a brief description of what had happened. With the report sent and stored he returned into the recreation area of the crew module and poured himself another drink. The room was buzzing with chatter as the men guessed and second guessed as to the cause of the explosions. Several of them were looking out of the reinforced glass window which was set into one wall looking away from the superstructure, but there was nothing to see but snowflakes and darkness.

"Are we playing crash or what?" Big Gordon said as he approached the card table. The deck of cards had been left untidy and they were spread out across the table face down. "Who's left the cards in this state?"

"Tommy Young should have stacked them away but he's an idle bastard," one of the men shouted and raucous laughter broke out through the crew module.

"Oh stop crying will you, and don't call me idle," Tommy replied and the men laughed again. "I admit to being a bastard but never idle in a million years."

The five crewmen chuckled and pushed each other playfully as they sat around the card table in their respective seats. Everyone had their own seat at that table and no one dared to sit in another's chair. It was bad luck. Big Gordon picked up the deck and shuffled the cards without looking at them. He spilt them into two piles and then expertly flicked them into one deck before dealing out the regulation four hands. Four men could play at any one time with the loser making way for the next man.

"What do you think caused the explosion, Gordon?" the man to his immediate left asked. He was the only civilian member of the crew and they called him Chef because he was responsible for providing three square meals a day for the engineers and technicians.

"Probably one of your curries, Pat," Gordon teased him much to the amusement of the men. "The last time I went on shore leave I couldn't stop trumping after that Chicken Madras you made. I reckon some poor bloke has exploded on his way back to shore out there." The men laughed and the chef pulled a scowl for a brief second before joining in the mirth.

"Oh yes very funny, I didn't hear you moaning when you were all scoffing it, like pigs at a trough you are when I make curry," the chef scolded the card players as they continued to laugh at him.

"Highest card to deal," Gordon said sliding a card face up to each player before giving himself the last one. The red light on the shore line flashed which indicated that a call was coming in from the mainland from head office. Big Gordon cursed and stood up. His huge shoulders swayed as he walked into his office and he had to turn sideways to enter the room. He picked up the telephone with pudgy fingers.

"Gordon Morris," he spoke gruffly. He was annoyed by the interruption of his card game.

"Morris, this is Jackson at the port authority here," an unfamiliar voice said.

"How can I help?"

"You obviously heard the explosions?" Jackson had already read his incident report form.

"Yes we heard them but there's nothing much to report apart from what I have put in my report," Gordon explained grumpily.

"We need your lab rat to run some tests for the next hour or so, just to make sure there's no toxic fumes heading ashore, we can't be too careful," Jackson was curt when he spoke. Each rig had to take samples of the slurry created by the drilling from the waste filters at regular intervals. They were analysed in a small lab and the findings sent directly to the company's main laboratory via computer link. Everything was automated and so the lab technician was rarely aware of the results of his own tests.

"Okay, what tests would you like him to run?" Gordon was as polite as he could be under the circumstances.

"Air quality and moisture samples please every thirty minutes, and we need the results sent immediately to the following server address," Jackson reeled of a dot com address. "We also need thirty minute weather reports please."

"Anything else I can do for you?" Big Gordon asked sarcastically.

"That's all for now, thank you," Jackson hung up. Big Gordon swore at the hand set and slammed it back into its receiver as the first tendrils of a strange mist engulfed the rig. It had been carried on a light breeze and it had the slightest scent of garlic to it.

CHAPTER 28
'Two Hours Later'/the Evacuation

The Major and a combined government reaction team had set up the evacuation communications centre. They had taken refuge in the network of sandstone tunnels which made up the secret government bunker beneath the city. It had been purpose built to cope with a nuclear, chemical or biological attack from above, and was designed as a safe haven for the government, military leaders and the Royal Family in the event of an imminent invasion.

The Ministry of Defence and the Home Office had conspired with the taskforce to release a blanket news statement to the effect that there had been a petrochemical explosion of significant size in the gas field off Liverpool Bay. The story was that the explosion had damaged several of the drilling rigs and toxic gasses had been released into the atmosphere. The city centre was being evacuated as a precaution in the first instance. The evacuation of the inner city had begun in earnest and chaos reigned the streets of Liverpool. All modes of public transport had stopped. Air raid sirens had been sounded for the first time in decades and all television and radio stations were transmitting a pre-recorded set of evacuation instructions. Banks, jewellers, and cash rich businesses were being instructed to fasten down metal shuttering, and to set time locks and intruder alarms before sending their staff home. Armed police wearing ugly protective suits were patrolling the streets to prevent looting. The city centre was beginning to empty but the streets leading away from it were gridlocked. The snowstorm had intensified making all but the main arterial routes impassable.

"Is the perimeter functioning properly?" the Major asked his closest group of advisors. Many of the government employees were completely unaware of the real situation that they were facing.

"Yes Major. The motorways have been closed and all traffic leaving the city is being filtered to the decontamination areas. We already have five miles of queuing traffic at all the major junctions with the perimeter," the fat controller said. He didn't think that the perimeter idea was a sound one and he almost wanted it to fail just to prove that he'd been right all along.

"What about the decontamination process itself?"

"As far as we can tell it is working, but they are treating uninfected people at the moment," the fat controller shook his head and his double chins wobbled.

"We don't know that David," the Major countered sternly. "We cannot take any chances with people's lives. By the time we have confirmation of a blister agent being present it would be too late to help thousands of innocent men, women and children."

The fat controller was about to argue when Helen Walsh approached the desk at which they were sat. Her face was pale and she looked washed out. The pressure of becoming the resident blister agent expert was obviously getting to her.

"Helen?" the Major greeted her.

"I have very bad news Major," she replied and her eyes filled with tears.

"We have to deal with very bad news in this department everyday Helen, that's what we do, now please keep your voice down and tell me what you found out," the Major tried to encourage her a little.

"We have results in from the Explorer gas drilling rig," her voice choked as she spoke. "The laboratory on board tested moisture droplets which had been left behind by a fogbank which passed over them roughly two hours ago. It tested positive for concentrated 2-chloroethyl sulphide, the strongest blister agent that we know of."

"Okay give me your best guesstimate as to our situation," the Major prompted her without acknowledging her distress. He picked up a pen to jot down some notes as she spoke. He also loosened his tie which very rare indeed. The Major was always immaculate.

Helen took a moment to gather her thoughts before

continuing. "The moisture tested by the rig laboratory was taken from a sample of vapour which had been left on the metal handrails. The moisture would only have formed as several layers of the substance built up over a period of time. I'm guessing here obviously," she paused.

"Obviously," the fat controller sniped. He removed his glasses and breathed on the lenses before wiping them on his long suffering tie. The Major threw him a withering glance before prompting Helen to continue with her worst case scenario. The fat controller used the opportunity to letch at Helen's shapely legs.

"For a vapour to form on the rig then it must have been in contact with the 2-chloroethyl sulphide for a reasonable amount of time, which gives us an indication off the size of the blister cloud," she explained.

"Blister cloud?" the fat controller rolled his eyes to the ceiling and then looked at her behind.

"For want of a better description yes, blister cloud," Helen turned on him and caught him looking at her. She glared at him and blushed and looked away.

"It's perfectly obvious what Helen is talking about," the Major growled. "Please continue."

"If we imagine that the vapour took twenty minutes to develop into visible moisture droplets and then if we surmise that the blister agent would be at its most concentrated form in the centre of the cloud," she used her hands to aid her communication as she spoke. The Major had noticed that she did that a lot.

"Okay I'm with you so far," the Major said.

"Then the blister cloud or fog bank, whatever you want to call it could be over a kilometre wide already, and that means that when the centre of the cloud had past the rig then the periphery was already over the city centre."

"In which case we already have infected people?" the Major asked.

"Definitely," she nodded.

The Major looked at the fat controller for confirmation. He replaced his glasses, took a deep breath and nodded slowly in agreement with Helen's theory. It was a tough pill to swallow but it looked to all intents and purposes that he'd been wrong. It didn't help that she had caught him staring at her ass.

"What about the travellers at the airport?" the Major asked him.

"They haven't reported any fogbank encroaching as yet and we closed it to all incoming flights ninety minutes ago. It has since been evacuated so it would have been closed in time to prevent any casualties there," he replied.

"What about the underground rail system?"

"That could be touch and go. If there was already part of the blister cloud over the city, then the stations nearest to the river could have been affected before we managed to close them," the fat controller looked at Helen. "What do you think the actual strength of the periphery vapour would be Helen?"

"It would be much weaker than it is at the centre, obviously it would be dissipated by the wind and diluted with atmospheric gasses," Helen blushed a little as she replied. It was the first time the fat controller had asked her a serious question. "I think that infected people may display mild symptoms, redness of the skin, sore throat, stinging eyes and maybe rashes or slight blistering of exposed skin tissue. It certainly wouldn't be life threatening unless they were severely asthmatic."

"Okay we need to react to the time scale that Helen has suggested and react quickly. Anyone in the city centre two hours ago may be infected," the Major said to the wider group of advisors as he picked up the telephone. "Get onto it immediately."

"Major, there is an urgent priority here that we are overlooking," Helen said. Everyone stopped and looked at her.

"Quickly Helen, if you have a point then let's hear it," the Major tucked the handset underneath his chin as he listened.

"The men on that gas rig have been exposed to a concentrated form of 2-chloroethyl sulphide, and they have no idea that they are infected yet," Helen's voice cracked again. "Given the amount of time that has past and the strength of the chemical I would anticipate the first symptoms of infection to begin any time now."

The Major stood up and walked across the open desk area to his makeshift private office. He opened the door, stepped into the room and switched the light on. He summoned the fat controller to join him and Helen moved to follow them.

"That'll be all for now Helen, thank you," the Major didn't look at her as he spoke. He stepped aside as the fat controller approached and then closed the door behind them.

Helen was aghast for a moment but no one paid her any attention as they set about their business. The bunker was now being used by all the law enforcement divisions involved in the evacuation and the place was a hive of activity.

The Major leaned against the door and took a deep breath. "What's going to happen on that rig?" the Major asked David Bell. He loosened his tie further.

"The crew will be split into those who were off shift when the cloud past over and a smaller number of men who would make up the maintenance gang on board. Depending on who was outside and exposed to the concentrate then the symptoms should start to appear at varying degrees very soon," he looked at his watch for effect as he spoke. He had a chronograph dial which he set running. He was interested to time the imminent series of events.

"We have to stop all communication from that rig," the Major said. "Anyone making a mobile phone call from the Explorer could blow this whole thing wide open and we will have a national disaster on our hands."

"I can have all their signals jammed immediately, but you do realise that we are cutting them loose with no way off that rig don't you?"

"Of course I do you fool, look at the weather conditions out there. We can't a send a helicopter to extract them, if we send a ship then they will become infected too. When men start getting sick onboard that rig they will call home on their mobiles. All merry hell will break loose and we don't have any choice," the Major looked tired as he spoke.

The fat controller picked up the telephone and made a call to the intelligence agency's listening post. He asked for details of all recent communications from the rig, and ordered them to jam everything coming from it. "That's done Major. Shall we order the crew on the rig to follow the emergency drill and remain secured in the crew module?"

"No David," the Major face was ashen. "If the prognosis for infected victims is as bad as we think it is then I wouldn't want to be locked in that pod with the infected men when the drinking water runs out."

CHAPTER 29
Uri

Uri kept the Bentley on the beach and headed toward the city lights. His progress along the sand would be much quicker than it would be if he'd chosen to use the snow packed roads. He tried to stay on the flat compacted sand away from the softer sand near the dunes, but all the time he was wary that there were shifting pools of quicksand dotted all across the bay. The snow was thick enough to stop him determining a clear path, but the salt content was melting it quickly and made driving at speed relatively easy. The Bentley tore down the wide sand flats at speed toward Seaforth docks. Uri turned the windscreen wipers onto full speed as the snow piled up on the glass. He looked into the rear view mirror and caught the glint of headlights behind. They were far away in the distance but they were there none the less. It couldn't be Victor, he was too stupid to follow him along the bay and Uri had his car after all. That meant that the government spook must have escaped and was now in pursuit. It would only be a matter of time before he caught up; the snow was making it impossible to travel without leaving any tracks. He didn't want another face to face encounter with that government man, Uri was tough but he also knew his own limitations, and that agent would have destroyed him if it weren't for his mace spray.

Uri drove past a junction with the coast road. There was a wide access ramp which led to a barrier and the road beyond it. He had driven past two similar entrances to the beach already and had expected the police to be there waiting for him but he had not encountered anyone at all. Uri turned up the radio and realised why he hadn't been stopped by a police roadblock. The radio was broadcasting a recorded transmission advising everyone to evacuate the city centre immediately. For those adamant that they weren't leaving, then they were instructed to remain in doors and close all the windows and doors. There was a brief link about a petrochemical explosion onboard a rig in the Bay of Liverpool but Uri knew better. He had also seen firsthand what the effects of the chemicals were on a human being. Headlights glinted in the wing mirror again but they were still miles behind him. He lowered the electric window and sighed deeply. This situation had gone pear shaped and he wanted out of it right now. The problem was that he hadn't had a penny of the ridiculous financial reward he had been promised by Christopher Walsh. He needed to get to him quickly and insist on some of the money upfront then he could disappear and leave the lunatic to his crackpot plans.

Uri was beginning to stiffen up and feel the bruising that he'd incurred during his fight with the government gorilla. He knew that he would be black and blue in the morning and that he'd feel ten time worse too. He lit a cigarette and breathed deeply. Underneath the soothing tobacco was an aroma that he recognised only too well. It had been etched into his brain as he'd cleaned up Christopher's experiments onboard the lightship. It was the unmistakable smell of garlic. Uri realised the implications of being able to smell it and slammed the Bentley into a high speed hand brake turn. Snow and sand sprayed across the beach dozens of yards in a huge fan shape as he floored the accelerator and headed back toward the access ramp that he'd just past. The Bentley swerved violently as it left the sand and hit the tarmac road. Snow had coated the roads and turned them into lethal skidpans. He approached the beach barrier and brought the Bentley to a sliding stop in front of it. The vehicle had barely stopped moving when he was out of the driver's door and running to the barrier. He held his breath all the time and his lungs screamed for air. The barrier was a fifteen feet long metal pole with a heavy concrete block on one end. Uri pushed the concrete and the bar raised up. He was back into the Bentley in a flash and the vehicle fishtailed up the ramp and onto the deserted coast road.

Uri was in a flap as he flicked through the radio channels searching for more information but there was nothing but static or the pre-recorded message. It was too much of a coincidence for there to have been a petrochemical incident as well as his employer's own personal disaster. The odour on the breeze confirmed it to Uri that one of the wrecks had exploded releasing some of the blister agent.

"How did I get into this shit?" Uri said to himself. The coast road was coming to a junction about a half a mile ahead. On the right were the sand dunes which separated the coast road from the beach. They were like a never ending mountain range of sand that went on and on into the darkness. On his left were salt flats and acres of green marsh land before the lights of civilization could be seen. Ahead of him the lights of the city were becoming obscured by a murky fogbank. The closer he drove to the city the stronger the odour of garlic became and the more his resolve was weakened. Uri flicked the headlights onto main beam and tried to work out what was happening up ahead.

There was an army jeep parked on the kerbside facing him with its lights on. There were four figures in the road setting out traffic cones to block off the route into the north of the city. The figures were bulky and grotesque and bright green in colour. Uri realised that they were wearing protective clothing of the type he'd only ever seen in the movies. He slowed as he neared them and one of the men waved his arm in a circular motion instructing him to turn around and go back the way he had just come from. The insignia on the jeep identified it as a territorial arm vehicle. They were part time soldiers who must have been drafted in to assist in the evacuation of the city. There had been several massive exercises carried out all over the country in the years following the September 11th attacks on the Twin Towers, New York. The Territorial Army were a key part of any reaction plans that the government had. Uri had met some of the part time soldiers at a football game a few years earlier and he remembered being told by them that the territorial soldiers did not carry loaded weapons on exercises. He smiled in the darkness as he approached the road block.

"There's no way through I'm afraid sir," the nearest soldier shouted. Uri flicked his cigarette through the open window and eyed the army jeep. It had thick treads and wide tyres, and would be much easier to drive in the snow than Victor's Bentley.

"My wife and children are at home on their own two miles

down the road there. They have no way of leaving the city unless I get them. Please they are my children," Uri played the role of terrified father very well. The soldier turned to his companions who were still placing cones across the road. As far as they were concerned this was a precautionary evacuation and thus no one was expecting any trouble. The rumours were that the government had exploited the situation and blown it out of all proportion in order to practice their disaster management procedures again.

"Sergeant," the soldier shouted. His voice was muffled by his respirator and protective suit. "This bloke only lives two miles down the road and his wife and kids are home alone."

"Orders are orders, Corporal," another suited form replied. "No one enters the city for any reason and that's that."

The soldier turned to Uri and was about to repeat what his sergeant had said when a nine millimetre soft nosed bullet smashed through his clear visor and ripped a hole the size of a ten pence piece below his right eye. The dumdum round hit the back of his skull where it flattened before bouncing around inside his cranium. The grey matter that was once his brain was liquidised in seconds and the soldier crumpled onto the floor beside the Bentley. The gunshot alerted the others but their movements were hampered by the cumbersome protective suits. Uri moved out of the car and held the Glock at arm's length level with his eye line. He squeezed the trigger twice and the sergeant was lifted off his feet as two bullets punched through his suit and hit him in the chest. His lungs and liver were shredded as the slugs ricocheted inside his ribcage.

There were two soldiers remaining. One of them held his hands above his head in a gesture of surrender and the other one bolted for the jeep. Two high velocity rounds hit him in the back as he ran, knocking him clean over. He landed face down and tried to crawl away. There was a deep red smear in the snow as he inched forward, desperately trying to escape. Uri stood over him and fired a single shot into the back of his head and the soldier became still.

"Don't shoot," the remaining soldier said as Uri turned to face him.

"Take off the suit and the respirator," Uri trained the gun on him.

"What?" the soldier asked confused.

"The suit," Uri shouted. "Take off the fucking suit."

"Okay, okay please don't shoot me, I'm taking it off, here you'll have to do the back," the soldier turned his back to Uri and he began to unfasten a series of zips and Velcro fixings. Uri unclipped the tag which fixed the head mask to the back of the suit and the soldier peeled himself out of the lime green material. He pulled off his respirator which was worn beneath the suit and handed it toward Uri with a shaking hand.

"Put it down on the floor," Uri instructed him. He kept the soldier at a safe distance.

"Let me go, I don't know anything, and I certainly haven't seen anything. I'll say you knocked me out and I didn't see anything, just don't kill me," the soldier rambled as Uri began to climb into the green suit.

"I have three children, Mary, Natalia and little Susan, she's the youngest, little monkey she is," he began to shake as a mixture of the subzero temperature and fear hit him. Uri pulled the suit over his shoulders and zipped up the front panel.

"My wife, Stacy her name is, she'll be really worried about me being out here in the snow, she's always worrying about me, heart of gold she has. I don't know what I'd do without my girls. Have you got kids?" the soldier tried to smile but it looked more like a grimace because the muscles in his face were frozen with terror. Uri pulled the respirator over his head and then pulled the head mask over that. There was a clear flat visor to see through but it was very uncomfortable inside the suit and the field of vision was impaired.

"Mary, she's the oldest, she wants to be a ballerina, Marina Ballerina I call her, makes her laugh when I call her that," tears ran down the soldiers face. The man with the gun hadn't flinched all the time he was talking.

"Where do your family live?" Uri asked. His voice was alien like through the mask and the respirator.

"What?"

"Where do your family live?" Uri repeated slowly.

"Toxteth, Liverpool eight we call it, why?" the soldier stuttered.

"Is it near the river?" Uri asked.

"Yes, it's on the edge of the city centre next to the river," the soldier thought that maybe he'd made a connection with the gunman.

"You'll see your girls sooner than you think then," Uri said. He raised the Glock and fired one shot through the soldiers left eyeball. A large blob of blood and vitreous humour hit Uri's mask as the eyeball exploded. He tried to wipe it off with a gloved hand but only succeeded in smearing it across his visor. The soldier fell onto his back and his body twitched violently. Uri fired again into his forehead and he stopped moving.

"Your girls will die a much slower death than you did, soldier," Uri said as he climbed into the jeep. He started the engine and engaged first gear. The wind blew in from the sea and the snowfall became a blizzard as he turned the army jeep onto the tarmac and headed toward the docks.

CHAPTER 30
Grace Farrington

Grace Farrington scanned the beach ahead through night vision glasses. The vehicle that they were following had turned back toward them for a few seconds and then disappeared. The glare of the headlights had appeared as a luminous green smudge and then darkness had returned. As they approached the turning point they could see tyre tracks in the snow which ran in a wide circle across the beach and then headed up an access ramp toward a narrow pass between the sand dunes. The pass was virtually a single track lane which joined the main coast road and the other side of the huge sand hills. Judging by the way the snow had fallen into the tracks Grace reckoned that they were about five to ten minutes behind their quarry.

"Take the exit road, he's gone that way," Grace ordered her driver. The driver was a corporal from the Royal Marines called Barnes by his colleagues. Her voice was muffled by the respirator. "Take it easy when we hit the ramp."

"Roger that," Barnes answered. It was difficult driving at speed with the mask on so he slowed the vehicle as it mounted the ramp. When they reached the top of the ramp there was a small hut in which a parking attendant would sit during the daytime hours manning the barrier. The barrier had been left up and they drove straight on. He followed the tyre tracks through the sand dunes until they reached the coast road. The tracks turned right toward the city. "Why do you think he's left the beach?"

"That's what I'm asking myself, it doesn't make any sense, it's going to be much harder to make progress on the roads, and he's far more likely to run into the police," Grace replied. Barnes slipped the truck into four wheel drive and followed the tyre tracks. The tracks continued for about a mile when they saw something in the road up ahead.

"What the hell is that?" Grace said to herself. She peered through the night vision glasses and tried to make sense of the scene.

"What can you see," Barnes asked. He glanced at her as he spoke and the truck shimmied.

"Concentrate on the road corporal," Grace said without looking at him. "We have casualties in the road ahead."

"Shall I call it in?" Barnes asked.

"Wait until we know what we're dealing with," Grace answered. As the vehicle approached the scene it became clearer to her what had happened. There was a Bentley Continental parked in the road. The engine was running and the driver's door was open. There were traffic cones across the road and a number of unidentifiable shapes lying near the verge to the left. On the right hand side was what appeared to be the body of a man wearing camouflage trousers and a white tee shirt. There was a dark pool of liquid in the snow surrounding his head. They were one hundred yards away when Grace raised her hand and Barnes brought the truck to a stop.

"I'll check it out, cover me," she said as she opened the door and climbed out. She carried her Glock seventeen two handed and scanned the area before she moved. The truck's headlights illuminated the scene and Grace sprinted over to the Bentley and ducked down low as she approached the open door. She paused momentarily before checking inside the vehicle. The Bentley was empty. Grace closed the door and sprinted over to the unidentified shapes that were lying in the snow. She quickly realised that they were military personnel in nuclear, chemical and biological warfare suits, and that they were dead. Grace checked the area again and then moved over to the other body. All the time Barnes covered the perimeter with his Brugger and Thomet MP9 automatic machine pistol. It was capable of firing over nine hundred armour piercing rounds a minute. The dead man wasn't wearing any protective clothing and he certainly wasn't equipped for the snowstorm. He was wearing dog tags. Grace checked the tags and then sprinted back to the truck.

"Okay call it in," she said as she climbed back into the truck. "They're a unit of part timers. Territorial Army boys, and they're all dead. The x-ray has shot and killed four men and stolen one of their NBC suits. There are vehicle tracks heading away from the scene on the coast road toward the city," Grace slammed the door.

"Roger that," Barnes said and he picked up the coms unit and began to relay the incident to the taskforce headquarters. Grace signalled him to drive while she took the microphone from him. Barnes finished relaying the message and then engaged gear before moving the truck around the abandoned Bentley. He weaved it through the bodies and traffic cones and followed the fresh tracks.

"Is there any air support available," Grace asked the Major.

"Negative Grace, we can't get anything in the air because of the storm," the Major replied. "Where are you?"

"We are following the x-ray toward the north of the city. Tank seemed to think that he was connected to Christopher Walsh and now I'm certain of it," she explained.

"What makes you so sure?" the Major asked.

"The x-ray had a clear run along the beach to the docks and for some reason he chose to take an exit road. He's taken one of their NBC   suits Major which tells me he knows what's in the air," Grace checked her watch and wondered if Tank had made it into surgery yet.

"That makes sense to me. Grace, your respirators will not protect you from the blister agent on their own. You must wear an NBC suit as well," the Major said. "You cannot head back into the city without protective clothing."

Grace slammed her hand on the dashboard. "Stop the truck," she demanded.

"What?" Barnes said.

"Stop the truck Corporal," she looked at him sternly.

"Roger that, what's the score?" he brought the vehicle to a halt as he was ordered but he was confused.

"We need two of those suits, soldier," Grace said pointing to the bodies in the road behind them. Barnes looked at the bodies and recalled what the Major had just said. He understood and opened the door to exit the vehicle. In the blink of an eye he had disappeared from sight.

"We can commandeer two of the suits from the territorial soldiers, Major," Grace spoke quickly.

"Are they compromised?" the Major was referring to bullet holes.

"We can patch two of them up for now using the spare one Major," she said. "There's adhesive in the tool box on these trucks we'll have to make do for now. How's Tank, Major?"

"We're not sure yet, Grace?" the Major hesitated slightly.

"What is that supposed to mean?" Grace said flatly.

"He was taken straight to the casualty department in Southport. It was still functioning as normal as it's outside of the perimeter. He was taken down to see the doctors and cleaned up and they left him with the nurses to be prepped for theatre," the Major paused again.

"And what?" Grace had an idea what was coming.

"I'm afraid that he's disappeared, Grace," the Major coughed as he finished speaking. "We have absolutely no idea where he is."

CHAPTER 31
The Explorer

Brains rubbed his eyes with the back of his hands as he left the tiny laboratory for the umpteenth time that night. Big Gordon had asked for moisture samples to be processed and submitted to the mainland every thirty minutes, which was a real bummer because he had been winning at the card table until then. Brains wasn't his real name of course, his real name was Brian, but because he was a lab technician the crew called him the brain, or Brains for short. As far as night shifts went this was the weirdest he'd ever pulled. He was officially off duty when the explosions had occurred, but because head office wanted sample analysis completing he had to clock back on. Big Gordon told him that he would make sure that he was paid double time for his troubles. Brains didn't mind getting double bubble as he called it, and taking moisture samples was hardly rocket science. The funny thing was that the samples he'd been taking were going off the PH scale completely. The last three sets off tests that he had submitted were showing an alkali level that he had never seen before outside of a laboratory environment. He couldn't explain it. One thing for sure was that his eyes were sore and his throat was dry as a bone.

Brains walked into the recreation room to a barrage of abuse from the card players.

"Hey Brains, how come you've pulled a double bubble shift and we get Jack shit?" said an engineer called Smokey Pete.

"If you want to go and run some moisture samples then be my guest, Pete. You know where the lab is," Brains retaliated and headed for the drinks machine. He slotted a fifty pence piece into the machine and selected a tin of diet coke. His eyes were feeling gritty and he rubbed them again.

"Ooh! Moisture samples is it?" Smokey Pete teased him.

"I hear that your missus collects moisture samples while you're away on the rigs," Chef shouted.

"Yes I've heard that too. She collects moisture samples from the milk man all over your bed sheets," Smokey Pete added to the verbal abuse. The men around the table laughed loudly. "She likes to collect as much moisture as she can while you're working away!"

"All right Chef," Big Gordon growled. Sometimes the men's banter could become too sharp. "That's a bit below the belt."

"Well that's where all the moist bits are boss," Smokey Pete retorted. The beer had been flowing and there was little room for sympathy on board the rigs. Big Gordon always told his men that if they wanted sympathy then they could find it in the dictionary in between 'shit and syphilis'.

Brains didn't feel like laughing much and he opened his can of coke and put it to his lips. He took a long swig on the cold fizzy liquid and it eased the soreness in his throat. The men continued to laugh and tease each other but Brains had switched off to the sound of their voices. He tipped the can backward again and drained the liquid until it was empty.

The door which led from the platform into the crew module opened and snowflakes rushed into the room. The three men from the maintenance watch entered in a flurry of wind and white powder. The card table became silent as the men brushed snow off their high visibility coats. Leaving the platform unmonitored was a taboo.

"What's the problem boys?" Big Gordon stood up from the table and walked toward them.

"We've been trying to ring down here for twenty minutes," an electrician called Sparks growled. He turned his back to the others and headed for the kitchen.

"The telephone hasn't buzzed once, has it lads?" Gordon turned to the card table and shrugged his huge shoulders.

"No it hasn't rung at all honestly," Smokey Pete said. He stood up and walked over to the recreation room handset which was fitted next to the drinks machine. Pete put the telephone receiver to his ear and listened. He frowned when all he could hear was static. "This thing is as dead as a doornail."

Big Gordon walked into his office and followed suit. The handset was dead. He punched a few buttons but only got the same result. There was nothing on the line but silence.

"The system must be down boys I'm sorry. What's the problem anyway?" Big Gordon asked sternly. Leaving the banks of gauges unmanned was dangerous, and more to the point it was gross misconduct. "You know that you shouldn't leave your posts."

"Twenty minutes we have been trying to get relief from you shower of selfish bastards," Sparks shouted as he walked out of the kitchen into the recreation room with a bottle of mineral water in his hand. He lifted the bottle to his lips and swallowed hard. Big Gordon noticed that the skin on the back of his hands had reddened. He looked at the electrician's face and noted the same thing there. His face was red and the whites of his eyes were bloodshot.

"There something in the air out there, my throat feels like I've swallowed broken glass, and all you lot can do is sit on your fat arses and play cards," Sparks was getting angry. Gordon could see the veins in his forehead pulsing. The electrician drained the mineral water and tossed the empty bottle toward the card table. It landed in the middle of the players with a clatter and then bounced onto the floor.

"Calm down Sparks or I'll put you down," Chef stood up and tensed his muscles ready for conflict. He was deeply offended by Sparks throwing the bottle at him, but he wasn't sure why he was so offended. Seeing the water bottle had made him thirsty. He just felt angry all of a sudden.

"Sit down, Chef my boy. No one will be fighting on my watch do you understand me?" Big Gordon seemed to inflate as he spoke.

"Sorry boss, but he was out of order chucking that bottle at me," Chef looked wounded as he apologised.

"Apologise to the Chef," Gordon gave Sparks a friendly clip behind the ear but the electrician didn't acknowledge it.

"Fuck him, I hate his cooking anyway," Sparks said calmly. "I'm feeling very thirsty." Sparks seemed to stop and think about the situation for a second before turning around and heading back into the kitchen. Big Gordon looked at the other two members of the maintenance shift and saw that they too had reddened eyes.

"How are you two feeling?" he asked concerned. "Get them a drink." Brains went to the coke machine and fed three coins into it. He selected fizzy orange because the coke just hadn't touched his thirst. The machine spewed three tins out and he gave the maintenance men one each and opened the remaining one himself.

"I'm not feeling good, Boss," a pipe fitter called Harvey said. He rubbed his eyes and they reddened even more. "My eyes are burning and my throat is red raw. Look at my hands."

"Get these men to the first aid room. You need some eye drops," Gordon said. Harvey's cheeks looked yellowish in patches as if water blisters were forming. He grabbed Brains by the elbow and pushed him toward the office. The technician shrugged off Gordon's grip on his arm and looked annoyed that he'd been touched in the first place.

"Get off me," he complained. He drained some of the fizzy orange from the tin.

"What have your test results been like?" Gordon whispered.

"Odd to say the least," Brains said. He paused to gulp some of the orange down. "Sorry Boss, but my throat is bad too. The moisture samples are off the scale. They are indicating that there is a very strong alkaline substance in the atmosphere."

"There must be something from those explosions in the atmosphere," Gordon was no scientist but it appeared to be the only explanation. "Get hold of head office and ask them what their test results are showing. Do you think that the moisture in the air could affect the men?"

"I'm no doctor Boss, but me eyes and throat have been affected from going outside every thirty minutes to collect samples. The maintenance crew have been out there all the time," Brains said.

"Okay, get the mainland on the blower and find out what their results are showing," Gordon walked toward the office door.

"The system is dead," Brains reminded him before he could leave.

"Use e-mail, your mobile telephone or fucking smoke signals, but I want to know what is wrong with my men," Big Gordon slapped a pudgy hand on the technician's back as he walked out of the office and into the recreation room. "I want three volunteers to cover the maintenance shift while we sort these guys out. Put respirators on in case there is something in the smoke from those explosions. I don't want you lot suing the ass off the company when we get home."

Three of the crew from the card table stood up without questioning the order.

"Are we on double bubble, Boss," one of them joked as they pulled on their platform clothes and high visibility jackets. Gordon forced a smile as they put on their yellow hard hats and opened the platform door. The wind rushed in and blew the cards off the table as the men stepped out into the strange smelling mist. The ace of spades landed face up on the floor next to Big Gordon's safety boot.

"Hey Boss," Brains shouted from the office.

"What now, Brains," Big Gordon said under his breath.

"The e-mail is down, in fact there is no internet connection at all, and my mobile is dead as a dodo."

Big Gordon reached into his jeans and pulled out his Samsung. The lights were on but the screen displayed that there was no signal.

"What the bloody hell is going on?" he whispered to himself. He swallowed and realised that his throat was sore too. He was still staring at his cell phone when Sparks stepped out of the kitchen into the recreation room. He had a full tray of bottled mineral water under one arm, and a three foot fire axe in the other. His lips were chapped and cracked and his eyes looked bloodshot and sore. There was a skittish look in his eyes as he looked around the room from one man to another, but there wasn't any recognition in them until he focused on Chef. Sparks dropped the tray of water onto the floor. He raised the fire axe above his head with both hands and launched himself across the rig.

"Come on Chef, let me see you put me down!" he screamed as he swung the axe down in a wicked arc.

CHAPTER 32
The Terrorist Task Force

Chen and his team approached the docks and were presented with a scene of absolute chaos. He had two teams of six men who had been split into three Land Rovers. The Land Rovers were kitted out with enough hardware to conquer a small country. The mechanics that serviced the machines had fitted snow chains to the tyres before they had left the bunker. It was a journey of less than five miles from the headquarters to the docks. When they arrived there was a line of traffic leaving the port as far as the eye could see. Coaches packed with tourists who had been evacuated from the cruise liners that used the port, stood next to articulated lorries loaded with scrap metal. Hundreds of men trudged out of the gates through the snow on foot, sent home by their respective employers when the sirens had gone off and the evacuation orders had been broadcasted.

Chen and his teams were wearing black NBC suits over their combat gear. Communications were to be maintained via individual earpieces linked directly to the control centre beneath the city. Chen held a detailed plan of the harbour and its maze of docks and canals.

"Do we have any sightings of the lightship, Major?" Chen asked.

"The last sighting that we have was from a Russian container vessel which was leaving port. They reported automatic gunfire coming from the direction of Seaforth Docks," the Major answered.

"There is no hope of any air shots?" Chen asked hopefully but he already knew the answer. The cloud cover was too thick for satellite cameras to be of any use, and the snowstorm was too heavy for helicopters to fly.

"Nothing I'm afraid, you're on your own," the Major confirmed his doubts.

Inside the gates the Land Rovers approached a security hut which operated a barrier system. The men inside the hut were suited in NBC gear and were members of the Territorial Army drafted in to guard the evacuated shipping from looters. The driver of the Land Rover flashed his ID and the barrier was raised to allow them access onto the docks. Chen studied the plans and decided to head for the smaller births to the north of the harbour. He pointed to a fork in the road and when there was a gap in the traffic that was leaving the port, the two vehicles branched right.

It was nearly an hour later when they began to leave the commercial berths behind them. The section of the docks that they had entered was on the periphery of the cargo terminal. The evacuation was complete and it was deserted. Chen studied the plans and tried to correlate what he could see before him. To the left was the river and the quayside was lined with giant cranes. On the right hand side there were acres of derelict warehouses. They were five storeys high and built from dark sandstone blocks. Once upon a time they had been packed to the rafters with cotton bales and grain, timber and leather, and fine teas and spices from the Far East. Directly in front of them was a series of oblong inlets which had once been used to service the boatyards and the warehouses beyond them. Chen looked at the plans again and then raised his hand to signal the driver to bring the vehicle to a stop. He picked up a night sight and scanned the docklands and boatyards which were laid out in symmetrical patterns for a kilometre or so. There were ships and boats, barges and buoys of all shapes and sizes moored to the quaysides. Chen signalled both teams to exit the vehicles. He climbed out of his Land Rover and walked to the front of the vehicle where he spread the plans out on the bonnet.

"Red troop will take this section of harbour inlets here, and blue troop will take this section here and here," he outlined an imaginary meridian line to the taskforce troops. They nodded imperceptibly in their NBC masks. Chen couldn't see them nodding but he knew that if there had been any concerns then they would have been raised.

"Keep coms to a minimum and team leaders check in to me every five minutes. We will keep the Rovers at a backup distance of two hundred yards. Are there any questions?" Chen looked around the two teams but they remained silent. "Okay let's go."

The taskforce members peeled away from the group in two formations. They moved swiftly and silently like segments of a giant centipede, individual pieces moving as one tight unit. Chen and his unit headed to the right of the Land Rovers. The docks cut into the shoreline in a rectangular shape which formed a small harbour big enough for a dozen trawlers to be moored. To their right hand side the huge looming shapes of four derelict grain silos towered in the distance. The quayside was level concrete crisscrossed by railway lines which once carried steam powered engines up and down the docks towing thousands of tons of coke and coal. Chen pointed to their left which took them across a narrow walkway over a set of ancient lock gates. The team moved between the small harbours without a whisper. They could have been ghosts except for the footprints that they left behind them in the crisp white snow.

Chen rounded a wide section of the quay which was piled high with cargo containers of every colour. He kneeled down and held up his hand to stop his unit from proceeding and each one of them took up a defensive firing position, and made sure that they were covering the two men next to them. Their tactics had been rehearsed a thousand times on the training grounds so that it became second nature when they were thrust into the theatre of conflict. He thought that he'd heard a diesel engine close by, but when they broke clear of the containers there was nothing moving and the engine was silent. Chen scanned the harbour with his night sight. He trawled left and then right and then left again when something registered in his brain.

"Major, I need a confirmation description of the lightship that we are looking for," Chen was focused on a vessel two hundred yards to his right hand side as he spoke into the coms unit. The taskforce had requested digital images of the type of vessel which had been tackled by the river police launch. The water in the harbour looked like it had been disturbed recently by a boat.

Water was lapping gently up against the harbour walls as if it had been created by a wake. The ship that he was studying was in total darkness and a thick layer of snow covered the quayside next to it. There were telltale footprints in the snow and tyre tracks on the quay.

"Roger that, Chen," the voice of the fat controller answered. "The lightships are usually painted red. They have a plated metal superstructure and they have a large circular compartment fitted above the bridge which will look similar to the top of a lighthouse in appearance."

"Roger that. We are in contact range of a ship fitting that description. There are no signs of life at the moment, but there are tracks here. They look fairly recent," Chen reported what he could see despite his reservations about the suspect vessel being the one that he was hunting. "I need permission to eliminate her from our search?"

"Roger that, you have permission to proceed with caution," came the reply. This time it was the voice of Major Stanley Timms.

"Roger that, Major," Chen signalled his men to gather around and then he contacted red troop. "Did you get that, red troop?"

"Roger that, sir. We have the suspect vessel fifty yards to our left," the leader of red troop replied.

"Okay, we move in a pincer, red troop take the stern, blue troop will take the bow. Bring the Rovers up to the quay in five minutes from now, check your watches three, two, one, move," Chen waved a gloved hand and the taskforce men moved in unison toward the lightship. He thought that he could hear a diesel engine somewhere in the distance. They would have to investigate that later.

As Chen approached the lightship he could see that the footprints in the snow indicated that at least three people had exited from two vehicles. They had boarded the lightship and then climbed up a metal staircase before entering the bridge. Three sets of footprints had also left the vessel and returned to two vehicles. The tyre tracks headed back along the quayside the same way that they'd arrived. The depth and size of the footprints suggested that they belonged to men. Chen didn't think that the lightship had sailed anywhere for a long time. The bow and stern lines were covered in a thick layer of snow which supported his theory. The tracks in the snow could have been made completely innocently, but they had to investigate it.

Silently he gave the signal for the two teams to board the lightship, and within a few minutes they had secured the decks and entered the bridge. Two hatches had been opened and the taskforce penetrated the vessel in silence. Chen led red troop into the bowels of the ship. The further they progressed the more convinced he was that they were on a wild goose chase. He followed a trail of melted snow along a corridor, and then the footsteps headed down into the lower deck. There was nothing on the lowest level except the engines and the fuel tanks. Chen covered an open doorway as his men poured into the engine room. He was the last man into the room and he stopped dead. In the middle of the room was oval shaped box which was fitted with a small antenna. There was a flashing red light in the centre of the box, which was attached to a plastic type brick of C4. Blue troop entered the corridor behind him from the bow end of the ship. If the plastic explosive was detonated in such a confined space the taskforce men would not stand a chance.

CHAPTER 32
The Lightship

The Lightship edged toward the dockside. Cranes lined the harbour walls like giant metal sentinels guarding the city from invaders. The shoreline was a patchwork of busy cargo docks which serviced enormous deep sea tankers, huge berths for the many cruise liners that visited the historic port, and smaller boat repair yards. There were smaller inland harbours which could be reached via a network of canal locks. Along the farthest reaches of the docks there were several boatyards. Many of the boatyards had unused derelict berths on the periphery. Most of the canal locks were rusted shut by the lack of use over the years. They used to carry barges loaded with everything from cow hides for the tanneries, to Argentinean corned beef. All the cargo that was staying in Liverpool had to be transported from the container vessels to one of the hundreds of warehouses that were located further inland. The canal system was entered via a series of lock gates. It had become a mishmash of operational sections of water, and those canals which were unused and therefore remained sealed. About half of them were now mostly stagnant rubbish filled stretches of water that led nowhere. The largest part of the docks was owned by the port authorities but there were long tranches of it which were owned by a myriad of private shipping companies, and many of them had gone bust years ago. The majority of the deserted berths were not maintained at all and had been allowed to fall into dereliction. Christopher Walsh had acquired a covered dry dock that was once part of a boatyard repair business. The berth was covered by a large corrugated iron building which had once acted as a boatshed. Access to the

176

boatshed from the river was gained through lock gates that were nearly as old as the port itself. He had left the lock gates open when he'd set off on his salvage mission in order to save himself some time when he returned.

Across the rectangular harbour, through a flotilla of defunct trawlers on the port side, was another of his projects. He could barely make her out in the distance. She was a bright red lightship similar to the L2 but she'd been past repairing. Christopher had her bodywork repainted but the engines and superstructure had been condemned. He had decided to use her as bait in the event of a hiccup. As far as hiccups went this one was humongous. His plan had been to leak the details of a suspected terror attack on the London Olympics and then encourage governments all over the planet to buy a counter measure for blister agents. It was a simple plan and he wasn't sure how it had gone so badly wrong. He mulled it over as he steered the ship toward the abandoned boatyard.

Christopher sailed the L2 toward the lock gates and thrust the engines into reverse to slow her down. The berth was narrow and had been designed to be used as a dry dock which would have been utilised to repair ships that had hull damage below the waterline. He allowed the boat to bump up to the quay before turning the diesel supply off and shutting down the engines. He climbed down the steps from the bridge and unfurled the bow line and the stern line one at a time. The ropes were thicker than his arm. The metal gangplank clattered as he pushed it over the side onto the quay and it echoed loudly off the boatshed walls. Christopher ran down the gang plank and tied up the anchor ropes into rusted metal rings that were fixed into the crumbling concrete. He had expected at least two of Uri's men to be there guarding the boatyard but it was deserted. He looked to and fro at the shadows in the corners of the dark boatshed but there was no help to be seen.

The lock gates were massive and could not be closed manually by one man. Despite the fact that he was alone Christopher picked up a winding handle and ran to the gates. He was in a panic and had to hide the L2 from view. Across the harbour he could see the cargo docks and the cranes that belonged to the main port. On any normal night they would be teeming with men and forklift trucks. The job of unloading and loading the container vessels which used the port was a never ending one, but tonight the docks were quiet and the men that worked there were gone. The snow was piling up on the ships and their multicoloured containers and there was a mist drifting in the air. He slotted the handle into a metal cog and began winding the gates closed. With the gates closed the L2 could not be seen from the opposite quay or from the river. The rusty metal cog creaked and the gates groaned as they strained against the weight of the river. He breathed in deeply as the exertion began to take its toll. The familiar garlic smell of a blister agent cloyed in his nostrils. He stopped winding and sniffed the air again.

"Oh my god," he said out loud. He looked over at the deserted docks again and realised why they were silent. "The vapour has been blown ashore."

Christopher dropped the handle and it clanged heavily on the floor. The noise echoed through the dark boatshed. He ran toward the lightship in a panic desperate to get out of the mist and back into the ship where his antidotes were. The noise of a diesel engine approaching stopped him in his tracks and he looked around for somewhere to hide. There was an old oil drum ten yards away from him. It was big enough to hide behind and was in between him and the gangplank. He ran to it and ducked behind it. He saw headlights approaching the boatshed from the dock road and they were close, almost on him. The vehicle stopped outside the building but he could hear that the engine was still running. He heard the locks and chains being rattled and then heavy footprints stomping to and fro. The main doors which were big enough to fit a lorry through were locked and bolted, but there was a smaller pedestrian entrance at the side of them. He held his breath as he waited for the footsteps to retreat but they kept coming closer. The door opened and he heard the footsteps inside the boatshed. He was sure he'd locked it but maybe he'd forgotten. His breathing was laboured which panicked him further because he knew what it was that he was breathing in. He could hear three separate sets of footsteps. At least he thought that there were three but he daren't look around the oil drum to confirm it. From his hiding place he could see out of the lock gates and across the harbour. The mist was thickening and the mental images of swollen bloated bodies flickered through his mind as his experiments with blister agents returned to haunt him. The antidotes that he had developed were capable of treating any skin that had been exposed to the agents. The counter measure only worked if the subjects were treated in good time before the skin blistered. He had also developed a tonic which consisted of pure drinking water with eight to ten drops of a chlorine based serum added to each gallon. The water was turned slightly acidic which counteracted the alkaline effects of the blister agent and stopped the throat from becoming blistered. The only thing that he hadn't developed successfully was a treatment for the lungs. The tissue in the air sacks was so delicate that everything he had tried resulted in the death of the experimental subject. Christopher reckoned that he had half an hour at the most before his lungs were affected beyond repair. He had protective equipment on board the L2 but he couldn't move from his hiding place.

Across the harbour in the distance, he thought that he could see movement. He looked again through the darkness and the snow but it had gone. Suddenly it was there again. Brief shadows moving in the dark, almost unseen. He could see a flicker of movement and then nothing. The movement was on the quayside near to his defunct lightship. Someone was approaching the ship in a covert fashion. Christopher realised that there were other people on the docks, and that they were not people that he needed to have a close encounter with. He heard footsteps climbing the gangplank of the L2 and decided that he had to see who it was. He twisted his body around and pressed his face against the rusted drum. The metal felt cold against his skin and it smelled of must and decay. There were three shapes walking up the gangplank. Two of the men were wearing heavy black jackets and woollen hats, and they had gasmasks on. A third person was wearing a full NBC suit. He leaned further over trying to get a better view of the intruders. He leaned his weight onto his left hand and pressed down hard on a shard of broken glass which pierced his palm. He cried out and lost his balance.

Christopher ended up on his back looking in dismay at the three men on the gangplank. They were fifty yards away from him. He sucked the blood from his wounded hand and waved nervously at the men with his other one.

"Go and help him," Uri ordered the two men that had been left behind to guard the boatshed. The two men clomped down the quay toward their boss who was lying on his back in an embarrassing position.

"Uri?" Christopher asked. "Is that you?"

"Yes you fool. Get up!" Uri snarled at him. He had completely lost all patience with his eccentric employer.

"Where did you get that suit? I need to get into the boat and out of this mist. You're obviously one step ahead of me Uri, you're not as......," he trailed off his sentence.

"What Christopher?" Uri asked. "I'm not as, what were you going to say?"

"Nothing I was just surprised to see you in that suit," Christopher mumbled and sucked his cut again.

"I'm not as stupid as I look Christopher, am I?" Uri finished his sentence for him.

Christopher remained silent as the two men picked him up and helped him to gather himself. He looked back at the open lock gates. Uri followed his gaze and saw the lightship anchored across the harbour. There were flashlights being played over her and brief signs of movement although it was difficult to see any detail through the snowfall.

"Get your men to close the lock gates. I need to get inside and sort out some protection," Christopher sniped and walked away from the two hoodlums. "I think we have company across the harbour. We need to move quickly."

Uri pointed an Uzi nine millimetre machine pistol at him. The Uzi is the most common automatic machine pistol on the planet because they are so simple to manufacture. Christopher Walsh had purchased nine of them, plus enough ammunition to start a small war, prior to embarking on his salvage mission. Christopher stared at the machinegun and he froze in his tracks.

"What are you doing with my machinegun, Uri?"

"We need paying for what we have done so far, Christopher. This job has been one fuck up after another and now we need to be paid," Uri's voice was muffled by the respirator but Christopher could hear the venom in it none the less. "I'm going to borrow your machineguns for a while."

"We don't have time for this Uri. The torches over there across the harbour must belong to the police, and they're obviously looking for us," Christopher pointed through the lock gates at the lightship.

"I've been across there myself tonight Christopher, while we were waiting for you to bring the L2 back. I can buy us some time, but as I said earlier we need to see some hard cash or this ends here," Uri kept the gun pointed at him. "I think that you should help to close the gates with my men. Now move it!"

"I need to get out of this mist Uri, now I'll pay you as much as you like when we are out of here with those shells intact," Christopher tried to sound assertive but he failed miserably.

"The longer you argue the more of that shit you are breathing in," Uri shrugged.

"Okay for fuck's sake okay, hurry up," Christopher turned and ran toward the winding mechanism and the two burly men followed him. Uri watched them turning the winding mechanism which closed the gates slowly and smiled. He could see more torch beams flicking about on the deck of the defunct lightship and there were two sets of headlights on the quayside. There was a lot of activity being focused on that part of the docks. Uri reached into his pocket and removed a remote detonator. He'd taken it from a container next to the boatshed which had the dive team's equipment inside. There was plenty of explosive in there and he'd made the best use of it while he'd been waiting for Christopher Walsh to reach the boatyard. He wasn't sure who was on the condemned lightship but he did know that they were looking for them. It could be the police, the army, the port authorities or even Special Forces, but it wouldn't matter because they would all die the same way. Uri was going to take Christopher's money and then blow both the lightships to pieces to cover his escape.

CHAPTER 33

The Government Bunker

Helen Walsh put down the telephone and rushed to her feet. She had just had a very interesting conversation with an eminent scientist from China about a suspected mustard gas incident in the Northern provinces. He had come to several conclusions following his investigation of the issue. One was that he could never work directly for the Chinese government again without being in fear of his life, and those of his family. The second thing was that the concentration levels of the blister agent varied greatly as the distance from the release site increased. He also had some detailed information about how some of the victims had been treated.

"Major I have some very important information," Helen approached a huddle of government employees who represented several different agencies.

The Major looked at her and decided that it would be prudent to talk to her in the privacy of his temporary office. He made his excuses and left the group.

"I think we should go into my office," he guided her gently by the arm. He opened the door where the fat controller was already sat working at his desk. "Now, what is your good news?"

"I have been talking to another scientist about his experiences with a chemical gas incident in the Northern Provinces of China five years ago," she began excitedly. She was about to carry on when she realised that the Major's facial expression had turned to thunder. "Please Major hear me out, I haven't mentioned anything to him about what is happening here."

"Okay, we'll discuss the protocol of seeking outside help later. It's not important now what context you broached the matter with him. For now tell me what information he had for us," the Major looked seriously concerned about Helen's naivety.

"Well, the short version of events is that there was an alleged government attack on a rebel town in the northern territories of China. The inhabitants displayed terrible burn injuries which couldn't be explained because there were no fires. Some of the local doctors swabbed their patients to try and determine exactly what was causing their skin to blister. The swabs showed that they had come into contact with a vapour or gaseous substance with a very high alkaline PH reading," she was desperately trying to get to the point. "They had no idea what it was that had caused the injuries, but they simply applied a mild acidic solution to the burns and discovered that it gave the victims relief, and in some cases it stopped any further blistering."

"It would make perfect sense that a solution of an acidic nature would neutralise the effects of the alkaline somewhat," the fat controller jumped in with his professional opinion. "That is simple basic chemistry," he added.

"Exactly," she continued. "We are using the decontamination units to apply a mild acid to all the evacuees at the moment, which is causing major tailbacks across the city's main arterial routes, but we have over a dozen facilities near to the perimeter where we could speed things up dramatically."

"I'm not sure that I follow, Helen," the Major said. He pinched the skin on his nose between his finger and thumb and squeezed his eyes closed tightly. The events of the last few days were catching up on him.

"Swimming pools!" the fat controller shouted. He stood up and patted Helen on the back. He was grinning insanely and there was a blob of spittle at the corner of his mouth which indicated that he was excited about the concept.

"What?" the Major asked confused.

"Swimming pools, public baths, they're all laced with chlorine to purify the water. Chlorine in its pure form is a powerful acid which we use every day of the week in some shape or form, therefore we have a certain inbuilt tolerance to it already," the fat controller grasped the idea by the horns enthusiastically.

The Major looked from Helen back to David Bell and then back to Helen again. He shrugged at her for some kind of confirmation but she was grinning like an idiot too.

"Helen?" the Major said.

"Yes, Major," she nodded excitedly. "We could open all the public baths and speed up the decontamination process tenfold at least, and the information also gives us an indication as to how we can help those who are affected by vapour internally too."

"Salt water," the fat controller anticipated what she was going to say, and he clapped his hands together.

"Yes Major, salt water seemed to help the Chinese victims because it is sodium chloride and we eat it every day, therefore..." she began.

"We already have a tolerance to it?" the Major finished off the sentence. "I get the picture."

"I'll get onto it straight away, Major," the fat controller said excitedly. He picked up the telephone and dialled the number of the perimeter commander. The information would need to be passed on to every member of the evacuation teams and also to every institution which had not been evacuated. The city's hospitals and prisons could become proactive by treating their patients and prisoners before they displayed any symptoms.

Helen felt elated that her information had the fat controller in a spin. It had been a difficult initiation into the world of counter terrorism for her, and she would only prove her worth by providing useful solutions to the traumas that presented themselves.

"The Doctor was instructed by the Chinese Government to disprove that any chemical weapons had been used against the rebels, but his investigation proved the opposite," Helen paused and sipped a mouthful of tepid tea before continuing. "His tests showed that there was an area of the town where the blister agent was present in a concentrated form. He also explained that as the blister agent passes over the land, especially buildings, it becomes weaker and weaker very quickly indeed. The moisture in the vapour seems to be absorbed by brick and concrete structures weakening the blister agent considerably with every few hundred yards that it travels," Helen had gathered herself now and was speaking in the role of the rational well balanced expert that she had been employed as.

The Major looked at the digital screen on the wall. It was

displaying an aerial view of the city. Like many historic ports around the globe Liverpool's waterfront was lined with high buildings. Behind them was mile after mile of shops, multi-storey car parks and the retail and commercial quarters that they serviced. There were millions of tons of concrete and stone on every city block.

"Do you think that the vapour will dissipate as it progresses across the city?" the Major asked.

"Yes I do, Major," Helen answered in an assured manner. "I also think that the snowfall will have an effect."

"What do you mean?"

"The Chinese scientist told me that his test results showed that the agent is easily absorbed into whatever chemical elements it comes into contact with. Therefore fresh snowflakes will absorb the vapour as they pass through it."

"What do you think the effect will be then?" the Major waved his hand over the image of the city.

"The good news is that I think that the contamination could be limited to the riverbank and the city centre," she explained. "The bad news is that the men on that gas rig have been exposed to the chemical in a very concentrated state. We have to send them a communiqué advising them what to do, it's the only chance that they have. They are surrounded by seawater, and I think that could slow down the effects of the blister agent by immersing themselves in the sea."

The Major glanced at the fat controller and he shook his head almost imperceptibly. "That's impossible I'm afraid we have imposed a communication blanket on the rig. We cannot risk anyone working out there to contact their families on the mainland. The slightest mention of burn victims and the press would be full of speculative disaster stories."

"Okay, I can understand that you have to block their telephones, but let me send one e-mail, that's all it will take," Helen Walsh looked the Major directly in the eye as she spoke. She couldn't stand by and let the gas workers die if there was the slightest chance that they could be saved. The Major looked at the fat controller again and this time he shook his head emphatically.

"If we turn their e-mail back on to send a message then

everything that is sat in the rig's outbox, waiting to be sent, will upload automatically. There could be a dozen messages to family and friends describing god only knows what," the fat controller spoke quietly. "We cannot take the risk I'm afraid."

He turned back to his telephone calls and the Major blushed red with embarrassment. Helen stared at the Major trying to provoke a crisis of conscience within him.

"We can stop their out mail at the main server," Helen spluttered. She wasn't sure if they could but it seemed to make sense. If it wasn't possible then it should be. The fat controller turned back to her and removed his glasses.

"You might be right, Helen," he said rubbing his eyes. "There could be a way."

CHAPTER 34
The Explorer

As Sparks swung the fire axe down, Chef back peddled as fast as he could. He had taken a few steps backward when he toppled over the deserted card table, and he landed on his rear end with a thump. The axe missed its target and cleaved a six inch dent into the metal floor. Everyone in the recreation room froze in shock as they tried to comprehend that the resident electrician had just attempted to hit the rig's cook with a fire hatchet. Sparks wiped spittle from his cracked lips and his breathing became shallow. He was panting like a dog. He turned around quickly and glared at Big Gordon. Gordon didn't recognise the man that was stood in front of him, his face was twisted into a snarl and his eyes were blood red. Sparks seemed to be confused. He looked down and saw the tray of mineral water on the floor, and something flashed behind his eyes. There was a flicker of recognition. He stooped and picked up the water as if it was a baby, and he cradled it lovingly in his arms. Gordon took a step toward him and the twisted snarl reappeared on the electrician's face. Sparks swung the axe one handed in a lateral arc perpendicular to the floor, and Big Gordon jumped backwards out of its path.

"Sparks! Put the axe down man," Gordon shouted at the electrician. Sparks looked at his foreman, and then he looked at the axe as if it was the first time he had seen it. He dropped the hatchet onto the floor and backed away from it like it was a poisonous snake.

"Brains," Big Gordon shouted. He needed to regain some control. He shouted instructions to his men and spurred them into action. "Get Sparks to the sickbay immediately, and make sure that you put him into isolation."

Brains looked shocked by what had just happened, but he responded quickly to the order. He approached Sparks warily and placed his hand gently on his arm. Sparks looked confused and clasped the tray of mineral water tightly to his chest. Brains didn't see the point in trying to take it from him. It would only provoke more violence judging by what had already taken place. Gordon had told him to put Sparks into isolation, which was the only room in the crew module that could be used as a cell. It was designed to be used as either a secure facility in the event of a heinous crime, or as quarantine quarters. The explorer had been drilling off shore for over a decade and the isolation cell had only ever been used as a mortuary. Brains had never witnessed it being used as a cell before, but then no one had ever tried to hit the Chef with an axe before tonight either. Brains swallowed and his throat felt like there was broken glass sliding down it.

"Come on with me Sparks," Brains said gently. "Let's get you to bed and then we can sort your eyes out my friend. They look sore. Mine are a little sore too. We can get some drops from the sickbay."

Sparks looked at Brains and he nodded his head. Brains led him toward the door without any fuss. Big Gordon picked up the hatchet and stared at it in disbelief. It had been a very strange night so far and something told him that it wasn't over by a long way yet.

"Are you okay?" Gordon asked Chef. The cook had turned an unusually pale colour, all the blood had drained from his cheeks. He patted himself down and shook his head from side to side.

"I think I've shit my pants," the chef answered shakily.

"You're not the only one," Big Gordon said. He turned and headed toward his office. Smokey Pete looked into the kitchen area and saw Harvey pouring half a bottle of water over his head before swallowing the rest of it in two gulps. The skin on Harvey's face had begun to blister and there was a fat yellow sack of fluid beneath his left eye.

"Hey boss," Smokey Pete tapped Big Gordon on the shoulder. "Harvey looks really sick. What the fuck happened to them out there?"

Gordon approached the kitchen area cautiously and he

watched Harvey closely. Harvey took another bottle of mineral water from a large refrigerator and twisted the top from it with his teeth. He spat the plastic cap onto the floor and put the bottle to his lips. Gordon winced as blood dribbled from the corner of Harvey's mouth. The skin there had blistered and then cracked as he drank from the water bottle. The skin on the back of the pipe fitter's hands was a deep purple colour.

"Harvey, we need to get you into the sickbay," Gordon stayed in the doorway as he spoke, and didn't encroach on the injured man's space.

"I'm fine, I'm just really thirsty," Harvey turned to face Gordon, and the full extent of his injuries became visible. His lips were twice their usual size. They were swollen with blood and yellow puss. The whites of Harvey's eyes were blood red, and his eyelids had become dark and bloated. At the corner of his mouth a blister had burst and bloody mucus ran from the wound down his chin. Harvey looked like an extra from a zombie movie.

"Fucking hell!" Smokey Pete said under his breath. "We need to get him airlifted out of here boss." Pete ran toward Gordon's office. His intention was to use the telephone to summon a med vac helicopter.

"The system is down Pete, and nothing is going to fly through this snowstorm," Big Gordon shouted after him. "We need to deal with this situation ourselves until communications are back up and running. Help me get Harvey into the sickbay."

As Gordon turned back toward Harvey, the pipe fitter kicked the kitchen door closed in his face. Gordon stepped forward and twisted the handle but Harvey had locked it from within. He could hear furniture being dragged across the floor. To the right of the door was a large rectangular window, and Gordon looked through it with dismay. Harvey had jammed a chair beneath the door handle and then he'd returned to the sink where he began to pour bottled water over his head. Chef joined Gordon and Pete at the window and he stared in silence. His hands had started to shake with shock.

"What's going on Gordon?" Pete stood next to the giant foreman and Chef as they watched Harvey drink a litre bottle of mineral water in seconds.

"I don't know Pete, but I think that they have been exposed

to something outside which has burned them," Gordon faced his colleague. "It must have been something outside because we are okay so far. My throat is sore and Brains said that he was struggling with his, but he would be worse because he had been outside on the platform doing his moisture tests."

"My eyes are stinging and I'm getting a sore throat," Pete said, although he didn't know if the symptoms were purely psychological. He had read somewhere that rig workers often developed similar symptoms to their work mates, despite not being ill themselves. It was something to do with working in close proximity with one another.

"Maybe we're not affected to the same degree because we have been inside all night," Gordon speculated. He looked through the kitchen window again and gritted his teeth. Harvey had opened another bottle of water and he was drinking it greedily. He scratched furiously at the blister beneath his eye and the skin tore like tissue paper. Blood and puss exploded from the ruptured skin and Harvey dropped onto his knees.

"Oh my god! We have got to get hold of the mainland, and get the maintenance crew back inside quickly," Big Gordon shouted to Pete. Smokey Pete couldn't tear his eyes away from the horror beyond the kitchen window. "Now Pete, get the crew inside now!"

"What about the safety checks?" Pete move toward the platform door. It was second nature for rig workers to think safety first.

"Tell them to shut everything down, and get back inside this module," Gordon had no choice but to get his men inside.

"What about me boss?" Chef didn't want to be left alone.

"Try and open that fucking door," Gordon said. He was struggling to think straight. Gordon placed the fire hatchet on a side table which was next to the drinks machine, and he moved toward his office as fast as his lumbering bulk would allow him to. Smokey Pete opened the platform access door and snowflakes blew into the recreation module. Gordon could hear his voice bellowing for his work mates to get inside until the door slammed closed again. Chef was hitting the kitchen door with his shoulder in a futile attempt to break it down. Like the rest of the crew module it was almost indestructible.

Big Gordon Morris picked up the telephone in his office and listened for a tone. There was nothing but static. He pulled out his mobile and prodded the touch pad with a podgy finger but the screen responded with only two words, 'Limited Service'. Gordon sat at his desk and hit the keyboard return button. The computer screen saver disappeared and the home page popped up. He clicked on messaging and the icon box changed to 'System Error'. His inbox was reading that there was one message unread. When he'd checked earlier it had been empty. Gordon clicked on it and the header read, 'Urgent'. He opened the message and printed it off as he read it on the screen. There was a brief set of instructions attached to a very vague e-mail which would have made absolutely no sense under any other circumstances. Gordon read it twice on the screen before standing up and taking the printed copy from the tray. He had to move quickly if he were to save the lives of any of his men at all, including his own. As he reached his office door Brains was returning from the backups. Chef stopped battering the kitchen door and went to join the new arrival and his boss.

"Did you put Sparks into isolation?" Gordon asked the lab technician.

"Fuck off fatty," Brains said as he walked past the big foreman. Chef was open mouthed by the flippant comment. The lab technician's skin had yellowed significantly and his eyes looked red raw.

Gordon was about to lose his temper with the lab technician. Now was not the time to be hurling childish insults around the rig. He opened his mouth to speak, but then he noticed that Brains was leaving a trail of blood spots behind him. The blood appeared to be dripping from the technician's right hand, and Gordon immediately thought that he must have cut his fingers, until he noticed that two of his fingers were missing. Sticky crimson fluid oozed from the bloody stumps, but Brains seemed to be oblivious to it.

"Jesus Christ Brian, what happened to your hand?" Gordon reverted to using his real name. He reached back inside his office and grabbed a small green first aid box. There was one in every room on the rig and Gordon had a feeling that it would need more than an elastic bandage and some sticky tape to fix Brain's hand.

"I wanted a bottle of water from his tray but the greedy bastard wouldn't give me one, so he bit me," Brains muttered as he walked by.

"Brian I need to stop you from bleeding," Gordon followed him at a distance. Chef followed Gordon like a lapdog hiding from a bigger animal, and he peered at Brains around his massive shoulders.

The technician ignored his boss and continued on his way. He reached the drinks machine and stopped in front of it. Brains felt his trouser pockets looking for pound coins, and was frustrated by the lack of fingers on his right hand. All his loose change was in his right hand pocket but he had no fingers to reach it. He stared at the bloody stumps and he was totally confused by the fact that his two of his fingers weren't there anymore. He looked around and spotted the fire hatchet lying next to the machine. Using his left hand Brains picked up the hatchet and swung it at the machine. The curved facia shattered, and the lights which illuminated it flickered and then went out. He hit it twice more before the hole in it was big enough for him to reach inside and remove a cold can of diet cola. Now he was faced with the dilemma of picking up the cola with no fingers on his free hand. He looked at the hatchet and dropped it before using his good hand to get the tin. Yet another hurdle frustrated him as he held the coke in his left hand and tried to the grasp the ring pull with his right. Having no fingers was making him very angry indeed. Brains spun around three hundred and sixty degrees in his search for a solution to his problem. He focused his attention on Big Gordon.

"Could you open this please, fatty?" Brains held the can out toward his boss. Gordon had his mouth open and he was dumbfounded by the sequence of events which had unfurled as the shift progressed.

"Of course I will Brian. Let me strap up your fingers while you drink that," Gordon took the cola tin and opened it. The tin was covered in blood which made it slippery. He handed it back to the technician and reached gently for his injured hand. Brains drank thirstily from the can while Big Gordon tried to stop the bleeding.

"Tie a tourniquet around the top of his arm Chef," Gordon spoke quietly but with a stern quality in his voice. Chef looked blankly at him. "Get a tourniquet from the box and fasten it to the top of his arm, and do it now while he is still calm."

Chef took the first aid box and removed the strapping from it. He approached Brains as if he was a stray dog, and with quivering hands he fastened the tourniquet above the bicep muscle. By the time Gordon had strapped the stumps with elastic bandages the blood had seeped through them and was dripping onto the floor. Gordon could see that Brian's eyes were bloodshot in the corners, not as bad as Harvey's had been, but they were getting worse.

"Open another one please fatty," Brains said matter of factly. He pulled his injured hand away from Gordon. Gordon took a sling out of the first aid box.

"I'll open a can of coke for you, if you put your arm into this sling for me. We need to keep it elevated so that you don't bleed to death," Gordon looked into the technician's eyes. They were like those of an animal. There was intelligence behind them but there was also fear and anger. Brains seemed to be thinking about his options. If he did as he was asked he could drink to quench his terrible thirst. He placed his injured hand across his chest, next to his shoulder, and Gordon tied a reef not behind his neck to support the limb.

"I need a drink please," Brains said.

Gordon reached into the shattered machine and took out a cold can of diet cola. He opened it and handed it to Brains with a smile on his face.

"It has been a hell of a night," Gordon tried to contact the rational being that had once lived within Brian's body. "I need to get you some salt water to drink Brian. It will ease your throat."

"What are you talking about?" Chef asked.

"I've had an e-mail from someone on the mainland. It's a long story but basically there has been an accident which has released a cloud of very strong alkaline vapour," Gordon spoke in a whisper. Brains was calm and he wanted to keep him that way. They had to isolate each of the infected men, and then try to treat them one at a time. "According to the information that I've received, we have to try and isolate the badly affected men before they become violent. It's the thirst which affects their mental state."

"Are you telling me that they know what's gone on out here?" Chef asked angrily. Brains looked at him with frightened eyes. He could sense the aggression in his voice. Gordon saw the injured man's reaction and he grabbed Chef by the arm. He dragged him away from the drinks machine and the injured technician.

"Keep your voice down. I don't know who sent the fucking information through to me, but I do know that Sparks is in isolation after attacking you with an axe; Harvey has locked himself in the kitchen and he looks like a fucking zombie, and Brains has had his fingers bitten off and he looks like he is going to explode any second now, so what I need you to do is listen to me, answer my questions and do not give me any shit," Gordon had his nose pressed close to Chef's face. Chef was leaning backward to avoid his boss's ranting but Gordon held him tightly. There was no escape. "Do you understand me Chef?"

"Okay, okay, I understand. I'm just a bit blown away by everything that's happened," Chef tried to get a grip.

"We all are. Now where do you keep the salt? Apparently their delirium is caused by burns to the throat. We can ease it by giving them salt water to drink and gargle with. We can also slow down the skin damage by immersing them in the ocean," Gordon took the printed instructions from his pocket. He scanned them again. "We also need bleach."

Chef racked his brains as he processed the questions that he had been asked. It was a scary position to be in, and it was all the more frightening because none of it made any sense. He was used to the odd strange request from the crew. Some people were vegetarians, others were vegans, some had wheat allergies, and others had nut allergies, gluten allergies, low fat diets, high protein diets, bodybuilders, anorexics and bulimics. The longer he served at sea the more unusual scenarios he encountered, but nothing like this, nothing dangerous.

"Chef," Gordon growled at him. "I need you to get a grip and help me. We have been affected too. We have to move quickly."

"What has bleach got to do with anything?" Chef asked. He was confused and baffled by everything that was happening.

"I'm not a hundred percent sure, but the information says that because it's acidic it helps to treat the skin burns," Gordon shrugged his huge shoulders.

"It's in the kitchen," Chef gathered himself. He looked past Gordon at the rectangular window and into the kitchen area beyond it. The room was in darkness. Harvey must have turned the lights out.

"What is in the kitchen?" Gordon asked. He followed Chef's gaze and registered mentally that the lights had been turned off.

"The salt and the bleach are in the kitchen. I keep them in the store cupboard at the back of the kitchen," Chef waved a hand toward the kitchen door.

"Open this please fatty," Brains approached them with a diet cola in his outstretched hand. The sling was soaked with blood despite the limb being elevated. His eyes were swollen and his lips were cracked and bleeding.

"He is getting worse every few minutes," Gordon said quietly. He took the cola tin from his hand and opened it. Brains snatched it from him and drank from it greedily. He turned around and walked back toward the broken vending machine as happy as a man with his fingers bitten off fingers could be.

The door which led into the backup areas slammed open. Gordon and Chef turned to see who it was. Sparks stood in the doorway naked. His face and neck had turned into a mass of yellow blisters. The skin was stretched and swollen. There was blood smeared around his face and neck. The rest of his body appeared to be normal which only accentuated the damage to the parts of his body which had been exposed when he was on the platform. Sparks collapsed and toppled forward onto his front. There was a broken chair leg protruding from the back of his head. Dark congealed blood clung to the makeshift weapon. Gordon and Chef turned to each other, and then they simultaneously looked at Brains. Brains was staring at the dead electrician.

"He bit my fingers," Brains said. He turned around and reached into the drinks machine for another can.

The platform access door burst open and the impromptu maintenance crew tramped in one at a time. They were stunned by the bloody scene that met them in the recreation room.

"Every single one of us has been affected by something outside. It must be something to do with the explosions earlier. If we move quickly we may survive this, if we don't we're going to end up like Brains. Tie him up and follow my instructions, and do it now," Big Gordon and his crew were in a race against time, and the losers would become deranged before bleeding to death.

CHAPTER 35
Grace Farrington

Grace Farrington reached the deserted docks at Seaforth without any further incidents. Traffic had become thinner as they approached the city and the streets were empty. The snowfall was relentless and if it were not for the four wheel function of the pickup truck then driving would have been impossible. Barnes slowed the vehicle down as they approached the northern entrance of the cargo docks. The entrance led into the warehouse sectors of the old docks and was unused. The gates hadn't been unlocked for decades. There were thick wooden gates preventing access from the dock road.

"We need to get into the docks here," Grace said. Her voice was muffled inside her NBC suit. "This is the most northern point of access."

"The gates are chained up. How far is it to the next entrance," Barnes asked.

"It's at least a mile or so if my memory serves me correctly. Get those gates open soldier," Grace ordered. There wasn't time for protocol.

"Roger that," Barnes left the truck in idle and climbed out of the vehicle. He looked clumsy as he waddled through the deep snow. Grace watched as he fumbled with the rusted padlock and chain for a few seconds. He stepped back four paces and fired a short burst from his machinegun. The padlock disintegrated, and the chain dropped into the soft snow. Barnes reached through the gates and slipped the bolt from its keep. He pushed the huge gates with his shoulder but they refused to open. The wooden planks had swelled over the decades and they were jammed tight in the middle.

"They're stuck tight," Barnes shouted.

Grace slid over the centre console into the driver's seat. She engaged first gear and swung the truck into the centre of the road, pointing away from the entrance gates. The gearbox crunched as she slammed the vehicle into reverse, and snow sprayed high into the air as the wheels sought purchase in the deep white powder. Barnes had to move quickly to avoid being rundown as the pickup hurtled backwards toward the gates at speed. Grace kept her foot hard down on the accelerator as the back end of the truck connected with the centre of the gates with a deafening crunch. The rear lights exploded into a shower of coloured glass, and the gates splintered into pieces which were strewn across a large area. Only the hinges remained and they were left flapping in the wind.

"That'll do it every time," Barnes muttered to himself inside his helmet. He jogged over to the truck and then climbed into the passenger seat.

"What did you say soldier?" Grace said.

"Nothing ma'am, nothing at all," Barnes laughed.

Grace turned the steering wheel and span the vehicle through ninety degrees and they were faced with acres of warehouses and canals spread out in front of them. The snow and the Victorian warehouses gave the scene a look of a Dickens novel. The docks were empty and nothing moved.

"Now what?" Barnes said squinting through the windscreen.

"This will be like looking for a needle in a haystack," Grace mumbled. "I'll get the Major on the coms."

"Major, what is Chen's twenty?" Grace asked. Twenty was a citizens band radio code for position, and it is still often used by the military.

"He has two units moving in on a suspect vessel which is situated south of the warehouse sector," the Major replied.

"Is it the lightship?"

"It is a lightship, and there is evidence of activity around it, but we can't be sure," the Major was leaning on the side of caution. "Chen said that there are tyre tracks leading away from it. If you are coming in from the north then keep your eyes open for them. They could lead us to something."

"Roger that," Grace selected first gear and the pickup lurched forward through the storm. She steered the truck between two five storey grain silos which towered above them. The windows were made up of three columns of squares, but every pane of glass was long since smashed or reclaimed by unscrupulous scrap merchants. The snow was deeper between the buildings. The wind had formed deep snowdrifts against the silo walls. Grace kept the vehicle in the centre of the cobbled roads as they progressed from one block to another. Even with four wheel drive the vehicle was slipping and sliding.

At the end of the third block of warehouses they joined the quayside of the canal system. To the right they could see the perimeter walls which separated the docks from the main road. In front of them was a rectangular harbour which was flanked on two sides by boatsheds, and was completely open to the river on the opposite side. To the left was a series of narrow swing bridges which crossed the canals, and connected one harbour to the next. There was no sign of vehicle tracks in either direction.

"This is the most northern dock, if we head south toward the city then we should meet up with Chen and his units at some point," Barnes pointed to the left.

Grace drove the pickup onto the first narrow bridge and it rattled and groaned in protest at the weight as the vehicle crawled across it. On the right as they cleared the bridge another large harbour opened up. It had boatsheds on one side and there was a flotilla of trawlers anchored together in the middle of the inlet. The far side of the harbour was almost out of sight through the snowstorm but Grace could just make out narrow beams of light in the distance. She pointed across the harbour and brought the vehicle to a sliding stop.

"Over there, across the water," she said. "They are gun lights, it must be Chen's units."

"Never mind that, look there," Barnes pointed toward the quayside on their right. Tyre tracks had been left which crossed the swing bridge ahead of them and then went to the right toward a line of boatsheds where they disappeared.

"Pass me those night sights," Grace said. Barnes handed a pair of binoculars to her. She placed them against her visor and adjusted the focus so that she could see the activity across the harbour. There were two teams of men in protective clothing boarding a vessel which was anchored to the quayside. One of the teams swarmed the bow decks, and the second team took the stern. Thin beams of light played over the vessel as the men moved in well rehearsed formations. She couldn't see the bridge door being opened or the men entering it. Neither could she see them descending below the decks into the bowels of the lightship, but she knew that they had. Two men remained on deck as the taskforce men penetrated the vessel, and two sets of headlights appeared from behind a tall block of metal containers. Grace couldn't identify the vehicles but she knew from experience that they were the Land Rovers moving in as backup. She was about to look away when the lightship was illuminated by a massive explosion which ripped her mid-ships apart. A fireball climbed up into the night sky from the vessel and the flash blinded her for a second. She closed he eyes to protect them from the blinding light and turned her head away.

"Jesus," Barnes whistled as he spoke. "Please tell me our men weren't anywhere near that."

Grace swallowed hard and looked through the field glasses again. The remnants of the lightship were scattered like burning confetti across the quayside. With the upper decks blown clear the exposed hull looked more like a large rowing boat. A tower of flame burned fiercely from the hull. There was no sign of life, no sign of the two Land Rovers' headlights, and no sign of Chen and his men.

CHAPTER 36
Tank

John Tankersley was half a mile from Seaforth docks when the lightship exploded. He was driving a Territorial Army Hummer, which he had acquired outside of the Southport General hospital. Tank had stripped the taskforce pickup truck of its weapons and ammunition. His colleague had the only set of keys to the ignition, and he wasn't likely to hand them over to him without causing a fuss, and so the Hummer was the obvious choice. He'd watched from the casualty department window as the army vehicle had been parked at the rear of the hospital. Its occupants climbed out and entered the building leaving it unguarded. Two of the part-time soldiers were half dressed in protective suits, while the others were in standard fatigues. They didn't seem to be taking the evacuation training very seriously. Tank sneaked out and raided the taskforce vehicle for weapons and then headed for the abandoned Hummer.

Stealing the vehicle was a piece of cake. He'd driven back to the old funfair before searching the rear of the vehicle for equipment; there were half a dozen NBC suits stored in a crate. He checked the size of each suit in turn, and then climbed into the largest one. It was a tight fit to say the least.

Tank had followed the tyre tracks along the beach up to the point where they had exited it. He had driven past the dead soldiers, slowing down slightly to check their identities. None of them belonged to the taskforce, and more to the point none of them were Grace Farrington. The Hummer had a wide wheelbase and it made short work of the snowfall as he neared the city's docklands. The pain in his face had been reduced to a dull ache by the drugs he'd been administered. The nurses had applied an icepack to it to bring down the swelling, but he still resembled the elephant man. The gash in his cheek had been closed over with adhesive stitches, which had stemmed the bleeding for now. The fracture was a bad one but a cocktail of painkillers and adrenalin allowed him to function at eighty percent. The dock road had been empty as he neared the perimeter wall and that's when he'd seen the fireball climbing skyward from the river.

Tank turned up the volume control on the Hummer's coms unit. The set was buzzing with a dozen people talking at the same time. The Territorial Army had men stationed at the dock's main entrance. He could make that much out of the chatter but not much else. Nobody could identify where the explosion was located, except that it was on the docks somewhere. Grace would already be there, and there was a chance that chemical ordinance was there too. He slammed the Hummer into third gear and floored the accelerator. The road bent to the right following the perimeter wall and the vehicle slid sideways as he took the bend.

Tank saw a figure in the middle of the road but by the time it had registered it was too late to avoid hitting him. The bend obscured him until the last moment, by which time it was too late to stop. There was a thud as he bounced off the bonnet and a cracking sound as the windshield shattered into a thousand segments. Although it was fractured it remained in place which made it impossible to see through. He stamped on the brakes and the Hummer went into a three hundred and sixty degree spin. There were vehicles parked across the road, which was madness, but they were there anyway. Tank assumed that they had been abandoned by their owners in the blind panic of the evacuation. The Hummer careered toward them and all Tank could do was hold on tight and wait for the impact to come. When the impact came it was a bone crunching smash which sent vibrations through every inch of his being. The fracture in his face sent white needles through his brain and his upper teeth felt like every nerve ending was exposed. He held tightly to the steering wheel and waited for the pain to subside, but all the time his brain was processing the visual information that his eyes were gathering.

There were shapes moving amongst the abandoned cars. Dark

shadows and hooded figures flitted behind them like ghosts. At first he didn't comprehend what was happening, and then there was a loud crack as the passenger window cracked. There was a small hole in the reinforced pane and a spider web of fractures surrounded it. Another projectile smashed into the panel followed by others hitting the bodywork. Tank saw a shadowy figure climbing onto the bonnet of a dark Ford. The arms were extended like those of an archer. A steel ball bearing hit the damaged pane and Tank was showered with shards of glass. The figure reloaded his powerful hunting catapult and fired again. Hunting catapults can fire a ball bearing with enough velocity to penetrate a human skull like a knife cutting through butter. This time his aim was not as sure and the ball bearing slammed into the door before ricocheting fifty yards across the road.

Tank selected reverse with a crunch and hit the accelerator. The Hummer shot backwards as more projectiles pinged off the vehicle. There was a whooshing noise and Tank could see flames through the shattered windscreen. A glass bottle exploded on the bonnet and the Hummer was engulfed in flames. A second petrol bomb smashed against the passenger side of the vehicle. The Hummer sped backward and crashed into a two door saloon. The impact threw Tank sideways against the headrest and the pain in his face flared up again. A hooded figure appeared out of the darkness next to the driver's door. Tank glanced at the figure as he thrust the vehicle into first gear. This time there was no catapult in sight, but there was a silver revolver in the gloved hand. A fat forty five millimetre slug hissed past Tank's face as the Hummer roared away from the roadblock. He drove the vehicle a few hundred yards before yanking on the handbrake and pulling hard left on the steering wheel. The Hummer went into a slide and came to a halt facing the roadblock. Tank flicked the lights onto main beam and assessed the situation. His face was beginning to cause him severe pain again.

In the middle of the road was the body of the person that he'd rundown. Two hooded figures ran to the prone body and lifted the person to their feet. The wind gusted and the injured person's hood blew down to reveal long blond hair and a pretty feminine face. The girl couldn't have been more than sixteen. Her nose was bleeding but her eyes were open and she seemed to be talking to her helpers. The hooded figure with the revolver joined them and he raised the pistol and aimed it at the Hummer. Tank was aware of the drug gangs, and gun crime in that part of the city and it looked like the gang members had chosen not to leave. Whatever their reasons for building the roadblock were, Tank didn't have the time or the inclination to empathise. The hooded figure fired and a bullet hissed past the vehicle and pinged off the perimeter wall. Tank took out a nine millimetre Glock, which he had taken from the taskforce pickup. Firing it would alert the office to his whereabouts and they could then track him, but it was no longer an issue. Tank placed his elbow onto the door frame to steady his hand. He aimed the pistol through the shattered driver's window and fired once. The hooded gunman was knocked off his feet as if he had been hit by an invisible sledgehammer. His friends scattered in different directions like rats leaving a sinking ship.

There was a four foot gap between a Toyota and a Mini. Tank aimed the Hummer between them and stepped on the accelerator. The vehicle's five litre engine roared and the wheels skidded in the deep snow as it hurtled toward the roadblock. He braced himself for a fresh onslaught of bullets and ball bearings but none was forthcoming. The perpetrators had run for cover. Tank steered the huge front wheels of the Hummer over the body of the teenage gunman to further deter any would be attackers. The body burst beneath the immense weight and blood squirted across the snow in a fan pattern. Tank gritted his teeth as the Hummer smashed through the roadblock and sped on its way toward the docks.

CHAPTER 37
Barnes

Barnes jumped out of the pickup truck and inspected the tyre tracks that had been left in the snow. There was evidence of two vehicles. Grace Farrington drove the pickup at speed across the quayside toward the site of the explosion. She spoke into the coms unit as she approached the burning shell of the lightship.

"What's the situation Zulu chief?" the fat controller asked. The explosion had registered on the trackers at the taskforce bunker.

"The lightship is shredded," she shook her head in dismay as she surveyed the scene. There were pieces of metal strewn across the dockside, and the hull of the ship was still ablaze.

"Roger that, what about our men, is there any sign of survivors?"

"Negative, I'm going to check the Land Rovers now," Grace reported. She stopped the pickup fifty yards short of the burning ship, and put the vehicle into neutral before opening the door and climbing onto the quayside. The closest Land Rover was seventy yards to her left, next to a four high stack of cargo containers. The headlights and windscreen had been blown out, and the driver was hanging out of the door with his head on the dock. Grace crossed the dockside quickly. She was careful not to disturb any of the debris as she moved. The quay was littered with charred material, and she knew from experience that some of it was the remains of her taskforce colleagues. She was desperately hoping that Chen had been blown clear, or that he'd orchestrated the search from the Land Rovers, but she knew that he was gone. Grace reached the driver and moved the neck section of his NBC suit. She placed two fingers against the side of his neck. There was no pulse. His face had a swollen spongy appearance, which indicated that his internal organs and bone structure had been turned to pulp by the force of the concussion wave. Grace used a gloved hand to close his eyelids before moving away from the vehicle. She skirted the cargo containers and approached the second Land Rover. The driver was sat upright in his seat. There was a two foot metal pole protruding from his chest, and it had pinned him to his seat. His chest was heaving as he struggled to catch his breath.

"Red team driver is still breathing, but he is seriously injured," Grace called into the coms.

"Roger that, we have army medics en route. What about Chen and the others?" It was the Major's voice this time.

"Negative sir, they didn't have a chance," she replied. Her voice was breaking up as she choked back tears. Chen had been her close friend since the day she had been selected for the elite troop, and she would miss him badly.

"Is there any sign of Christopher Walsh and his men?" the Major asked.

"Barnes is following a set of tyre tracks on the opposite side of the harbour. They lead away from the site of the explosion along the quay toward an old boatyard. I'll back him up now I know that medics are on their way sir," Grace said as she ran toward the pickup. The snow was piling up and it was hard going making progress whilst wearing the clumsy NBC suit. She stumbled and fell onto her knees.

"Zulu one here," Barnes called into the system.

"Roger, Zulu one," the Major acknowledged his call sign.

"The tyre tracks run to the rear of a boatyard approximately five hundred metres along the dockside from where I left Zulu chief. There are a couple of vans and a Bentley Continental hidden in an annexe to the rear of the boatshed. I can see several sets of footprints from three people, maybe four, outside of the annexe leading to a side entrance. I want permission to move inside sir," Barnes was whispering.

"Negative Zulu one," wait for backup the Major instructed him. There was nothing but a static silence on the coms. "Zulu one, did you copy my command? Wait for backup."

Barnes had been selected for the Terrorist Task Force from the elite Paratrooper Regiment. He had joined the Paras at the tender age of seventeen and had served for thirteen years before joining the counter terrorist unit. Barnes had completed two tours of Iraq and three tours of Afghanistan. He had volunteered to stay on extended duty for every tour that he'd served on. Wherever there was action, Barnes wanted to be at the forefront of the conflict. His talent as a combat veteran had made him an obvious choice for several elite military units, but his gung ho attitude was bringing his decision making qualities into question.

"Major, this is Zulu chief," Grace interrupted the coms.

"Roger, Zulu chief, Zulu one is not responding," the Major said.

"I heard his request to enter the building. I'm two minutes away Major, if he's playing the role of a glory hunter then he's off my squad forthwith," Grace was frustrated and angry. Chen and two full teams of taskforce operatives were dead. The last thing that she needed now was a maverick running about thinking that he was Rambo.

"Zulu one, give me one click if you are compromised," Grace instructed him. If an operative was in close vicinity to an enemy agent, and their position could be compromised by speaking, then they could flick their coms unit and a single click could be heard at the other end. One click was affirmative, two was a negative response. Grace heard nothing but silence and static, which was created by the snowstorm. "I'm getting nothing from him on the coms, Major. I'm at the point where we split up, so I'll leave the pickup and follow his trail."

"Negative, Zulu chief, I want you to wait for backup. We have lost enough men today," the Major growled into the coms. "We have a weapon discharged signal from a Glock registered to us. It's been discharged about six hundred metres from the dock gates. It was assigned to Gomez."

"Where is he?" Grace asked.

"He's still at the hospital looking for Tank," the Major replied.

"Roger that, I think I know who fired that Glock, Major."

"Roger that, Zulu chief, I'm not a brain surgeon but I think I've a good idea who it was myself," the Major replied sarcastically. "We have green troop kitted up and ready to move. Wait for backup."

"Did you hear me, Zulu chief?" the Major asked gruffly.

"Zulu chief, are you receiving me?" he asked again impatiently, but there was no reply from Grace either. The only noise was the sound of the wind howling as the snowstorm became a blizzard.

CHAPTER 38
Uri

Uri pointed the Uzi at Christopher Walsh as he climbed up the metal ladder, which led into the bridge of the L2. Christopher was sweating from the exertion of closing the lock gates. He was also beginning to panic about the length of time he'd been exposed to the blister cloud without any protection. The damage to his lungs would become irreversible if he didn't use a protective mask of some description soon.

"Where is the money that you keep on the boat?" Uri asked him as they stepped onto the bridge. He could see over the top of the lock gates from the bridge, and out across the harbour. Thin beams of light were still moving across the old lightship. Someone was paying it more than a little attention.

"Uri, I need to put on a protective suit and treat my skin, and I need to do it now," Christopher folded his arms sulkily. His freckled cheeks had been affected by the blister agent, and although he felt no pain yet, they were beginning to redden. They made him look boyish.

"My men and I need to be paid, Christopher. Pay us what you owe us so far and then we can all get out of here. My men are loading your precious salvage into the vans as we speak," Uri peered over the stern of the L2. There was a white Ford van parked on the quay. One of his men was using a lifeboat winch to shift a sledge loaded with mustard gas shells onto the dock.

"I don't have that kind of money in my arse pocket Uri, I'll need to get it from my safe deposit box," Christopher lied.

"You have cash on the boat, Christopher," Uri looked toward the back of the boat again. "You don't have much time."

"I need to go below decks and treat my skin, Uri." Christopher walked past Uri with a defiant gait. Uri raised the black machine pistol and brought it down on the back of Christopher's head. Christopher howled and dropped onto his hands and knees. He had one hand on the back of his head and the other was flat on the deck supporting his weight. Uri slid off the safety catch and fired a short burst from the nine millimetre weapon. The Uzi is capable of firing nine hundred bullets a minute. In the fraction of a second that he'd activated the trigger, eight high velocity bullets had been fired. Five of them ripped through the flesh and sinew of Christopher's hand. He screamed and rolled onto his back. His little finger was hanging in tatters. It was still joined to his body at the wrist, but it was barely recognisable as a finger anymore.

"What you need to do Christopher, is pay myself and my men for what we have done, I'm not going to ask you again," Uri aimed the Uzi machine pistol at his bleeding employer.

Christopher had tears streaming from his eyes and he gritted his teeth against the pain in his ruined hand. Uri waved the machinegun over his face and Christopher squeezed his eyes closed tightly, trying to make the nightmare situation disappear. It didn't work. When he opened his eyes Uri was still standing over him. He looked completely inhuman in the NBC suit.

"There is a safe box beneath the bunk in the captain's quarters," Christopher cried as he spoke. "There are fifty thousand Euros in there, and two platinum credit cards. Take them and leave me alone."

Uri grabbed an oily rag from the window ledge and threw it to his wounded boss.

"Fifty thousand will do as a down payment. Wrap your hand with that rag before you bleed to death. You still owe me a lot of money Mr Walsh, so I don't want you dying on me before you settle your debt in full," Uri looked over the bow of the L2. He could see two sets of headlights parked on the opposite side of the harbour close to the quayside. There were torch beams flashing in the darkness. It wouldn't take them long to realise that they were on the wrong lightship. Uri removed his remote detonator and smiled in the darkness as he pressed the button. A huge explosion ripped through the night and he watched a tower of flame climbing skyward. Christopher Walsh was wide eyed and open mouthed. He curled up in a ball, shocked by the explosion, and frightened for is life.

"What have you done?" he whispered under his breath. Uri wasn't sure if he was talking to him, or to himself.

"Where is the key for the safe box?" Uri asked. He dropped the remote onto the bridge console. It had served its purpose and now it was just a useless pile of transistor parts attached to a nine volt battery.

"There is no key to it, it's just hidden under the captain's bunk," Christopher stared at his injured hand, and then he picked up the cloth and wrapped it tightly around his hand. His body was shaking with pain as he tightened the makeshift bandage. Uri waved the Uzi toward the stairs and Christopher tried to stand up. His knees were weak and he staggered across the bridge, before descending to the lower deck. Uri followed closely behind him with the weapon aimed at the back of his head. He wasn't sure why he hadn't already killed him. He was tempted to take the fifty thousand, and the credit cards, and then cut his losses. Maybe it was greed that kept him here, and maybe he liked the adrenalin rush.

"You know where the money is Uri, now let me get a protective suit at least," Christopher said as they reached the first deck. "They are stored in the room next to the captain's quarters."

"Shut up and keep moving," Uri shouted. He knew that blowing up the lightship had bought them some time to escape. He was estimating that they had an hour at least. Any emergency services that were functioning in the city would be focused on the site of the explosion, and the surrounding area. No one would search a derelict boatyard on a whim. There was too much chaos to deal with elsewhere.

"Don't ruin everything Uri, we could still be rich beyond your wildest dreams. We have the shells and the Olympics are an international incident just waiting to happen," he turned to face his employee. "Just think how much money the newspapers would pay for a sample shell. It would be worth millions. Every government in the world would buy my counter measures. We would be rich Uri."

Uri stopped for a moment and then punched him in the

mouth for his troubles. Christopher bent double and began to moan. He spat blood onto the floor.

"I told you to keep moving, I suggest that you do as you are told if you want to live," Uri snarled and grabbed his injured hand. Christopher screamed and recoiled from his attacker. He broke free and staggered down the corridor toward the captain's quarters.

"You'll be sorry Uri. You'll be so sorry. Just you wait and see if you're not," Christopher shouted at the top of his voice. He ran past the captain's quarters and rattled the handle of the cabin next to it. The door opened and he stumbled inside. A burst of machinegun fire hammered harmlessly into the walls behind him. He locked the door latch and leaned against it. His breath was coming in short gasps. Blood loss and fear were taking their toll. He waited for Uri to begin barging down the door but he didn't. The door was constructed from the same reinforced steel as the rest of the superstructure. They were built to be watertight in the event of the hull being breached. He had time to treat himself and to put on an NBC suit, if he was quick. There was a thumping noise from the captain's cabin next door, and Christopher knew that Uri had tossed the mattress aside to gain access to the safe box. He smiled and held his breath as he waited.

Uri stepped over the bedding, and the mattress that he had strewn across the cabin. Built into the base of the bunk was a compartment which was used as safe storage for charts and important documents, as well as the captain's valuables. The lid was a simple metal square with two finger holes drilled into it. Uri had to wiggle his fingertips into the narrow holes because of his protective gloves. He lifted the lid and noticed a fine filament of twine. Before he had understood what it was attached to, it was too late. Christopher had fitted a sawn off shotgun beneath the captain's desk, and then strung fishing twine to the trigger, before attaching it to the safe box. He had been involved in criminal operations all over the planet, and thus he had developed a good understanding of how untrustworthy human beings could be.

The shotgun roared as it spat its deadly load of twelve gauge buckshot. The lead spray hit Uri in the back of his left thigh and buttock. It tore through his NBC suit and ripped a two inch chunk of muscle from his leg. He dropped to the floor and cried out loud.

It was a cry of pain and anguish, partly because of the agony from his leg, and partly because he'd fallen into his employer's trap. Uri picked up the discarded blanket and ripped a strip from it. He pressed the material against his wounds and tried to stem the bleeding. There were dozens of individual metal pellets deep inside his muscle tissue, and the pain was excruciating. He leaned over the bunk and reached inside the safe box. It was empty. Uri screamed in frustration and he stood on his feet shakily. Blood was running down his thigh as he stumbled toward the door. He flung the door open and it clattered against the metal hull. The door into the next cabin was flapping open. Christopher Walsh was nowhere to be seen.

Uri heard heavy footsteps coming through the bridge and down the stairs. He pointed the Uzi toward the approaching footsteps but lowered it immediately. It was one of his gorillas called Marco. Marco was an Albanian hoodlum. His reputation for violence was so renowned that even the Russian Mafioso wouldn't employ him. He had left a trail of death and destruction behind him wherever he had been. Uri had given him the opportunity to work on several occasions over the past few years, and so far he had never let him down. Marco was a squat hairy man with thinning black hair which was always greased tightly to his pale scalp. Uri thought that he looked, and walked, like a shaved ape.

"Are you ok, Boss?" Marco asked in a guttural Albanian accent.

"No, I've been shot in the ass," Uri complained. He stepped into the cabin that Christopher had been in. There was pile of crumpled clothes and a pair of Ralph Lauren sneakers in the corner. "Did Mr Walsh pass by you?"

"No boss, I heard gunshots and came straight in here," Marco's hands were beginning to redden. "We've finished loading the shells, Boss."

"Good, check out the lower deck. He can't have gotten far away," Uri knew that the lower decks were where Christopher had carried out his experiments. He turned right and headed toward the stern of the boat. Marco stomped down the steps to the bowels of the vessel. Uri could hear his heavy boots clomping in and out of the cabins. The deck below that one was where the engines and fuel tanks were situated. At the stern of the ship Uri entered a wide open space which had once been converted into a tea room. There was no sign of Christopher Walsh. He ran back into the cabin where he had disappeared and kicked over the pile of clothes. There was a large cardboard box next to the cabin bunk, which contained protective clothing. They had been used during Christopher's experiments. Uri pulled it to one side and cursed under his breath.

The box was covering a square opening that had been cut into the floor of the cabin. There was a narrow metal ladder tacked to the hull with small neat welds. It seemed that Christopher Walsh had adapted the lightship with a few customised features of his own design while she was being refurbished. Uri banged his fist on the side of the hull in frustration. He was about to step onto the ladder to follow his slippery employer when he realised that the cabin door had been left open. It had not been locked from the inside.

"Why would you unlock the cabin door, Christopher?" Uri said out loud. He looked back at the opening that had been cut into the floor. "Why would you open the door unless, of course you wanted me to follow you, that is." Uri walked back to the hatch and kneeled down. He peered into the darkness of the lower deck. There was a length of fine fishing twine stretched across the opening, about three feet down the ladder. Uri followed it with his eyes. It was tied to yet another sawn off shotgun, which was welded to the hull of the ship between the rungs of the ladder. If he had descended the ladder he would have taken twin barrels of shot in the chest.

"Not twice in one day, Mr Walsh. Marco!" Uri shouted through the hatch. His voice echoed around the lower decks. "Marco," he shouted again.

"Yes Boss," the Albanian replied from the depths of the ship.

"He escaped down this ladder. Is there any sign of him down there?"

"No Boss, there's nothing down here," Marco replied.

It was then that they heard automatic gunfire from outside.

CHAPTER 39
Christopher Walsh

Christopher placed four vials of his counter measure solutions into a canvas bag. Then he took a full magazine which contained thirty nine millimetre bullets, and he slotted it into a brand new Uzi. The weapon had never been used and it was still sleek with gun oil. He stuffed a handful of spare bullet clips into his bag and then slipped the bolt on the hatch in front of him. He was in a compartment on the lower deck. It had been built into the space between two fuel tanks, and unless you were familiar with the ship's original design then it couldn't be detected. The hatch was a new addition to the superstructure, which he had built into his lightship to be used in the event of an emergency. He had changed into a protective suit and pulled on a gasmask. His hand was causing him pain and he was losing lots of blood. He couldn't hold anything with it as it was virtually useless. He opened the hatch silently and then reached out to the ladder which was in front of him. The ladder was attached to the boatyard wall and was used for engineers to access the hull of damaged ships, once the water had been drained from the dock. He stepped out of the lightship onto the ladder and pushed the hatch closed again.

Christopher struggled up the ladder and peered over the top into the boatshed. To his right he could see the flames across the harbour, where the fractured hull of the derelict lightship was still burning. To the left he could see one of his vans stood on the quayside. One of Uri's gorillas was closing the back doors. He slammed the van doors shut and then jogged along the quayside past Uri's hiding place, and onto the gangplank. Christopher waited until he had heard the bridge door being closed before climbing onto the dockside. He secured the bag over his shoulder and ran to the van. The back doors were unlocked and he pulled them open and looked inside. The cargo sledge had slotted neatly into the back of the Ford. There were at least fifty brass shells stood erect in neat lines on the sledge. Christopher reached inside and touched one of the shells gently. He picked it up and placed it gently into his bag. Christopher caressed the nose cone with the palm of his hand and he relished the coldness of the metal through his glove. He wished that it was against his skin.

There was movement to his right near the main doors of the boatshed. He looked toward the doors but he couldn't see anything. There had been just a fleeting glance in the corner of his peripheral vision but it was gone. It was probably a rat, he thought. Christopher closed the doors quietly and then ran around to the driver's door. He pulled the handle but the door was locked.

"Shit," he hissed. He looked through the window to see if the passenger side was locked too. It was. One hundred and fifty yards away, at the back of the boatshed near the lock gates, there was a door which led into an annexe. They had used the annexe as a garage for their vehicles while preparing the salvage operation. Christopher ran clumsily across the boatshed toward the annexe door. His footsteps echoed loudly as he ran. He was half way across the dock when he heard the bridge door crashing open. The gorilla that had past him earlier obviously hadn't gone down to the lower decks, and he had heard Christopher stomping across the quayside like a baby elephant. A volley of nine millimetre bullets whizzed over his head and blasted fragments of concrete off the dock wall. Christopher froze and raised his hands in surrender.

CHAPTER 40
Tank

Barnes was watching proceedings from the annexe as Christopher Walsh raised his hands. The Major had refused him permission to enter the boatshed, but Barnes felt that he had no option now. The Major couldn't see what he could see, and therefore he wasn't in any position to be giving orders. Barnes was a member of the elite Terrorist Task Force, and as far as he was concerned the men in front of him were terrorists. They were also responsible for the deaths of an unknown number of his unit. I was just them and him now, and that suited Barnes fine.

"Zulu one, this is Zulu chief, are you receiving me?" Grace said into his earpiece. There was no way that Barnes was going to stop now, it was payback time. He flicked the coms unit volume control to zero, and raised the Brugger and Thomet MP9 sub machinegun to his shoulder. The Brugger is used by Special Forces units all over the world because of its low recoil action, which makes it accurate up to about a hundred metres. The x-ray who had just fired his Uzi was standing at one hundred and thirty metres away. At that range even an expert shot would struggle to hit the target with a Brugger, unless they emptied the full magazine, in which case the percentages come right down. Firing a full magazine would compromise his position. Barnes lined up the red dot sight on the x-ray's chest and tensed his trigger finger. The man with his hands raised stepped into the line of his shot.

Barnes lowered the weapon and scanned the boatshed for another position. He needed to be somewhere that he could make an accurate shot, and maintain a covered position. The dockside was too open and there were no hiding places to be had. Barnes turned round and looked toward the vehicles which were in the annexe behind him. There was one white van and a sleek Bentley parked side by side. He kept low and moved toward them. Another man appeared on the bridge of the lightship. Barnes looked inside the van to see if the keys had been left in the ignition. They hadn't. He moved stealthily around the van to the Bentley, and then he tried the driver's door.

"Bingo," he whispered to himself as he opened the door. A set of keys dangled from the ignition. He slid into the driver's seat and peered over the steering wheel into the boatshed.

There were now three men on the bridge of the lightship. Two of them were wearing bog standard gasmasks, and the other had a Territorial Army NBC suit on. Barnes knew that it was the same as the one that he was wearing, and that would explain who had shot the part time soldiers at the roadblock. Barnes decided that the man in the suit would die last, and he would die slowly. The man with his hands raised was walking toward the lightship, while the three men on the bridge covered him with their weapons. Suddenly there was a chink of light at the opposite side of the boatshed, behind the lightship. It was barely noticeable, but there was no doubt that it had been there. A strip of light about six feet high, and two feet wide had appeared and then disappeared just as quickly. Barnes deuced that someone had entered the building through a doorway. It was someone swift, and silent.

Barnes opened the door and climbed out of the Bentley Continental. He crouched low as he scoured the floor around him for something that he could use to press the accelerator pedal down. Three yards away to the right was a thick block of wood. It was three feet long, and six inches square, and it was almost black in colour. Barnes reckoned that it had been used to hold engine blocks off the floor while they were worked on by boat mechanics. From the colour of the wood it had been underneath engine sumps for years. He slid across the floor silently and grabbed it. Barnes jammed the oily block between the driver's seat and the accelerator pedal. It was about three inches too short.

"You have got all the bells and whistles, so we might as well use them," he whispered to himself as he turned the ignition key one click. The system lights on the dashboard illuminated, and he pressed a lever at the side of the driver's seat near the floor. The seat slid backwards driven by an electric motor. The block of wood slipped off the pedal and thumped onto the floor pan of the Bentley.

"Oops, that was the wrong way," he hissed as he pushed the lever the other way. This time the seat slid forward toward the steering wheel and the block became firmly jammed. The accelerator pedal was pressed wide open at full throttle.

"Here goes nothing, Chen my friend, this one's for you and the boys," Barnes whispered as he turned the ignition key. The engine roared to life and the needle on the rev counter shot around the clock into the redline segment. Barnes leaned over and released the handbrake. He knocked the gear stick into drive and then dived out of the way as the huge motorcar hurtled forward into the boatshed. The tyres were spinning wildly, and there was thick black choking smoke and an ear piercing squealing, as the torque from the powerful engine was transferred to the wheels. The Bentley shot forward like a rocket toward the lightship.

The man who had his hands raised turned around as the Bentley screamed across the dock. It was only metres away from him when he dived out of its path. The three men on the bridge of the lightship opened fire with their Uzi nine millimetre machineguns. Each magazine clip holds thirty fat nine millimetre rounds and their weapons clicked empty in less than thirteen seconds. The windscreen of the Bentley was blown to smithereens and the luxurious leather interior was ripped into shreds by the hail of bullets. Despite the deadly maelstrom of machinegun fire, the empty vehicle continued on its final journey at breakneck speed.

Barnes used the vehicle as a decoy and rushed forward behind as it careered across the quay. He crossed fifty metres of the dock, and waited for the Uzi's to run empty before kneeling down and taking aim. The red dot sight settled on the heart of one of the x-rays and he squeezed off four rounds. The x-ray moved sideways to reach for a new magazine and the bullets smashed into the windows of the lightship. The three men realised that they were under fire and they retreated into the bridge. Barnes stooped low as he crossed another thirty yards of the dock. The Bentley hit the edge of the dry dock at about sixty miles an hour and it was launched into the air. Such was its momentum it sailed across the narrow gap between the dockside and the lightship and it smashed onto the bow of the vessel. The boat was rocked violently by the impact and the three men in the bridge were thrown to the floor like ragdolls. The Bentley's fuel tank ruptured and the flammable liquid inside it leaked onto the red hot exhaust pipe. The vehicle was blown into the air where it somersaulted before crashing back down onto the lightship once more.

Barnes saw the man on the dockside running toward the rear of the boatshed. He disappeared into the dark shadows before Barnes could get a shot off. There was movement on the bridge and one of the terrorists looked through the window. Barnes raised his weapon in a flash and switched it to automatic. He emptied a thirty round clip into the bridge before running across the dock to the ship. Barnes was covered by the hull of the ship, and he could see the bridge through the bowline porthole. He removed his empty magazine and slid in a fresh clip. The Bentley was burning fiercely and one of the tyres exploded. Barnes turned his head away from the explosion instinctively, and ducked beneath the porthole. When he looked through it again an avalanche of nine millimetre bullets greeted him.

Uri fired a volley at him and then jumped from the Bridge onto the deck. The bullets pinged off the metal hull and ricocheted across the boatshed loudly. Barnes tried to return fire but as soon as he peeped through the porthole he was met with a maelstrom of bullets. Marco emptied a full clip through the porthole to keep Barnes pinned down, while Uri closed the gap between himself and the taskforce man.

Barnes was running low on ammunition, and he wished that he'd waited for backup. He had three magazines left, when suddenly another machinegun joined the fray. This time it was the familiar sound of a Brugger and Thomet. It was a taskforce weapon for sure. Barnes couldn't see who was firing it, or where they were, but he was very glad that they were there. He waited two seconds after the Brugger had become silent, and then he peeped through the porthole and prepared to fire at the men on the bridge. Barnes was hoping that the Brugger had pinned them down long enough for him to set himself. He was partly right in his assumption because Marco and the other man had ducked out of the line of fire, but Uri had not. Uri was aiming at the porthole and was waiting patiently for Barnes to show his head. When he did Uri emptied the magazine into his face. Barnes took thirteen bullets in the head, face and neck area in the space of just a few seconds. Three molars and one of his eyeballs were found intact seventy yards away from his body. The remains of the rest of his head were completely unidentifiable.

Uri leaned against the ship's rail and looked over into the darkness. A second Brugger had joined in the fire fight but he hadn't seen where it had been fired from. He could hear Marco on the bridge wittering angrily in Albanian. The man with him was Marco's cousin, a man called Davida. Uri wasn't sure if he was really his cousin as the Albanians had a habit of calling everyone their cousin, especially if they were vouching for them for a job.

"Marco, are you hit?" Uri shouted.

"No Boss, but I'm very angry," Marco answered. From Uri's experience Marco said that a lot.

"Can you see where the other shooter is?" Uri asked in Albanian. He wasn't fluent but he could speak a pigeon version when he needed to communicate to them in secret.

"On the opposite side," Marco replied in his native tongue. At least that was what it sounded like.

Uri moved away from the burning car and headed for the stern of the ship. The rails were higher there, and he could crouch down to use it as cover, and move below it easily.

"We're coming down Boss, cover us," Marco shouted in Albanian. Uri could hear them opening the bridge door behind him. He lifted his Uzi over the rail and fired blindly into the dark corners of the boatshed. Thirty nine millimetre bullets raked the darkness without any reply. The boatshed was silent. Marco climbed down the steps first and ducked low when he reached the deck. Davida followed him and was half way down when a muzzle flash lit up the darkness. The shooter was on the other side of the boatshed now. They had used the darkness to move silently around the dockside. Davida cried out as four fat hollow points smashed into his back. The soft nosed bullets bounced around inside his ribcage and ripped his internal organs to pieces. He was dead before he hit the deck.

Marco flipped. He ran the full length of the boat cursing and snarling like a lunatic, while firing one magazine after another around the boatshed. Uri though that Davida may actually have been related to Marco because of all the fuss he was making. Uri crossed the stern and waited patiently for the shooter to take Marco down. It would be a loss, but only a small one and the shooter would reveal their position. The boatshed remained silent. Whoever was out there was good in fact they were very good. They certainly weren't as impetuous as the man he had just killed. His bravado had cost him his life. Marco had returned to his dead cousin and Uri thought that he was going to break down into an emotional wreck, until he started rifling through his pockets to steal the dead man's wallet, and his wrist watch. Uri smiled as his faith in human nature was once again restored, and then he stopped smiling when he saw a red dot on the back of Marco's skull. Uri was about to shout a warning but he was too late.

Three shots rang out and Marco's skull exploded as the bullets ripped through his brain. There was only one exit wound which was around the forehead area, and there was a hole in it the size of a melon. Marco's brains were sprayed over his dead cousin, and in a wide circular pattern across the deck. Uri couldn't work out where the shot had come from until he mentally worked out the trajectory in reverse. He looked upward into the roof beams and saw a flicker of movement. He raised the Uzi and squeezed the trigger. The machinegun jerked violently and then clicked empty when the bullets were spent, and he ejected the clip and inserted another one with an expert's touch.

He was about to fire again when a body fell from the ceiling. It was a fifty feet drop from the beams to the dockside and the body hit the floor with a thump. A Brugger and Thomet sub machinegun clattered across the concrete. Uri ran across the deck and jumped onto the gangplank. He cleared the gangplank in a few long strides and leapt onto the quayside. The body was dressed in an NBC suit and was laid still on the concrete. Uri ran to the prone body and looked through the visor. The face was black skinned. He leaned over and tugged at the facemask. It came off in his hands as he tugged and he stared into the pretty face of a black woman. There didn't seem to be any bullet wounds anywhere, Uri surmised that she had probably lost her balance when he'd fired. She was unconscious but she was still breathing.

"It's a real shame that I haven't got more time or I'd take you with me pretty lady," Uri's face twisted into an evil grin as he imagined the brutal debauchery that he could carry out on handcuffed woman in a quiet location. Especially one that was as tough as this one. She would probably live for a month.

"There's not much call for pretty women were you're going," a deep voice came out of the darkness and Uri turned to look into the swollen face of Tank. Tank hit Uri square on the jaw with an iron fist. All the power generated by seventeen stone of muscle was transferred through four knuckles. The visor shattered and long shards pierced Uri's face. Uri's jaw was shattered by the crushing blow. His hands dropped to his sides and his knees buckled beneath him. Tank hit him again on the bridge of the nose. The fragile bone splintered and a sharp fragment of bone protruded from beneath Uri's right eye. Uri toppled backward onto the dockside and Tank stood over him. He raised the Glock and fired the entire clip. The first six were head shots and the remainder of the seventeen bullets were fired into his chest. Despite being dead Uri's body twitched for a while. Tank always found that amusing.

CHAPTER 41

Blister

Grace Farrington had a broken leg, concussion and damaged pride. Tank had saved her life in the boatshed, which he reminded her of as often as he could. If he had listened to sense then he would have been in a warm hospital bed when she was shot dead with a terrorist's Uzi.

The Terrorist Task Force was devastated by the loss of twelve men that day on the docks, but the threat to the 2012 Olympics never materialised in the terrible manner that it had been planned. Chen's remains were buried with his family in a leafy graveyard which overlooked the river. There was very little of Chen in the coffin as it was carried through the graveyard, and the undertakers had used bricks to add some weight to the proceedings. It seemed fitting that he'd spent the best years of his working life overlooking the flowing waters of the River Mersey, and now he'd been laid to rest there too.

The men aboard the Explorer shared mixed fortunes. Big Gordon had survived virtually unscathed, although his skin was always sensitive to heat and sunlight and his lungs were prone to frequent infections. Although he was plagued by nightmares he lived a long and happy life with his wife and two daughters. By the time he'd become a grandfather for the fourth time he had mellowed somewhat. Brains died from a combination of third degree burns and blood loss, as did Harvey. The crew of the Explorer had to strap them to their bunks as the thirst drove them mad and the blister agent burnt slowly through their skin. Despite the crew's desperate efforts they could not ease the suffering of their workmates and it was a blessed relief when they finally stopped clinging to life. The other members of the crew suffered varying degrees of lung damage and skin burns. None of them ever returned back to sea, and the truth about what happened to them that night was never revealed. They were all paid six figure sums in compensation for their injuries, although some of them did not live long enough to spend it all as complications from their lung injuries beat them in the end.

The taskforce was returned to full strength within three months, and though they exist to rid the world of the scourge that is terrorism, their work load was never done. It probably never would be as long as human beings are the dominant species on planet Earth. Man's determination to dominate other men means that there will always be another terrorist around the corner. They may have different coloured skin and speak in different tongues, but they will always be there.

Christopher Walsh was never apprehended, but he was known to have supplied blister agent formulas to several rogue states that support terrorism. Nuclear, chemical and biological terrorism is still the biggest threat to Western society, and there are plenty of Christopher Walsh characters out there with the money and the know how to utilise their deadly potential. The mustard gas shells which were manufactured by the allies in 1943 really did exist, and the shocking events that took place in the Italian port of Bari are well documented. The exact locations of the dump sites will never be revealed, but they are out there, somewhere, waiting to be salvaged.

Author's Notes

My father Congellous Sydney Jones won the Italy Star medal for service with the Royal Navy during World War II. I didn't realise that he'd been so close to Bari, despite having polished his medals more times than I can remember. I was incredibly proud as a child that my dad had medals for fighting in the war, and he was my hero even when he lost his final battle against cancer. It's strange how I was drawn to the events which happened in the Italian Port of Bari, without realising the connection, perhaps Dad was guiding me to the source of a good story. Many men died there, and others were affected badly. Congellous came home from the war and fathered Pamela, Catherine, Libby, Graham, Jeanette, myself and Stanley (Tim to me!), so I don't think he suffered any long term effects himself.

Thanks to my beautiful long suffering wife Ruth for her never-ending support and encouragement, even when her own demanding job is taking its toll. It will be worth it one day.

To my son Ryan, Mum and all my friends, thank you for making me laugh and constantly asking when the next colouring book will be finished. X